S0-EIV-365

THE THIRD Galaxy READER

The Third
Galaxy READER

EDITED BY H.L. GOLD

DOUBLEDAY & COMPANY, INC., GARDEN CITY, N. Y.

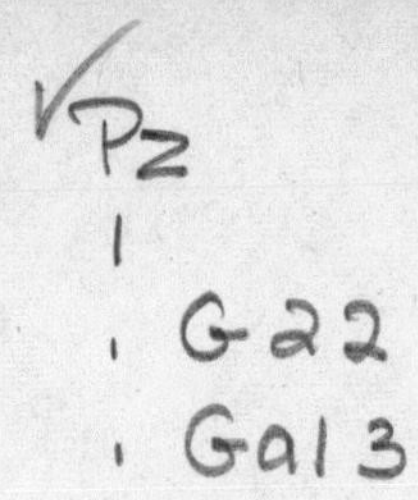

All of the characters in this book are fictitious, and any resemblance to actual persons, living or dead, is purely coincidental.

PRINTED IN THE UNITED STATES OF AMERICA

An Editor's Best Friend Is His Publisher

– If That Publisher Happens to Be

ROBERT M. GUINN

To Whom This Book Is Dedicated

CONTENTS

PROGRAM NOTES

There is no way of setting the birth date of science fiction. Some authorities claim that Plato was the father. Other authorities trace paternity back to Homer, the Bible.

All authorities on science fiction are not authorities to all other authorities.

When the haystacks are finally scattered and the shining needle bearing the birth date of science fiction is triumphantly held aloft, it will stay aloft only long enough to be thrust into one footnote or another.

No matter. We're not concerned with that dim-distant event. What counts is that, unlike any form of literature, science fiction can specify year, month, day, hour, minute, and second as The Moment When Science Fiction Came True.

It was October 4, 1957, the date of the launching of Sputnik I. The Russians have yet to announce the exact time—it's been determined by astronomers calculating backward from the statement that Sputnik was allowed to orbit twice, to make sure it would stay up, before the news was released, but that calculation is dependent on hitherto unreliable sources.

Since then, news break has followed news break. Whenever one lands on the front pages, my phones ring and reporters say: "Well, congratulations! Another prediction panned out!" And I say: "Thanks on behalf of the writers and readers, but science fiction isn't in the prediction business." And they say amiably: "Of course not. But what else are you guys working on these days?"

And I tell them.

And they make notes and ask questions that are explained.

And the write-ups appear, and each succeeds in its quest for color—my face turns red with embarrassment and frustration.

If interviews are called for—and they are—science editors and not reporters should be assigned the job. It's not that science fiction is difficult or dull or intimidating, only that regular newsmen have to be briefed all the way and find themselves with more to say than they have room for and are forced to condense the sense out of their material. If you read any articles that quote me in laughable fashion, please credit me with being only half as much of an ass as I sound in the newspapers, and don't blame the reporters; they're laymen sent to do an expert's job.

But this is not a complaint against journalistic malpractices. It's an alert, a distant early warning, so to speak, that newspapers—and the public—can expect more such startling headlines, and still more, and more and more, as science makes science fiction come true at greater and greater speed, and so be less startled or shocked or alarmed when the headlines appear.

For this is the I.G.Y.—the International Geophysical Year—perhaps the most important handful of months in the history of mankind, when the countries of the world are uniting in the most massive assault yet on the mysteries of this planet of ours.

The land and the air and the sea are being invaded in force, and the chill and challenging void above the air and the fiery metal under the land and the restless black deeps beneath the sea, and the news of victories will explode on the front pages like daily communiqués in a war that can only accelerate, never slow down.

The casualties will be laws that were never quite laws, comfortable dogmas that "stood to reason" and don't stand at all when tested, all sorts of notions of what is and isn't possible or true, plus things that will come as blinding surprises to people who never even thought of them.

Few of those stunned people will be writers or readers of science fiction.

For those headlines will not explode out of nothingness, as though unthought of, unspoken of, unwritten of until they burst. They began as ideas, and ideas are the heart of the matter in science fiction.

But I said that science fiction is not in the prediction business and yet I am saying here that if we check back through the files we will discover that all or practically all the discoveries to be announced have appeared in one or more stories. There is no contradiction. To see why there is not and to prepare for the coming headlines, we need a working definition somewhat like this:

Science fiction is fiction based upon scientific speculations that have not been proved untrue.

The key, of course, is "that have not been proved untrue." Any speculation that complies with this definition is legitimate, however outrageous it may seem. Once an idea has been thought of, the biggest step has been taken toward realization. So:

First comes the thought . . .

Then speculation . . .

Then experiments . . .

All of which fail . . .

Except the one that succeeds . . . either in proving or disproving, for disproof is also a success; the dead ends have to be explored before they can be signposted, and, like a maze whose dead ends have been sealed off, the disproofs often make the next trip swift and sure to the logical new exit.

Mostly, the proofs that something cannot be achieved show merely that it cannot be achieved with existing methods or an orthodox approach. A breakthrough is needed. Breakthroughs are never comfortable and tidy. They wreck structures of theory, convictions, skills, turn costly machinery to obsolete junk, stockpiles and inventories and know-how to deadly sea-anchors that must be cut even sooner than possible. And all because of an idea that someone thought of.

If not for these wrenches, though, we would still be living in caves and using stone implements—the finest and most luxurious, to be sure, the absolute ultimate in polished tunnels and eversharp flints, for improvement is the easiest part of invention. But improvement can be carried only as far as perfection, and then, when you want something better, a wholly new approach is called for.

It may be human to try to salvage as much as you can of the old ways, but it isn't good economics or sound thinking. Airplane design, for example, was refined to the last seam and curve, and motors beefed up until the old standard of one horsepower per pound was a pathetically modest requirement—and the propeller, no matter how feathered and faired, began actually holding back the plane.

There was only one thing to do and it had to be the most radical solution. The propeller was creating the holdup; scrap it.

It's not surprising that the research had already been done and so jet motors were available. As far as theoretical reasoning was concerned, jets too were outmoded and rocket motors were to be had. They still are. We just have to adapt them to human tolerances of acceleration and deceleration. Being improvement, it will be done quite quickly.

But we in science fiction and scientists in basic research can see, even now, before manned rockets are a reality, that there are—to us—intolerable limitations to rocket travel:

They need an enormous amount of fuel to lift a small payload.

They will take a great time to slow down enough to land, either for intercontinental or interplanetary travel.

They are only good enough for right now in lumbering from one inner planet to another at no more than tens of miles a second; when we head for the outer planets, the trips will last years, which is downright poor economy, besides the inhuman burden that would impose on the crews.

Improved to the last imaginable—or unimaginable—ton of thrust per microgram, rocket ships would nevertheless be held to just under the speed of light, 186,000 miles a second. That's good enough for getting around in our solar system, but it's disastrously slow for interstellar travel. At the speed of light, Alpha Centauri is four and a half years away, and other star systems in this one little galaxy of ours are as distant as 100,000 light-years. The speed of light won't do. Impractical.

But what are the practical answers? In every single instance, the most impractical solution has been to cling to what has been practical. The converse is true: The most practical solution is the seemingly most impractical. The more ruthlessly and totally the accepted theories and methods are routed out, the more swiftly and satisfactorily the new will be found.

Regard you, by way of substantiation:

Jules Verne knew, of course, that such antique notions for getting to the Moon as rising with the dew, being towed by birds or with balloons under the armpits, were in keeping with the knowledge of their day, when it was not even suspected that no air lay between Earth and her first and largest satellite. He had an excellent idea of the thrust needed to break free of Earth's gravity, the distance to be traveled, and the conditions and hazards of travel. So, working with slide rule, sky maps, firing tables, and such, and adhering devoutly to the science of his own day, he shot his passengers from a gigantic cannon braced deep in the ground. Naturally, they couldn't land on the Moon and take off again, so he contented himself with a sweep around it and back again.

H. G. Wells, on the other hand, being, as Verne said, a completely impractical visionary, simply abolished gravity with cavorite, a wondrous substance that he didn't bother to analyze or justify; he couldn't, because it wasn't known to the science of his day.

Nor is it known to ours—but there never was and never will be a Verne-type Earth-Moon cannon, while researchers are in business-like fashion checking in every day to work on a well-financed, well-directed anti-gravity project. They expect to have it solved in forty years. If they are wrong at all, it is on the side of conservatism; nearly every sound conjecture in science fiction and basic science has been too cautious.

Anti-gravity is the answer to the unacceptable, wasteful ratio of fuel to payload. And it will go right on being visionary and impractical—until the day it hits the headlines—to those who don't read science fiction, or science journals, which sound remarkably like science fiction in all but entertainment value.

But anti-gravity combined with rocket thrust, even if they reach the speed of light, cannot overcome the limitation set by the Lorenz-Fitzgerald Contraction. I have to add: "pending actual test." But if we find it does not hold up, which appears unlikely, and anti-grav rockets *can* multiply the speed of light, that still means years to reach the closest stars, not to mention stopover time and return trip.

So science fiction abolishes the concept of straight-line travel, just as Wells abolished gravity because it was an obstinate nuisance, and we go by way of sub-space, hyper-space, inter-dimension, and the like, arriving in less time than it would take to travel from one planet to another in our solar system by conventional means. We don't have to justify our radical measures any more than Wells did his; the science doesn't yet exist to support more than a hypothesis. That, however, is a good bit more substantial than Wells's was.

Will interstellar travel come about just as it is described in science fiction? If it does, it would be remarkable, almost miraculous—the one example of such long-range speculation, dependent on principles and techniques and materials that we can only guess at, proving out in practice. We know the problems and we know in advance what won't work, so we try to find those that might.

Might, mind you, not *will.* That is why science fiction is not in the prediction business.

Planes, submarines, ground cars, air conditioning date back—in ideas laid out in detail drawings—to Leonardo da Vinci. He was restricted to muscle and spring-drive power. He needed the internal-combustion engine—but think of the theoretical work, lab testing, geology, chemistry, metallurgy, and all the industries required to mine, smelt, forge, deep-soil drill, refine, pipe, and ship—just to get him that modest engine and a supply of fuel and lubricant. And a fat lot of good all that would do him without a storage battery, the development of which took still more research and interrelated industries.

But assume those were possible and, had we not gone past his original thinking, we would fly in flap-wing planes that could only outfly birds by some now negligible multiple; travel in submarines with self-contained air, like the diving bells of his period; bump along on ground cars with wooden wheels; smother in soaked air conditioning because his collant was running water.

Some crust, eh, daring to speculate on inventions that lay centuries in the future? No, ideas are living things when they are born, and someone has to give birth to them, whether prematurely or not is not the standard to apply. Ideas are always born prematurely, in the sense that turning them into reality takes time and work and money.

And what of serendipity—the happy accident, like the discovery of penicillin? It's an outsize factor in discovery and invention, and will become more so rather than less. But so will the promptness of recognition, and science fiction can take credit for that—our greatest proportion of sale to population is in towns where scientific installations are the principal industry—and science fiction is the sharpest goad to speculation when a serendipitous event takes place. Because of it, a lag of a full decade, as with penicillin, is highly unlikely.

But will the conjectures in this anthology come about? Maybe, maybe not—they haven't been proved untrue yet. More important, they're fun to read, an enjoyable way of getting a brain massage.

H. L. GOLD

THE THIRD Galaxy READER

Limiting Factor

By THEODORE R. COGSWELL

Is there a Homo superior in the audience? This story is printed primarily for you!

The beautiful girl slammed the door shut behind her and for a moment there was silence in the apartment. The blond young man in baggy tweeds looked at the closed door uncertainly, made a motion as if to follow her, and then stopped himself.

"Good boy," said a voice from the open window.

"Who's there?" The young man turned and squinted out into the darkness.

"It's me. Ferdie."

"You didn't have to spy on me. I told Karl I'd break off."

"I wasn't spying, Jan. Karl sent me over. Mind if I come in?"

Jan grunted indifferently and a short stocky man drifted in through the window. As his feet touched the floor, he gave a little sigh of relief. He went back to the window, leaned out, and looked down the full eighty stories to the street below.

"It's a long way down there," he said. "Levitation's fine, but I don't think it will ever take the place of the old-fashioned elevator. The way I look at it is that if man was intended to fly, he'd have been born with wings."

"Man, maybe," said Jan, "but not superman. Want a drink? I do."

Ferdie nodded. "Maybe our kids will take it as a matter of course, but I just can't relax when I'm floating. I'm always afraid I'll blow a neuron or something and go spinning down." He gave a shudder and swallowed the drink in one gulp. "How did it go? Did she take it pretty hard?"

"Tomorrow will be worse. She's angry now and that acts as a sort of emotional anesthetic. When that wears off, it's really going to hurt. I don't feel so good myself. We were going to be married in March."

"I know," said Ferdie sympathetically, "but if it's any consolation, you're going to be so busy from now on that you won't have much time to think about it. Karl sent me over to pick you up because we're pulling out tonight. Which reminds me, I'd better call old Kleinholtz and tell him he'll have to find himself a new lab technician. Mind if I use your phone?"

Jan shook his head mutely and gestured toward the hallway.

Two minutes later, Ferdie was back. "The old boy gave me a rough time," he said. "Wanted to know why I was walking out on him just when the apparatus was about ready for testing. I told him I had a sudden attack of itchy feet and there wasn't much I could do about it." He shrugged. "Well, the rough work's done, anyway. About all that's left is running the computations and I couldn't handle that if I wanted to. It's strange, Jan—I've spent a whole year helping him put that gadget together, and I still don't know what it's for. I asked him again just now and the tight-mouthed old son-of-a-gun just laughed at me and said that if I knew which side my bread was buttered on I'd get back to work in a hurry. I guess it's pretty big. It's a shame I won't be around to see it." He moved toward the window. "We'd better be on our way, Jan. The rest will be waiting for us."

Jan stood irresolute and then slowly shook his head. "I'm not going."

"What?"

"You heard me. I'm not going."

Ferdie went over to him and took him gently by the arm. "Come on now, boy. I know it's hard, but you've made your decision and you've got to stick to it. You can't pull back now."

Jan turned away sullenly. "You can all go to hell! I'm going after her."

"Don't be a fool. No woman is worth that much."

"She is to me. I have been a fool, but I'm not going to be any longer. I was a pretty happy guy before you people came along. I had a job I liked and a girl I loved and the future looked good. If I backtrack fast enough, maybe I'll be able to salvage something. Tell the rest I've changed my mind and I'm pulling out."

The short stocky man went over and poured himself another drink. "No, you're not, Jan. You aren't enough of a superman to be able to forget those poor devils down there." He gestured at the peaceful city that spread out below them.

"There won't be any trouble in our time," Jan said.

"Or in our children's," agreed Ferdie, "but there will be in our grandchildren's and then it will be too late. Once the row starts, you know how it will come out. You've got an extra something in your brain—use it!"

Jan looked out into the night and finally turned to answer. Before he could, an angry voice suddenly boomed inside his head.

"What's holding you up over there? We haven't got all night!"

"Come on," said Ferdie. "We can argue later. If Karl is wound up enough about something to telepath, it must be important. Me, I'll stick to the telephone. What's the point to having a built-in transceiver, if you have to put up with a splitting headache every time you use it?" He stepped to the window and climbed up on the sill. "Ready?"

Jan hesitated and slowly climbed up beside him.

"I'll go talk to Karl, anyway," he said. "Maybe you're right, but it still hurts like hell."

"The head?"

"No, the heart. All set?"

Ferdie nodded. They both closed their eyes, tensed, and drifted slowly up into the night.

Karl was stretched out on the couch with his head in Miranda's lap and a look of suffering on his face. She was gently massaging his temples.

"Next time use a telephone," said Ferdie as he and Jan came in.

Karl sat up suddenly. "What took you so long?"

"What do you mean, so long? An aircab would have got us here a lot quicker, but we're supermen—we've got to levitate."

"I'm not amused," said Karl. "Are you all set?"

Ferdie nodded. "All ties broken and everything prepared for a neat and tidy disappearance."

"And him?" Karl looked narrowly at Jan.

"He's all right."

"Yeah, I'm fine," said Jan. "Girl and job dumped down the drain. Do you want the details? Ferdie's boss figured he'd be back. He said Ferdie knew which side his bread was buttered on. My girl didn't say anything; she just slammed the door in my face. And now that that's over, if you'll just detail me a female I'll start breeding little supermen for you. How about Miranda? She's one of the elect."

"Climb off it, Jan," Karl said sharply. "We know it wasn't easy, but dramatics won't help."

Jan threw himself sullenly into an overstuffed chair and stared morosely at the ceiling.

Karl pulled himself to his feet and made a quick survey of

the room. ". . . thirty-seven, thirty-eight—I guess we're all here. Go ahead, Henry. You've got the floor."

A tall, prematurely gray man began to speak quietly. "It's got to be tonight. There is heavy cloud cover over Alta Pass that goes up to twenty thousand feet. If we're careful, we should be able to take off without detection. I suggest we leave at once. It'll take some time to move the ship out of the cave and we want to be on our way before the weather clears."

"Check," said Karl. He turned to Miranda. "You know your job. The ship will be back to pick up the new crop in ten months or so."

"I still think you should leave somebody else behind," she objected. "I can't listen twenty-four hours a day."

"You're just looking for company," Karl said impatiently. "The unconscious mental signals that mark the *change* go on for a week or more before the individual knows anything is happening. You'll have plenty of time to make contact."

"Oh, all right, but don't forget to send a relief back for me. It's going to be lonely with all of you gone."

Karl gave her a short but affectionate kiss. "Okay, gang, let's go."

The engine room of the ship consisted simply of an oval table with ten bucket seats spaced equidistantly around it. At the moment, only one of them was occupied. Ferdie sat there, his eyes closed and his face pale and tense. As a hand touched his shoulder, he jumped, and for a moment the ship quivered slightly until the new mind took over.

Ferdie ran his hands through his hair and then pressed them against his aching temples. Then he stood up. There was a slight stagger to his walk as he pulled himself up the ladder into the forward observation room.

"Rough shift?" said Jan.

Ferdie groaned. "They're all rough. If I'd known how much work was going to be involved in this superman stuff, I'd have arranged to be born to different parents. You may think there is something romantic about dragging this tin ark through hyperspace by sheer mental pressure, but to me it feels like the old horse-and-buggy days with me as the horse. Mental muscle, physical muscle—what's the difference? It's still plain hard work. Give me an old-fashioned machine where I can sit back and push buttons."

"Maybe this was your last turn at the table." Jan looked out at the gray nothingness on the other side of the observation port. "Karl says we're due to pull out of warp this evening."

"And by the time we look around and find that Alpha Centauri has no suitable planets, it'll be my turn to pull us back in again."

Late that evening, a bell clanged through the ship. A moment later, all ten seats in the engine room were occupied.

"Brace yourself and grab hold," snapped Karl. "This is going to take a heap of twisting."

It did. Three times, figures collapsed and were quickly replaced by those waiting behind them, but at last they broke through into normal space. With a sigh of relief, they all relaxed. Karl reached over and switched on the ship intercom.

"How does she look up there, Ferdie?"

"Alpha Centauri blazing dead ahead." There was a slight pause. "Also there's a small man in a derby hat directly off the starboard bow."

Those in the engine room deserted their posts and made a mad dash for the forward observation compartment. Ferdie was standing as if transfixed, staring raptly out into space. As Karl came up and grabbed his arm, he pointed with a shaking finger.

"Look!"

Karl looked. A plump little figure wearing a severely cut business suit, high-buttoned shoes, spats, and a derby hat was floating a scant five yards from the observation port. He waved cheerily at them and then opening the briefcase he carried, removed a large sheet of paper. He held it up and pointed to the words lettered on it in large black print.

"What does it say?" demanded Karl. "My eyes don't seem to be working."

Ferdie squinted. "This is insanity."

"It says that?"

"No, I do. It says, 'May I come on board?' "

"What do you think?"

"I think we're both crazy, but if he wants to, I say let him."

Karl made a gesture of assent to the figure floating outside and pointed aft to the airlock. The little man shook his head, unbuttoned his vest, and reached inside it. He twiddled with something for a moment and then disappeared. A split second later, he was standing in the middle of the observation compartment. He took off his hat and bowed politely to the jaw-dropped group.

"Your servant, gentlemen. My name is Thwiskumb—Ferzial Thwiskumb. I'm with Gliterslie, Quimbat and Swench, Exporters. I was on my way to Formalhaut on a customer service call when I noted an odd disturbance in sub-ether, so I stopped for a moment to see what would come out. You're from Sol, aren't you?"

Karl nodded dumbly.

"Thought so," said the little man. "Do you mind if I ask your destination?"

He had to repeat the question before he was able to get a coherent answer. Ferdie was the first to recover enough from shock to say anything.

"We were hoping to find a habitable planet in the Alpha Centauri system."

Mr. Thwiskumb pursed his lips. "There is one, but there are difficulties. It's reserved for the Primitives, you see. I don't know how the Galactic Council would view settlement. Of course, the population has been shrinking of late and there's practically nobody left on the southern continent." He stopped and thought. "Tell you what I'll do. When I get to

Formalhaut, I'll give the Sector Administrator a call and see what he has to say. And now if you'll excuse me, I don't want to be late for my appointment. Gliterslie, Quimbat and Swench pride themselves on their punctuality."

He was reaching inside his vest again when Karl grabbed his arm. The flesh felt reassuringly solid.

"Have we gone insane?" begged the leader.

"Oh, dear me, of course not," said Mr. Thwiskumb, disengaging himself gently. "You're just a few thousand years behind on the development cycle. The migration of the Superiors from our home planet took place when your people were still in the process of discovering the use of fire."

"Migration?" repeated Karl blankly.

"The same thing you're off on," said the little man. He removed his glasses and polished them carefully. "The mutations that follow the release of atomic power almost always end up in the evolution of a group with some sort of control over the *terska* force. Then the problem of future relations with the Normals comes up, and the Superiors quite often decide on a secret migration to avoid future conflict. It's a mistake, though. When you take a look at Centauri III, you'll see what I mean. I'm afraid you'll find it a depressing place."

Placing his derby firmly on his head, he gave a genial wave of farewell and disappeared.

A wild look was in Karl's eyes as he held up his arms for silence.

"There's just one thing I want to know," he said. "Have I or have I not been talking to a small man in a derby hat for the past five minutes?"

Forty-eight hours later, they pulled away from Centauri III and parked in free space until they could decide what they wanted to do. It was a depressed and confused group that gathered in the forward observation compartment to discuss their future.

"There's no use wasting time now talking about what we saw down there," said Karl. "What we've got to decide is whether we're going to push on to other solar systems until we find a planet that will suit our needs, or whether we are going to return to Earth."

A little redheaded girl waved her hand.

"Yes, Martha?" Karl said.

"I think we *are* going to have to talk about what we saw down there. If our leaving Earth means that we are condemning it to a future like that, we're going to have to go back."

There was an immediate objection from a tense young man in horn-rimmed glasses.

"Whether we go back or ahead will make little difference in our lifetimes, so we can't be accused of personal selfishness if we don't return to Earth. The people it will make a difference to are our descendants. That strange little man who materialized among us two days ago and then vanished is a concrete demonstration of what they can be—if we stay apart and develop the new powers that have been given us. I say the welfare of the new super-race is more important than that of the Ordinaries we left behind!"

There was a short muttering of agreement as he sat down.

"Next?" Karl asked.

Half a dozen people tried to get the floor at once, but Ferdie managed to get recognized.

"I say go back!" he stated. "And since the previous speaker was talking about accusations, let me say that I can't be accused of personal bias, either. As far as I'm concerned, I would just as soon spend the next several years cruising around to the far corners to see what's up. But the longer we're gone, the harder it will be to fit ourselves back into normal society.

"Look, we left Earth because we thought it was the best thing for mankind. And when I say *mankind*, I mean the Normals, the parent race. What we saw down there"—he gestured in the direction of Centauri III—"is dramatic proof that we were wrong. It would seem that a scattering of Superiors is somehow necessary to keep human society from collapsing. Maybe we act as a sort of essential catalyst or something. Whatever it is, we're needed. If we walk out on Man, we'll never be able to live with ourselves in our brave new world."

Karl looked worried. "I think I agree with you," he said, "but if we go back, we'll be dumped into the old problem of future relations again. Right now there are so few of us that if we were found out, we'd be looked upon as freaks. But what's going to happen when our numbers start to shoot up? Any group that has special powers is suspect, and I don't relish the thought of condemning our descendants to a world where they'll have to kill or be killed."

"If worst comes to worst, they can always take off the way we did," replied Ferdie. "But I'd like to point out that migration was the first solution proposed and the one we've given all our attention to. There must be other ways out, if we look for them. We've got to give it a try, anyway." He turned to the young man in the horn-rimmed glasses. "How about it, Jim?"

The other nodded reluctantly. "I'm dubious, but maybe we should go back and make the try you've been talking about." His voice sharpened. "Under one condition, though. If the Normals start to give us any trouble, we get out again!"

"I'll agree to that," said Ferdie. "How about the rest of you?"

"Let's make it official," said Karl. "All in favor of returning?"

The *ayes* had it.

There was a sound of polite applause from the doorway. Mr. Thwiskumb had returned. "A very wise decision," he said, "very wise. It demonstrates a commendable social maturity. I am sure your descendants will thank you for it."

"I don't know what for," said Karl sadly. "We're robbing them of all the things that you have. Instantaneous teleportation, for example. It's no particular sacrifice for us—

we're just starting to develop the powers within us—but it will be for them. I don't know if we are right, asking them to pay such a price."

"What about the other price?" demanded Ferdie. "What about that scrawny grimy gang down on Centauri III, sitting apathetically in the hot sun and scratching themselves? We also have no right to condemn the Ordinaries to a future like that."

"Oh, you wouldn't be doing that," said Mr. Thwiskumb mildly. "Those people down there aren't Ordinaries."

"What!"

"Dear me, no. They weren't the ones that were left behind. They are the descendants of those who migrated. Those poor devils down there are pure-blooded Superiors. When they ran into the limiting factor, they just gave up."

"Then what accounts for you? You're obviously a Superior."

"That's a very kind thing to say," answered the little man, "but I'm just as ordinary as anyone can be. We're all Ordinaries where I come from. Our Superiors left a long time ago." He chuckled. "It's a funny thing—at the time, we didn't know they were gone, so we didn't miss them. We just went about business as usual. Later we found them, but it was already too late. You see, the big difference was that we had an unlimited area of development and they didn't. There's no limit to the machine, but there is to the human organism. No matter how much training you have, there is a limit to how loud you can shout. After that, you have to get yourself an amplifier.

"A slight neural rearrangement makes it possible for you to tap and control certain sources of physical energy that aren't directly available to the ordinary man of your planet, but you are still dealing with natural forces . . . and natural organic limits. There is a point beyond which you can't go without the aid of the machine, an organic limiting factor. But after several generations spent in mastering what is inside your heads, rather than struggling for control of the world around you, and the time comes when your natural limits are reached, the very concept of the machine has been lost. Then where do you go from there?"

He waited for an answer, but nobody offered one.

"There is an old story in our folklore," he continued, "about a boy who bought himself an animal somewhat like your terrestrial calf. He thought that if he lifted it above his head ten times a day while it was little, he would build up his strength gradually until he would still be able to lift it over his head when it was a full-grown animal. He soon discovered the existence of a natural limiting factor. Do you see what I mean? When those people down there reached their natural limits, there was no place for them to go but backward. We had the machine, though, and the machine can always be made smaller and better, so we had no stopping point."

He reached inside his vest and pulled out a small shining object about the size of a cigarette case. "This is hooked by a tight beam to the great generators on Altair. Of course I wouldn't, but I could move planets with it if I wanted to. It's simply a matter of applying a long enough lever, and the lever, if you'll remember, is a simple machine."

Karl looked dazed. In fact, everyone did.

"Yeah," he muttered, "yeah, I see what you mean." He turned to the group. "All right, let's get back to the engine room. We've got a long flight ahead of us."

"How long?" asked the little man.

"Four months if we push it."

"Shocking waste of time."

"I suppose you can do better?" Karl inquired belligerently.

"Oh, dear me, yes," said Mr. Thwiskumb. "It would take me about a minute and a half. You Superiors dawdle so—I'm glad I'm normal."

Jan was doing a happy little dance through his apartment

when his buzzer rang. He opened the door and Ferdie stepped in.

"I came up on the elevator," he said. "It's a lot easier on the nerves. My, you look pleased with yourself. I know why, too—I saw her coming out of the lobby when I came in. She walked as if she were wearing clouds instead of shoes."

Jan did a little caper. "We're getting married next week and I got my job back."

"I got mine back, too," said Ferdie. "Old Kleinholtz gave me a little lecture about walking out on him when work was at its heaviest, but he was too pleased with himself to do more than a perfunctory job. When he took me back into the lab, I saw why. He's finally got his gadget running."

"What did it turn out to be? A time machine?"

Ferdie grinned mysteriously. "Something almost as good. It lifts things."

"What kind of things?"

"Any kind. Even people. Old Kleinholtz had a little set of controls rigged up that he could strap to his chest. He turned the machine on and went flying around the lab like a bird."

Jan's jaw dropped. "The way we do?"

"Just the same, boy. He's found a way to tap the *terska* force. Really *tap* it, not suck little driblets out, as we do. Another ten years and the Ordinaries will be able to do anything we can do, only better. And a good thing, too. Telepathy gives us headaches, and levitation is a pleasant Sunday afternoon pastime, but hardly something to build a civilization on. As Mr. Thwiskumb said, the machine has no natural limits, so I guess our worries about the future are over. Nobody is going to be unhappy about us being able to fly thirty miles an hour when they can make it instantaneous. Looks like superman is obsolete before he even had a chance to get started."

He stretched his arms and yawned. "Guess I'd better get home and hit the sack. It's going to be a busy day at the lab tomorrow."

He walked over to the open window and looked out.

"Flying home?" asked Jan.

Ferdie grinned and shook his head. "I'm waiting until the new improved model comes out."

Protection

By ROBERT SHECKLEY

I had the finest bodyguard on any world to protect me . . . but what was it that watched him?

There'll be an airplane crash in Burma next week, but it shouldn't affect me here in New York. And the feegs certainly can't harm me. Not with all my closet doors closed.

No, the big problem is lesnerizing. I must not lesnerize. Absolutely not. As you can imagine, that hampers me.

And to top it all, I think I'm catching a really nasty cold.

The whole thing started on the evening of November seventh. I was walking down Broadway on my way to Baker's Cafeteria. On my lips was a faint smile, due to having passed a tough physics exam earlier in the day. In my pocket, jingling faintly, were five coins, three keys, and a book of matches.

Just to complete the picture, let me add that the wind was from the northwest at five miles an hour; Venus was in the ascendancy and the Moon was decidedly gibbous. You can draw your own conclusions from this.

I reached the corner of Ninety-eighth Street and began to cross. As I stepped off the curb, someone yelled at me, "The truck! Watch the truck!"

I jumped back, looking around wildly. There was nothing

in sight. Then, a full second later, a truck cut around the corner on two wheels, ran through the red light, and roared up Broadway. Without that warning, I would have been hit.

You've heard stories like this, haven't you? About the strange voice that warned Aunt Minnie to stay out of the elevator, which then crashed to the basement. Or maybe it told Uncle Joe not to sail on the *Titanic*. That's where the story usually ends.

I wish mine ended there.

"Thanks, friend," I said and looked around. There was no one there.

"Can you still hear me?" the voice asked.

"Sure I can." I turned a complete circle and stared suspiciously at the closed apartment windows overhead. "But where in the blue blazes are you?"

"Gronish," the voice answered. "Is that the referrent? Refraction index. Creature of insubstantiality. The Shadow knows. Did I pick the right one?"

"You're invisible?" I hazarded.

"That's it!"

"But *what* are you?"

"A validusian derg."

"A what?"

"I am—open your larynx a little wider please. Let me see now. I am the Spirit of Christmas Past. The Creature from the Black Lagoon. The Bride of Frankenstein. The——"

"Hold on," I said. "What are you trying to tell me—that you're a ghost or a creature from another planet?"

"Same thing," the derg replied. "Obviously."

That made it all perfectly clear. Any fool could see that the voice belonged to someone from another planet. He was invisible on Earth, but his superior senses had spotted an approaching danger and warned me of it.

Just a plain, everyday supernormal incident.

I began to walk hurriedly down Broadway.

"What is the matter?" the invisible derg asked.

"Not a thing," I answered, "except that I seem to be standing in the middle of the street talking to an invisible alien from the farthest reaches of outer space. I suppose only I can hear you?"

"Well, naturally."

"Great! You know where this sort of thing will land me?"

"The concept you are subvocalizing is not entirely clear."

"The loony bin. Nut house. Bug factory. Psychotic ward. That's where they put people who talk to invisible aliens. Thanks for the warning, buddy. Good night."

Feeling lightheaded, I turned east, hoping my invisible friend would continue down Broadway.

"Won't you talk with me?" the derg asked.

I shook my head, a harmless gesture they can't pick you up for, and kept on walking.

"But you *must*," the derg said with a hint of desperation. "A real sub-vocal contact is very rare and astonishingly difficult. Sometimes I can get across a warning, just before a danger moment. But then the connection fades."

So there was the explanation for Aunt Minnie's premonition. But I still wasn't having any.

"Conditions might not be right again for a hundred years!" the derg mourned.

What conditions? Five coins and three keys jingling together when Venus was ascendant? I suppose it's worthy of investigation—but not by me. You never can prove that supernormal stuff. There are enough people knitting slipcovers for straitjackets without me swelling their ranks.

"Just leave me alone," I said. A cop gave me a funny look for that one. I grinned boyishly and hurried on.

"I appreciate your social situation," the derg urged, "but this contact is in your own best interests. I want to protect you from the myriad dangers of human existence."

I didn't answer him.

"Well," the derg said, "I can't force you. I'll just have to offer my services elsewhere. Good-by, friend."

I nodded pleasantly.

"One last thing," he said. "Stay off subways tomorrow between noon and 1:15 P.M. Good-by."

"Huh? Why?"

"Someone will be killed at Columbus Circle, pushed in front of a train by shopping crowds. You, if you are there. Good-by."

"Someone will be killed there tomorrow?" I asked. "You're sure?"

"Of course."

"It'll be in the newspapers?"

"I should imagine so."

"And you know all sorts of stuff like that?"

"I can perceive all dangers radiating toward you and extending into time. My one desire is to protect you from them."

I had stopped. Two girls were giggling at me talking to myself. Now I began walking again.

"Look," I whispered, "can you wait until tomorrow evening?"

"You will let me be your protector?" the derg asked eagerly.

"I'll tell you tomorrow," I said. "After I read the late papers."

The item was there, all right. I read it in my furnished room on 113th Street. Man pushed by the crowd, lost his balance, fell in front of an oncoming train. This gave me a lot to think about while waiting for my invisible protector to show up.

I didn't know what to do. His desire to protect me seemed genuine enough. But I didn't know if I wanted it. When, an hour later, the derg contacted me, I liked the whole idea even less, and told him so.

"Don't you trust me?" he asked.

"I just want to lead a normal life."

"If you lead any life at all," he reminded me. "That truck last night——"

"That was a freak, a once-in-a-lifetime hazard."

"It only takes once in a lifetime to die," the derg said solemnly. "There was the subway, too."

"That doesn't count. I hadn't planned on riding it today."

"But you had no reason *not* to ride it. That's the important thing. Just as you have no reason not to take a shower in the next hour."

"Why shouldn't I?"

"A Miss Flynn," the derg said, "who lives down the hall, has just completed her shower and has left a bar of melting pink soap on the pink tile in the bathroom on this floor. *You* would have slipped on it and suffered a sprained wrist."

"Not fatal, huh?"

"No. Hardly in the same class with, let us say, a heavy flowerpot pushed from a rooftop by a certain unstable old gentleman."

"When is that going to happen?" I asked.

"I thought you weren't interested."

"I'm very interested. When? Where?"

"Will you let me continue to protect you?" he asked.

"Just tell me one thing," I said. "What's in this for you?"

"Satisfaction!" he said. "For a validusian derg, the greatest thrill possible is to aid another creature evade danger."

"But isn't there something else you want out of it? Some trifle like my soul, or rulership of Earth?"

"Nothing! To accept payment for Protecting would ruin the emotional experience. All I want out of life—all any derg wants—is to protect someone from the dangers he cannot see, but which we can see all too well." The derg paused, then added softly, "We don't even expect gratitude."

Well, that clinched it. How could I guess the consequences? How could I know that his aid would lead me into a situation in which I must not lesnerize?

"What about that flowerpot?" I asked.

"It will be dropped on the corner of Tenth Street and McAdams Boulevard at eight-thirty tomorrow morning."

"Tenth and McAdams? Where's that?"

"In Jersey City," he answered promptly.

"But I've never been to Jersey City in my life! Why warn me about that?"

"I don't know where you will or won't go," the derg said. "I merely perceive dangers to you wherever they may occur."

"What should I do now?"

"Anything you wish," he told me. "Just lead your normal life."

Normal life. Hah!

It started out well enough. I attended classes at Columbia, did homework, saw movies, went on dates, played table tennis and chess, all as before. At no time did I let on that I was under the direct protection of a validusian derg.

Once or twice a day, the derg would come to me. He would say something like, "Loose grating on West End Avenue between Sixty-sixth and Sixty-seventh Streets. Don't walk on it."

And of course I wouldn't. But someone else would. I often saw these items in the newspapers.

Once I got used to it, it gave me quite a feeling of security. An alien was scurrying around twenty-four hours a day and all he wanted out of life was to protect me. A supernormal bodyguard! The thought gave me an enormous amount of confidence.

My social life during this period couldn't have been improved upon.

But the derg soon became overzealous in my behalf. He began finding more and more dangers, most of which had no real bearing on my life in New York—things I should avoid in Mexico City, Toronto, Omaha, Papeete.

I finally asked him if he was planning on reporting every potential danger on Earth.

"These are the few, the very few, that you are or may be affected by," he told me.

"In Mexico City? And Papeete? Why not confine yourself to the local picture? Greater New York, say."

"Locale means nothing to me," the derg replied stubbornly. "My perceptions are temporal, not spatial. I must protect you from *everything!*"

It was rather touching, in a way, and there was nothing I could do about it. I simply had to discard from his reports the various dangers in Hoboken, Thailand, Kansas City, Angkor Vat (collapsing statue), Paris, and Sarasota. Then I would reach the local stuff. I would ignore, for the most part, the dangers awaiting me in Queens, the Bronx, Staten Island, and Brooklyn, and concentrate on Manhattan.

These were often worth waiting for, however. The derg saved me from some pretty nasty experiences—a holdup on Cathedral Parkway, for example, a teen-age mugging, a fire.

But he kept stepping up the pace. It had started as a report or two a day. Within a month, he was warning me five or six times a day. And at last his warnings, local, national, and international, flowed in a continual stream.

I was facing too many dangers, beyond all reasonable probability.

On a typical day:

"Tainted food in Baker's Cafeteria. Don't eat there tonight."

"Amsterdam Bus 312 has bad brakes. Don't ride it."

"Mellen's Tailor Shop has a leaking gas line. Explosion due. Better have your clothes dry-cleaned elsewhere."

"Rabid mongrel on the prowl between Riverside Drive and Central Park West. Take a taxi."

Soon I was spending most of my time not doing things, and avoiding places. Danger seemed to be lurking behind every lamp post, waiting for me.

I suspected the derg of padding his report. It seemed the only possible explanation. After all, I had lived this long before meeting him, with no supernormal assistance whatsoever, and had gotten by nicely. Why should the risks increase now?

I asked him that one evening.

"All my reports are perfectly genuine," he said, obviously a little hurt. "If you don't believe me, try turning on the lights in your psychology class tomorrow."

"Why?"

"Defective wiring."

"I don't doubt your warnings," I assured him. "I just know that life was never this dangerous before you came along."

"Of course it wasn't. Surely you know that if you accept protection, you must accept the drawbacks of protection as well."

"Drawbacks like what?"

The derg hesitated. "Protection begets the need of further protection. That is a universal constant."

"Come again?" I asked in bewilderment.

"Before you met me, you were like everyone else and you ran such risks as your situation offered. But with my coming, your immediate environment has changed. And your position in it has changed, too."

"Changed? Why?"

"Because it has *me* in it. To some extent now, you partake of my environment, just as I partake of yours. And, of course, it is well known that the avoidance of one danger opens the path to others."

"Are you trying to tell me," I said, very slowly, "that my risks have increased *because* of your help?"

"It was unavoidable," he sighed.

I could have cheerfully strangled the derg at that moment, if he hadn't been invisible and impalpable. I had the angry feeling that I had been conned, taken by an extraterrestrial trickster.

"All right," I said, controlling myself. "Thanks for everything. See you on Mars or wherever you hang out."

"You don't want any further protection?"

"You guessed it. Don't slam the door on your way out."

"But what's wrong?" The derg seemed genuinely puzzled. "There are increased risks in your life, true, but what of it? It is a glory and an honor to face danger and emerge victorious. The greater the peril, the greater the joy of evading it."

For the first time, I saw how alien this alien was.

"Not for me," I said. "Scram."

"Your risks have increased," the derg argued, "but my capacity for detection is more than ample to cope with it. I am *happy* to cope with it! So it still represents a net gain in protection for you."

I shook my head. "I know what happens next. My risks just keep on increasing, don't they?"

"Not at all. As far as accidents are concerned, you have reached the quantitative limit."

"What does that mean?"

"It means there will be no further increase in the number of accidents you must avoid."

"Good. Now will you please get the hell out of here?"

"But I just explained——"

"Sure, no further increase, just more of the same. Look, if you leave me alone, my original environment will return, won't it? And, with it, my original risks?"

"Eventually," the derg agreed. "If you survive."

"I'll take that chance."

The derg was silent for a time. Finally he said, "You can't afford to send me away. Tomorrow——"

"Don't tell me. I'll avoid the accidents on my own."

"I wasn't thinking of accidents."

"What then?"

"I hardly know how to tell you." He sounded embarrassed. "I said there would be no further quantitative change. But I didn't mention a *qualitative* change."

"What are you talking about?" I shouted at him.

"I'm trying to say," the derg said, "that a gamper is after you."

"A what? What kind of a gag is this?"

"A gamper is a creature from *my* environment. I suppose he was attracted by your increased potentiality for avoiding risk, because of my protection."

"To hell with the gamper and to hell with you."

"If he comes, try driving him off with mistletoe. Iron is often effective, if bonded to copper. Also——"

I threw myself on the bed and buried my head under the pillow. The derg took the hint. In a moment I could sense that he was gone.

What an idiot I had been! We denizens of Earth have a common vice: We take what we're offered, whether we need it or not.

You can get into a lot of trouble that way.

But the derg was gone and the worst of my troubles were over. I'd sit tight for a while, give things a chance to work themselves out. In a few weeks, perhaps, I'd——

There seemed to be a humming in the air.

I sat upright on the bed. One corner of the room was curiously dark and I could feel a cold breeze on my face. The hum grew louder—not really a hum, but laughter, low and monotonous.

At that point, no one had to draw me a diagram.

"Derg!" I screamed. "Get me out of this!"

He was there. "Mistletoe! Just wave it at the gamper."

"Where in the blazes would I get mistletoe?"

"Iron and copper then!"

I leaped to my desk, grabbed a copper paperweight and looked wildly for some iron to bond it to. The paperweight was pulled out of my hand. I caught it before it fell. Then I saw my fountain pen and brought the point against the paperweight.

The darkness vanished. The cold disappeared.

I guess I passed out.

The derg said triumphantly, an hour later, "You see? You need my protection."

"I suppose I do," I answered dully.

"You will need some things," the derg said. "Wolfsbane, amarinth, garlic, graveyard mold——"

"But the gamper is gone."

"Yes. However, the grailers remain. And you need safeguards against the leeps, the feegs, and the melgerizer."

So I wrote down his list of herbs, essences, and specifics. I didn't bother asking him about this link between supernatural and supernormal. My comprehension was now full and complete.

Ghosts and spirits? Or extraterrestrials? All the same, he said, and I saw what he meant. They leave us alone, for the most part. We are on different levels of perception, of existence, even. Until a human is foolish enough to attract attention to himself.

Now I was in their game. Some wanted to kill me, some to protect me, but none cared for *me*, not even the derg. They were interested solely in my value to the game, if that's what it was.

And the situation was my own fault. At the beginning, I had had the accumulated wisdom of the human race at my disposal, that tremendous racial hatred of witches and ghosts, the irrational fear of alien life. For my adventure has been played out a thousand times and the story is told again and again—how a man dabbles in strange arts and calls to himself a spirit. By so doing, he attracts attention to himself—the worst thing of all.

So I was welded inseparably to the derg and the derg to me. Until yesterday, that is. Now I am on my own again.

Things had been quiet for a few weeks. I had held off the feegs by the simple expedient of keeping my closet doors closed. The leeps were more menacing, but the eye of a toad seemed to stop them. And the melgerizer was dangerous only in the full of the Moon.

"You are in danger," the derg said yesterday.

"Again?" I asked, yawning.

"It is the thrang who pursues us."

"Us?"

"Yes, myself as well as you, for even a derg must run risk and danger."

"Is this thrang particularly dangerous?"

"Very."

"Well, what do I do? Snakeskin over the door? A pentagon?"

"None of those," the derg said. "The thrang must be dealt with negatively, by the avoidance of certain actions."

By now, there were so many restrictions on me, I didn't think another would matter. "What shouldn't I do?"

"You must not lesnerize," the derg said.

"Lesnerize?" I frowned. "What's that?"

"Surely you know. It is a simple, everyday human action."

"I probably know it under a different name. Explain."

"Very well. To lesnerize is to——" He stopped abruptly.

"What?"

"It is here! The thrang!"

I backed up against a wall. I thought I could detect a faint stirring of dust, but that might have been no more than overwrought nerves.

"Derg!" I shouted. "Where are you? What should I do?"

I heard a shriek and the unmistakable sound of jaws snapping.

The derg cried, "It has me!"

"What should I do?" I cried again.

There was a horrible noise of teeth grinding. Very faintly I heard the derg say, *"Don't lesnerize!"*

And then there was silence.

So I'm sitting tight now. There'll be an airplane crash in Burma next week, but it shouldn't affect me here in New York. And the feegs certainly can't harm me. Not with all my closet doors closed.

No, the problem is lesnerizing. I must *not* lesnerize. Absolutely not. If I can keep from lesnerizing, everything will pass and the chase will move elsewhere. It must! All I have to do is wait them out.

The trouble is, I don't have any idea what lesnerizing might be. A common human action, the derg had said. Well, for the time, I'm avoiding as many actions as possible.

I've caught up on some back sleep and nothing happened, so that's not lesnerizing. I went out and bought food, paid for it, cooked it, ate it. That wasn't lesnerizing. I wrote this report. *That* wasn't lesnerizing.

I'll come out of this yet.

I'm going to catch a nap. I think I have a cold coming on. Now I have to sneez

The Vilbar Party

By EVELYN E. SMITH

"Nuts to you!" was what Narli knew Earthmen would tell him . . . only it was frismil nuts!

"The Perzils are giving a vilbar party tomorrow night," Professor Slood said cajolingly. "You *will* come this time, won't you, Narli?"

Narli Gzann rubbed his forehead fretfully. "You know how I feel about parties, Karn." He took a frismil nut out of the tray on his desk and nibbled it in annoyance.

"But this is in your honor, Narli—a farewell party. You must go. It would be—it would be unthinkable if you didn't." Karn Slood's eyes were pleading. He could not possibly be held responsible for his friend's antisocial behavior and yet, Narli knew, he would somehow feel at fault.

Narli sighed. He supposed he would have to conform to public sentiment in this particular instance, but he was damned if he would give in gracefully. "After all, what's so special about the occasion? I'm just leaving to take another teaching job, that's all." He took another nut.

"That's *all!*" Slood's face swelled with emotion. "You can't really be that indifferent."

"Another job, that's all it is to me," Narli persisted. "At

an exceptionally high salary, of course, or I wouldn't dream of accepting a position so inconveniently located."

Slood was baffled and hurt and outraged. "You have been honored by being the first of our people to be offered an exchange professorship on another planet," he said stiffly, "and you call it 'just another job.' Why, I would have given my right antenna to get it!"

Narli realized that he had again overstepped the invisible boundary between candor and tactlessness. He poked at the nuts with a stylus.

"Honored by being the first of our species to be offered a guinea-pigship," he murmured.

He had not considered this aspect of the matter before, but now that it occurred to him, he was probably right.

"Oh, I don't mind, really." He waved away the other's sudden commiseration. "You know I like being alone most of the time, so I won't find that uncomfortable. Students are students, whether they're Terrestrials or Saturnians. I suppose they'll laugh at me behind my back, but then even here, my students always did that."

He gave a hollow laugh and unobtrusively put out one of his hands for a nut. "At least on Earth I'll know why they're laughing."

There was pain on Slood's expressive face as he firmly removed the nut tray from his friend's reach. "I didn't think of it from that angle, Narli. Of course you're right. Human beings, from what I've read of them, are not noted for tolerance. It will be difficult, but I'm sure you'll be able to—" he choked on the kindly lie—"win them over."

Narli repressed a bitter laugh. Anyone less likely than he to win over a hostile alien species through sheer personal charm could hardly be found on Saturn. Narli Gzann had been chosen as first exchange professor between Saturn and Earth because of his academic reputation, not his personality. But although the choosers had probably not had that aspect of the matter in mind, the choice, he thought, was a wise one.

As an individual of solitary habits, he was not apt to be much lonelier on one planet than another.

And he had accepted the post largely because he felt that, as an alien being, he would be left strictly alone. This would give him the chance to put in a lot of work on his definitive history of the Solar System, a monumental project from which he begrudged all the time he had to spend in fulfilling even the minimum obligations expected of a professor on sociable Saturn.

The salary was a weighty factor, too—not only was it more than twice what he had been getting, but since there would be no necessity for spending more than enough for bare subsistence, he would be able to save up a considerable amount and retire while still comparatively young. It was pleasant to imagine a scholarly life unafflicted by students.

He could put up with a good deal for that goal.

But how could he alleviate the distress he saw on Karn's face? He did not consciously want to hurt the only person who, for some strange reason, seemed to be fond of him, so he said the only thing he could think of to please: "All right, Karn, I'll go to the Perzils tomorrow night."

It would be a deadly bore—parties always were—and he would eat too much, but, after all, the thought that it would be a long time before he'd ever see any of his own kind again would make the affair almost endurable. And just this once it would be all right for him to eat as much as he wanted. When he was on Earth and out of reach of decent food, he would probably trim down considerably.

"I just *know* you're going to love Earth, Professor Gzann," the hostess on the interplanetary liner gushed.

"I'm sure I shall," he lied politely. She smiled at him too much, overdoing her professional cordiality; underneath the effusiveness, he sensed the repulsion. Of course he couldn't blame her for trying not to show her distaste for the strange creature—the effort at concealment was, as a matter of fact, more than he had expected from a Terrestrial. But he wished she would leave him alone to meditate. He had planned to get a lot of meditation done on the journey.

"You speak awfully good English," she told him.

He looked at her. "I am said to have some scholarly aptitude. I understand that's why I was chosen as an exchange professor. It does seem reasonable, doesn't it?"

She turned pink—a sign of embarrassment with these creatures, he had learned. "I didn't mean to—to question your ability, Professor. It's just that—well, you don't look like a professor."

"Indeed?" he said frostily. "And what do I look like, then?"

She turned even rosier. "Oh—I—I don't know exactly. It's just that—well . . ." And she fled.

He couldn't resist flicking his antennae forward to catch her *sotto voce* conversation with the co-pilot; it was so seldom you got the chance to learn what others were saying about you behind your back. "But I could hardly tell him he looks like a teddy bear, could I?"

"He probably doesn't even know what a teddy bear is."

"Perhaps I don't," Narli thought resentfully, "but I can guess."

With low cunning, the Terrestrials seemed to have ferreted out the identity of all his favorite dishes and kept serving them to him incessantly. By the time the ship made planetfall on Earth, he had gained ten grisbuts.

"Oh, well," he thought, "I suppose it's all just part of the regular diplomatic service. On Earth, I'll have to eat crude native foods, so I'll lose all the weight again."

President Purrington of North America came himself to meet Narli at the airfield because Narli was the first interplanetary exchange professor in history.

"Welcome to our planet, Professor Gzann," he said with warm diplomatic cordiality, wringing Narli's upper right hand after a moment of indecision. "We shall do everything in our power to make your stay here a happy and memorable one."

"I wish you would begin by doing something about the climate," Narli thought. It was stupid of him not to have realized how hot it would be on Earth. He was really going to suffer in this torrid climate, especially in the tight Terrestrial costume he wore over his fur for the sake of conformity. Of course, justice compelled him to admit to himself, the clothes wouldn't have become so snug if he hadn't eaten quite so much on board ship.

Purrington indicated the female beside him. "May I introduce my wife?"

"Oh-h-h," the female gasped, "isn't he *cute!*"

The president and Narli stared at her in consternation. She looked abashed for a moment, then smiled widely at Narli and the press photographers.

"Welcome to Earth, dear Professor Gzann!" she exclaimed, mispronouncing his name, of course. Bending down, she kissed him right upon his fuzzy forehead.

Kissing was not a Saturnian practice, nor did Narli approve of it; however, he had read enough about Earth to know that Europeans sometimes greeted dignitaries in this peculiar way. Only this place, he had been given to understand, was not Europe but America.

"I am having a cocktail party in your honor this afternoon!" she beamed, smoothing her flowered print dress down over her girdle. "You'll be there at five sharp, won't you, dear?"

"Delighted," he promised dismally. He could hardly plead a previous engagement a moment after arriving.

"I've tried to get all the things you like to eat," she went on anxiously, "but you will tell me if there's anything special, won't you?"

"I am on a diet," he said. He must be strong. Probably the food would be repulsive anyhow, so he'd have no difficulty controlling his appetite. "Digestive disorders, you know. A glass of Vichy and a biscuit will be——"

He stopped, for there were tears in Mrs. Purrington's eyes. "Your tummy hurts? Oh, you poor little darling!"

"Gladys!" the President said sharply.

There were frismil nuts at Mrs. Purrington's cocktail party and vilbar and even slipnis broogs . . . all imported at fabulous expense, Narli knew, but then this was a government affair and expense means nothing to a government since, as far as it is concerned, money grows on taxpayers. Some of the native foods proved surprisingly palatable, too—pâté de foie gras and champagne and little puff pastries full of delightful surprises. Narli was afraid he was making a zloogle of himself. However, he thought, trying not to catch sight of his own portly person in the mirrors that walled the room, the lean days were just ahead.

Besides, what could he do when everyone insisted on pressing food on him? "Try this, Professor Gzann." "Do try that, Professor Gzann." ("Doesn't he look cunning in his little dress suit?") They crowded around him. The women cooed, the men beamed, and Narli ate. He would be glad when he could detach himself from all this cloying diplomacy and get back to the healthy rancor of the classroom.

At school, the odor of chalk dust, ink, and rotting apple cores was enough like its Saturnian equivalent to make Narli feel at home immediately. The students would dislike him on sight, he knew. It is in the nature of the young to be hostile toward whatever is strange and alien. They would despise him and jeer at him, and he, in his turn, would give them long, involved homework assignments and such difficult examinations that they would fail. . . .

Narli waddled briskly up to his desk which had, he saw, been scaled down to Saturnian size, whereas he had envisioned himself struggling triumphantly with ordinary Earth-sized furniture. But the atmosphere was as hot and sticky and intolerable as he had expected. Panting as unobtrusively as possible, he rapped with his pointer. "Attention, students!"

Now should come the derisive babble . . . but there was a respectful silence, broken suddenly by a shrill feminine whisper of, "Oooo, he's so adorable!" followed by the harsh, "Shhh, Ava! You'll embarrass the poor little thing."

Narli's face swelled. "I am your new professor of Saturnian Studies. Saturn, as you probably know, is a major planet. It is much larger and more important than Earth, which is only a minor planet."

The students obediently took this down in their notebooks. They carefully took down everything he said. Even a bout of coughing that afflicted him halfway through seemed to be getting a phonetic transcription. From time to time, they would interrupt his lecture with questions so pertinent, so well thought out, and so courteous that all he could do was answer them.

His antennae lifted to catch the whispers that from time to time were exchanged between even the best-behaved of the students. "Isn't he precious?" "Seems like a nice fellow—sound grasp of his subject." "Sweet little thing!" "Unusually interesting presentation." "Doesn't he remind you of Winnie the Pooh?" "Able chap." "Just darling!"

After class, instead of rushing out of the room, they hovered around his desk with intelligent, solicitous questions. Did he like Earth? Was his desk too high? Too low? Didn't he find it hot with all that fur? Such lovely, soft, fluffy fur, though. "Do you mind if I stroke one of your paws—*hands*—Professor?" ("So cuddly-looking!")

He said yes, as a matter of fact, he was hot, and no, he didn't mind being touched in a spirit of scientific investigation.

He had a moment of uplift at the teachers' cafeteria when he discovered lunch to be virtually inedible. The manager, however, had been distressed to see him pick at his food, and by dinnertime a distinguished chef with an expert knowledge of Saturnian cuisine had been rushed from Washington. Since the school food was inedible for all intelligent life-forms, everyone ate the Saturnian dishes and praised Narli as a public benefactor.

That night, alone in the quiet confines of his small room at the Men's Faculty Club, Narli had spread out his notes and was about to start work on his history when there was a knock at the door. He trotted over to open it, grumbling to himself.

The head of his department smiled brightly down at him. "Some of us are going out for a couple of drinks and a gabfest. Care to come along?"

Narli did not see how he could refuse and still carry the Saturnian's burden, so he accepted. Discovering that gin fizzes and alexanders were even more palatable than champagne and more potent than vilbar, he told several Saturnine locker-room stories which were hailed with loud merriment. But he was being laughed *at*, not *with*, he knew. All this false cordiality, he assured himself, would die down after a couple of days, and then he would be able to get back to work. He must curb his intellectual impatience.

In the morning, he found that enrollment in his classes had doubled, and the room was crowded to capacity with the bright, shining, eager faces of young Terrestrials athirst for learning. There were apples, chocolates, and imported frismil nuts on his desk, as well as a pressing invitation from Mrs. Purrington for him to spend all his weekends and holidays at the White House. The window was fitted with an air-conditioning unit which, he later discovered, his classes had chipped in to buy for him, and the temperature had been lowered to a point where it was almost comfortable. All the students wore coats.

When he went out on the campus, women—students, teachers, even strangers—stopped to talk to him, to exclaim over him, to touch him, even to kiss him. Photographers were perpetually taking pictures, some of which turned up in the

Student Union as full-color postcards. They sold like Lajl out of season.

Narli wrote in Saturnian on the back of one: "Having miserable time; be glad you're not here," and sent it to Slood.

There were cocktail parties, musicales, and balls in Narli's honor. When he tried to refuse an invitation, he was accused of shyness and virtually dragged to the affair by laughing members of the faculty. He put on so much weight that he had to buy a complete new Terrestrial outfit, which set him back a pretty penny. As a result, he had to augment his income by lecturing to women's clubs. They slobbered appallingly.

Narli's students did all their homework assiduously and, in fact, put in more work than had been assigned. At the end of the year, not only did all of them pass, but with flying colors.

"I hope you'll remember, Professor Gzann," the President of the University said, "that there will always be a job waiting for you here—a non-exchange professorship. Love to have you."

"Thank you," Narli replied politely.

Mrs. Purrington broke into loud sobs when he told her he was leaving Earth. "Oh, I'll miss you so, Narli! You will write, won't you?"

"Yes, of course," he said grimly. That made two hundred and eighteen people to whom he'd had to promise to write.

It was fortunate he was traveling as a guest of the North American government, he thought as he supervised the loading of his matched interplanetary luggage; his eight steamer baskets; his leatherbound *Encyclopedia Terrestria,* with his name imprinted in gold on each volume; his Indian war bonnet; his oil painting of the President; and his six cases of champagne—all parting gifts—onto the liner. Otherwise the fee for excess luggage would take what little remained of his bank account. There had been so many expenses—clothes and hostess gifts and ice.

Not all his mementoes were in his luggage. A new rare-metal watch gleamed on each of his four furry wrists; a brand-new trobskin wallet, platinum key-chain, and uranium fountain pen were in his pocket; and a diamond and curium bauble clasped a tie lovingly hand painted by a female student. The argyles on his fuzzy ankles had been knitted by another. Still another devoted pupil had presented him with a hand-woven plastic case full of frismil nuts to eat on the way back.

"Well, Narli!" Slood said, his face swelling with joy. "Well, well! You've put on weight, I see."

Narli dropped into his old chair with a sigh. Surely Slood might have picked something else to comment on first—his haggardness, for instance, or the increased spirituality of his expression.

"Nothing else to do on Earth in your leisure moments but eat, I suppose," Slood said, pushing over the nut tray. "Even their food. Have some frismils."

"No, thank you," Narli replied coldly.

Slood looked at him in distress. "Oh, how you must have suffered! Was it very, very bad, Narli?"

Narli hunched low in his chair. "It was just awful."

"I'm sure they didn't mean to be unkind," Slood assured him. "Naturally, you were a strange creature to them and they're only——"

"*Unkind?*" Narli gave a bitter laugh. "They practically killed me with kindness! It was fuss, fuss, fuss all the time."

"Now, Narli, I do wish you wouldn't be quite so sarcastic."

"I'm *not* being sarcastic. And I wasn't a strange creature to them. It seems there's a sort of popular child's toy on Earth known as a—" he winced—"teddy bear. I aroused pleasant childhood memories in them, so they showered me with affection and edibles."

Slood closed his eyes in anguish. "You are very brave, Narli," he said almost reverently. "Very brave and wise and good. Certainly that would be the best thing to tell our people. After all, the Terrestrials are our allies; we don't want to stir up public sentiment against them. But you can be honest with *me*, Narli. Did they refuse to serve you in restaurants? Were you segregated in public vehicles? Did they shrink from you when you came close?"

Narli beat the desk with all four hands. "I was hardly ever given the chance to be alone! They crawled all over me! Restaurants begged for my trade! I had to hire private vehicles because in public ones I was mobbed by admirers!"

"Such a short time," Slood murmured, "and already suspicious of even me, your oldest friend. But don't talk about it if you don't want to, Narli. . . . Tell me, though, did they sneer at you and whisper half-audible insults? Did they——"

"You're right!" Narli snapped. "I *don't* want to talk about it."

Slood placed a comforting hand upon his shoulder. "Perhaps that's wisest, until the shock of your experience has worn off."

Narli made an irritable noise.

"The Perzils are giving a vilbar party tonight," Slood said. "But I know how you feel about parties. I've told them you're exhausted from your trip and won't be able to make it."

"Oh, you did, did you?" Narli asked ironically. "What makes you think you know how I feel about parties?"

"But——"

"There's an interesting saying on Earth: 'Travel is so broadening.' " He looked down at his bulges with tolerant amusement. "In more than one way, in case the meaning eludes you. Very sound psychologically. I've discovered that I *like* parties. I *like* being *liked*. If you'll excuse me, I'm going to inform the Perzils that I shall be delighted to come to their party. Care to join me?"

"Well," Slood mumbled, "I'd like to, but I have so much work——"

"Introvert!" said Narli, and he began dialing the Perzils.

End as a World

By F. L. WALLACE

Prophets aplenty foretold the end—but not one ever guessed just how it would come about!

Every paper said so in all the languages there were, I guess. I kept reading them, but didn't know what to believe. I know what I wanted to think, but that's different from actually knowing.

There was the usual news just after Labor Day. The Dodgers were winning or losing, I forget which, and UCLA was strong and was going to beat everybody they met that fall. An H-bomb had been tested in the Pacific, blowing another island off the map, just as if we had islands to spare. Ordinarily this was important, but now it wasn't. They put stuff like this in the back pages and hardly anybody reads it. There was only one thing on the front pages and it was all people talked about. All I talked about, anyway.

It began long before. I don't know how long because they didn't print that. But it began and there it was, right upon us that day. It was Saturday. Big things always seem to happen on Saturdays. I ate breakfast and got out early. I had the usual things to do, mowing the lawn, for instance. I didn't do it, nor anything else, and nobody said anything. There wasn't any use in mowing the lawn on a day like that.

I went out, remembering not to slam the door. It wasn't much, but it showed thoughtfulness. I went past the church and looked at the sign that was set diagonally at the corner so that it could be read from both streets. There it was in big letters, quoting from the papers: THIS IS THE DAY THE WORLD ENDS! Some smart reporter had thought it up and it seemed so true that that was the only way it was ever said. Me? I didn't know.

It was a bright day. People were out walking or just standing and looking at the sky. It was too early to look up. I went on. Paul Eberhard was sitting on the lawn when I came along. He tossed me the football and I caught it and tried to spin it on my finger. It didn't spin. It fell and flopped out with crazy bounces into the street. The milk truck stopped, while I got it out of the way. I tossed the football back to Paul. He put his hand on it and sat there.

"What'll we do?" he said.

I made a motion with my hands. "We can throw the ball around," I said.

"Naw," he said. "Maybe you've got some comic books."

"You've seen them all," I said. "You got some?"

"I gave them to Howie," he said, thoughtfully screwing the point of the ball into the center of a dandelion. "He said he was going to get some new ones, though. Let's go see." He got up and tossed the ball toward the porch. It hit the railing and bounced back into the bushes. That's where he usually kept it.

"Paul," called his mother as we started out.

"Yeah?"

"Don't go far. I've got some things I want you to do."

"What?" he said patiently.

"Hauling trash out of the basement. Helping me move some of the potted plants around in front."

"Sure," he said. "I'll be back."

We went past another church on the way to Howie's. The sign was the same there. THIS IS THE DAY THE WORLD

ENDS! They never said more than that. They wanted it to hang in our minds, something we couldn't quite touch but we knew was there.

Paul jerked his head at the sign. "What do you think of it?"

"I don't know." I broke off a twig as we passed a tree. "What about you?"

"We got it coming." He looked at the sky.

"Yeah, but will we get it?"

He didn't answer that. "I wonder if it will be bright?"

"It is now."

"It might cloud over."

"It won't matter. It'll split the sky." That was one thing sure. Clouds or anything weren't going to stand in the way.

We went on and found Howie. Howie is a Negro, smaller than we are and twice as fast. He can throw a football farther and straighter than anyone else on the team. We pal around quite a bit, especially in the football season.

He came out of the house like he was walking on whipped cream. I didn't let that fool me. More than once I've tried to tackle him during a practice game. Howie was carrying a model of a rocket ship, CO_2 powered. It didn't work. We said Hi all around and then he suggested a game of keep-away. We'd left the football at Paul's and we couldn't, so we walked over to the park.

We sat down and began talking about it. "I'm wondering if it will really come," said Paul. We all squinted up.

"Where'll the President watch it from?" I said. "He should have a good view from the White House."

"No better than us right here," said Howie.

"What about Australia? Will they see it there?" I said.

"They'll see it all over."

"Africa, too? And what about the Eskimos?"

"It doesn't matter whether they actually see it or not. It will come to everyone at the same time."

I didn't see how it could, but I didn't feel like an argument.

That's what they were saying on TV and you can't talk back to that.

"Everybody," said Howie. "Not just in this town, but all over. Wherever there are people. Even where they're not."

"You read that," said Paul.

"Sure," said Howie. "You lent me the comic books. It's even in them."

We didn't say much after that. I kept thinking of the man who made the H-bomb. I bet he felt silly and spiteful, blowing up an island. Somebody might have wanted to live on it if he'd just left it there. He must have felt mean and low when something really big like this came along.

We talked on for a while, but we'd talked it out long ago. There was really nothing new we could say. Every so often we'd look up at the sky, but it wasn't going to come until it got here.

Finally we drifted apart. There wasn't anything left to do. We walked home with Howie and then I went with Paul, leaving him to come back to my house. I looked at the lawn and without thinking about it got busy and mowed it. I surprised myself.

It was hot, or it seemed to me it was. I went in to eat. Ma came by and shut off the sound of TV. I could still see the picture in the other room. The announcer was making faces, but, of course, I didn't hear what he said. He looked pretty funny, I thought. I thought we were all probably pretty funny, moving our mouths and blinking our eyes and waving our hands. Only nothing real was coming out. Not yet, anyway.

"Sit still," said Ma. "It will happen without your help. It's going to be all right."

"Think so?" I said. She would have told me anything to keep me quiet. She gets nervous when I fidget.

"I think so," she said, giving me my allowance. It was early for that. Usually I didn't get it until after supper. "Why don't you run uptown and watch it from there?"

"Maybe I will," I said, dabbling my hands in the water at the sink. "Are you going to go?"

"Of course I'm not. Why should I get into that mob? I can watch it just as well from here."

Sure she could. But it was not the same. Everybody I knew was going to be there. I changed shirts before I left. I took a rag and wiped the dust from my shoes. I wasn't trying to be fussy or dressed up or anything. I just thought I should do it.

There was shade and sun on the streets and a few big clouds in the sky.

A car slowed up and stopped beside me. The window rolled down and Jack Goodwin leaned toward me. "Going uptown?"

"Yeah."

"Want a lift?"

"Sure." Actually I didn't. I'd rather have walked, looking around as I went.

Jack Goodwin grinned as I got in. He's got gray hair, where he has hair. The rest is bald. He looked me over. "I don't see any comets on your shoulders," he said gravely.

"I never had any," I said. Some people seem to think everyone under seventeen is a kid.

"You'll be needing them," he said.

"Maybe," I said. I ought to have walked.

I never knew how slow a day could pass. I suppose I should have slept late and kept busy doing something. This was worse than putting on a uniform and waiting until gametime. At least there was a coach on the field to tell you what to do as you ran through the drill.

Jack Goodwin stopped at a light. I had a notion to get out. But I didn't. Goodwin grinned again as the light changed and we started up. "I don't blame you for being edgy," he said. "It's the suspense. If we only had some way of knowing for sure, radio maybe."

"There's no radio," I said. "The calculations have been checked."

"Sure, but maybe there's something we forgot. Or don't know. All sorts of things can go wrong."

He must have talked on and on, but I didn't listen. Howie and me and Paul had gone over everything he was saying.

"Thanks," I said as he stopped and I got out.

"Don't mention it," he said. He nearly scraped the rear fender of the car as he drove off. It was a new car, too. He wasn't so bad. Maybe he was just worried.

I wandered to the newsstand and looked at magazines and pocketbooks. Old lady Simpson didn't ask me if I was going to buy and didn't chase me away. She was busy arguing with some customers. Even so it was the first time she didn't pay attention to me when I came in. I had a good chance to look at things I never buy. There was nothing in them I wanted to see. I was thirsty. I had a coke and was still thirsty. I asked for a glass of water, drank half of it and went out.

Down the street there was a TV set in a store window. I watched it. They were showing a street in India, people looking up. They flashed all around, to Italy, China, Brazil. Except for their clothes, it wasn't much different from here. They were all looking up.

I did the same. For the first time I noticed there was a slight overcast. Big billowing clouds had passed, but this was worse. I hoped it would clear away in time. Not that it really mattered.

It was more crowded than usual for Saturday, but at the same time it was quiet. People were shopping, but they weren't really buying much or else they bought it faster. Nobody wanted to miss it. They all seemed to have one eye on their lists and another on the clock.

Howie and Paul came up the street and we nodded and said something. A few other boys from the school passed by and we stopped. We gathered together. It was getting closer —and the space between the minutes was growing longer and longer.

I looked at Paul's watch. He said it was on the minute. I

decided there was time to go in and get a candy bar. All of a sudden I was hungry. I didn't know where it came from. I'd had to stuff down lunch not long ago. And now I was hungry.

I went to a store and had to fight my way in. People were coming out. Not just customers, but the clerks and owner, too. There was a big television screen inside, but nobody wanted to see it on that. They wanted to be outside where it would happen to them. Not just see it, have it happen. The store was empty. Not closed—empty.

I turned and rushed out to join the others. I couldn't miss it. There were still minutes to go, but suppose there *had* been a miscalculation. I knew what that would mean, but even so I had to be there. I would almost die, too.

Now we were all looking up—all over the world people were, I suppose. It was quiet. You could hear them breathing.

And then it came, a flash across the sky, a silver streak, the biggest vapor trail there ever was. It went from this side to that side in no time. It split the sky and was gone before the shock blast hit us. Nobody said anything. We stood there and shivered and straightened up after the rumbling sound passed.

But there was the vapor trail that stretched farther than anyone could see. It would go around the world at least once before it came to an end somewhere in the desert. I saw my science teacher—he was trying to smile, but couldn't. And then there was the pharmacist who had wanted to be a research chemist, but wasn't good enough.

In front of me, old Fred Butler, who drives the bus to Orange Point and King City, cracked his knuckles. "He did it," he whispered. "All the way to Mars and back. Safe and right on schedule." He jumped up in the air and kept jumping up. He hadn't been that high off the ground in several years. He never would be again unless he took an elevator. And I knew he hated elevators.

Factory whistles started blowing. They sounded louder

than Gabriel. I wondered if he heard them. I grabbed hold of the nearest person and started hugging. I didn't know it was the snooty girl from the next block until she hugged back and began kissing me. We yelled louder than the factory whistles. We had a right.

It was just like the papers said: This was the day the world ended——

And the Universe began.

Time in the Round

By FRITZ LEIBER

Poor Butcher suffered more than any dictator in history: everybody gave in to him because he was so puny and they were so impregnable!

From the other end of the Avenue of Wisdom that led across the Peace Park, a gray, hairless, heavily built dog was barking soundlessly at the towering crystal glory of the Time Theater. For a moment, the effect was almost frightening: a silent picture of the beginning of civilization challenging the end of it. Then a small boy caught up with the dog and it rolled over enthusiastically at his feet and the scene was normal again.

The small boy, however, seemed definitely pre-civilization. He studied the dog coldly and then inserted a thin metal tube under its eyelid and poked. The dog wagged its stumpy tail. The boy frowned, tightened his grip on the tube, and jabbed hard. The dog's tail thumped the cushiony pavement and the four paws beat the air. The boy shortened his grip and suddenly jabbed the dog several times in the stomach. The stiff tube rebounded from the gray, hairless hide. The dog's face split in an upside-down grin, revealing formidable ivory fangs across which a long black tongue lolled.

The boy regarded the tongue speculatively and pocketed the metal tube with a grimace of utter disgust. He did not look up when someone called: "Hi, Butch! Sic 'em, Darter, sic 'em!"

A larger small boy and a somewhat older one were approaching across the luxuriant, neatly cropped grass, preceded by a hurtling shape that, except for a black hide, was a replica of Butch's gray dog.

Butch shrugged his shoulders resignedly and said in a bored voice: "Kill 'em, Brute."

The gray dog hurled itself on Darter. Jaws gaped to get a hold on necks so short and thick as to be mere courtesy terms. They whirled like a fanged merry-go-round. Three more dogs, one white, one slate blue, and one pink, hurried up and tried to climb aboard.

Butch yawned.

"What's the matter?" inquired Darter's master. "I thought you liked dog fights, Butch."

"I do like dog fights," Butch said somberly, without looking around. "I don't like uninj fights. They're just a pretend, like everything else. Nobody gets hurt. And look here, Joggy —and you, too, Hal—when you talk to me, don't just say Butch. It's the Butcher, see?"

"That's not exactly a functional name," Hal observed with the judiciousness of budding maturity, while Joggy said agreeably: "All right, Butcher, I suppose you'd like to have lived way back when people were hurting each other all the time so the blood came out?"

"I certainly would," the Butcher replied. As Joggy and Hal turned back skeptically to watch the fight, he took out the metal tube, screwed up his face in a dreadful frown and jabbed himself in the hand. He squeaked with pain and whisked the tube out of sight.

"A kid can't do anything any more," he announced dramatically. "Can't break anything except the breakables they give him to break on purpose. Can't get dirty except in the dirt-pen—and they graduate him from that when he's two. Can't even be bitten by an uninj—it's contra-programmed."

"Where'd you ever get so fixated on dirt?" Hal asked in a gentle voice acquired from a robot adolescer.

"I've been reading a book about a kid called Huckleberry Finn," the Butcher replied airily. "A swell book. That guy got dirtier than anything." His eyes became dreamy. "He even ate out of a garbage pail."

"What's a garbage pail?"

"I don't know, but it sounds great."

The battling uninjes careened into them. Brute had Darter by the ear and was whirling him around hilariously.

"Aw, *quit* it, Brute," the Butcher said in annoyance.

Brute obediently loosed his hold and returned to his master, paying no attention to his adversary's efforts to renew the fight.

The Butcher looked Brute squarely in the eyes. "You're making too much of a rumpus," he said. "I want to think."

He kicked Brute in the face. The dog squirmed joyously at his feet.

"Look," Joggy said, "you wouldn't hurt an uninj, for instance, would you?"

"How can you hurt something that's uninjurable?" the Butcher demanded scathingly. "An uninj isn't really a dog. It's just a lot of circuits and a micropack bedded in hyper-plastic." He looked at Brute with guarded wistfulness.

"I don't know about that," Hal put in. "I've heard an uninj is programmed with so many genuine canine reactions that it practically has racial memory."

"I mean if you *could* hurt an uninj," Joggy amended.

"Well, maybe I wouldn't," the Butcher admitted grudgingly. "But shut up—I want to think."

"About what?" Hal asked with saintly reasonableness.

The Butcher achieved a fearful frown. "When I'm World

Director," he said slowly, "I'm going to have warfare again."

"You think so now," Hal told him. "We all do at your age."

"We do not," the Butcher retorted. "I bet *you* didn't."

"Oh, yes, I was foolish, too," the older boy confessed readily. "All newborn organisms are self-centered and inconsiderate and ruthless. They have to be. That's why we have uninjes to work out on, and death games and fear houses, so that our emotions are cleared for adult conditioning. And it's just the same with newborn civilizations. Why, long after atom power and the space drive were discovered, people kept having wars and revolutions. It took ages to condition them differently. Of course, you can't appreciate it this year, but man's greatest achievement was when he learned to automatically reject all violent solutions to problems. You'll realize that when you're older."

"I will not!" the Butcher countered hotly. "I'm not going to be a sissy." Hal and Joggy blinked at the unfamiliar word. "And what if we were attacked by bloodthirsty monsters from outside the Solar System?"

"The Space Fleet would take care of them," Hal replied calmly. "That's what it's for. Adults aren't conditioned to reject violent solutions to problems where non-human enemies are concerned. Look at what we did to viruses."

"But what if somebody got at us through the Time Bubble?"

"They can't. It's impossible."

"Yes, but suppose they did all the same."

"You've never been inside the Time Theater—you're not old enough yet—so you just can't know anything about it or about the reasons why it's impossible," Hal replied with friendly factuality. "The Time Bubble is just a viewer. You can only look through it, and just into the past, at that. But you can't travel through it because you can't change the past. Time traveling is a lot of kid stuff."

"I don't care," the Butcher asserted obstinately. "I'm still going to have warfare when I'm World Director."

"They'll condition you out of the idea," Hal assured him.

"They will not. I won't let 'em."

"It doesn't matter what you think now," Hal said with finality. "You'll have an altogether different opinion when you're six."

"Well, what if I will?" the Butcher snapped back. "You don't have to keep *telling* me about it, do you?"

The others were silent. Joggy began to bounce up and down abstractedly on the resilient pavement. Hal called in his three uninjes and said in soothing tones: "Joggy and I are going to swim over to the Time Theater. Want to walk us there, Butch?"

Butch scowled.

"How about it, Butch?"

Still Butch did not seem to hear.

The older boy shrugged and said: "Oh, well, how about it—Butcher?"

The Butcher swung around. "They won't let me in the Time Theater. You said so yourself."

"You could walk us over there."

"Well, maybe I will and maybe I won't."

"While you're deciding, we'll get swimming. Come along, Joggy."

Still scowling, the Butcher took a white soapy crayon from the bulging pocket in his silver shorts. Pressed into the pavement, it made a black mark. He scrawled pensively: KEEP ON THE GRASS.

He gazed at his handiwork. No, darn it, that was just what grownups wanted you to do. This grass couldn't be hurt. You couldn't pull it up or tear it off; it hurt your fingers to try. A rub with the side of the crayon removed the sign. He thought for a moment, then wrote: KEEP OFF THE GRASS.

With an untroubled countenance, he sprang up and hurried after the others.

Joggy and the older boy were swimming lazily through the

air at shoulder height. In the pavement directly under each of them was a wide, saucer-shaped depression which swam along with them. The uninjes avoided the depressions. Darter was strutting on his hind legs, looking up inquiringly at his master.

"Gimme a ride, Hal, gimme a ride!" the Butcher called. The older boy ignored him. "Aw, gimme a ride, Joggy."

"Oh, all right." Joggy touched the small box attached to the front of his broad metal harness and dropped lightly to the ground. The Butcher climbed on his back. There was a moment of rocking and pitching, during which each boy accused the other of trying to upset them.

Then the Butcher got his balance and they began to swim along securely, though at a level several inches lower. Brute sprang up after his master and was invisibly rebuffed. He retired baffled, but a few minutes later he was amusing himself by furious futile efforts to climb the hemispherical repulsor field.

Slowly the little cavalcade of boys and uninjes proceeded down the Avenue of Wisdom. Hal amused himself by stroking toward a tree. When he was about four feet from it, he was gently bounced away.

It was really a more tiring method of transportation than walking and quite useless against the wind. True, by rocking the repulsor hemisphere backward, you could get a brief forward push, but it would be nullified when you rocked forward. A slow swimming stroke was the simplest way to make progress.

The general sensation, however, was delightful and levitators were among the most prized of toys.

"There's the theater," Joggy announced.

"I *know,*" the Butcher said irritably.

But even he sounded a little solemn and subdued. From the Great Ramp to the topmost airy finial, the Time Theater was the dream of a god realized in unearthly substance. It imparted the aura of demigods to the adults drifting up and down the ramp.

"My father remembers when there wasn't a Time Theater," Hal said softly as he scanned the façade's glowing charts and maps. "Say, they're viewing Earth, somewhere in Scandinavia around zero in the B.C.–A.D. time scale. It should be interesting."

"Will it be about Napoleon?" the Butcher asked eagerly. "Or Hitler?" A red-headed adult heard and smiled and paused to watch. A lock of hair had fallen down the middle of the Butcher's forehead, and as he sat Joggy like a charger, he did bear a faint resemblance to one of the grim little egomaniacs of the Dawn Era.

"Wrong millennium," Hal said.

"Tamerlane then?" the Butcher pressed. "He killed cities and piled the skulls. Blood-bath stuff. Oh, yes, and Tamerlane was a Scand of the Navies."

Hal looked puzzled and then quickly erased the expression. "Well, even if it is about Tamerlane, you can't see it. How about it, Joggy?"

"They won't let me in, either."

"Yes, they will. You're five years old now."

"But I don't feel any older," Joggy replied doubtfully.

"The feeling comes at six. Don't worry, the usher will notice the difference."

Hal and Joggy switched off their levitators and dropped to their feet. The Butcher came down rather hard, twisting an ankle. He opened his mouth to cry, then abruptly closed it hard, bearing his pain in tight-lipped silence like an ancient soldier—like Stalin, maybe, he thought. The red-headed adult's face twitched in half-humorous sympathy.

Hal and Joggy mounted the ramp and entered a twilit corridor which drank their faint footsteps and returned pulses of light. The Butcher limped manfully after them, but when he got inside, he forgot his battle injury.

Hal looked back. "Honestly, the usher will stop you."

The Butcher shook his head. "I'm going to think my way in. I'm going to think old."

"You won't be able to fool the usher, Butcher. You under-fives simply aren't allowed in the Time Theater. There's a good reason for it—something dangerous might happen if an under-five got inside."

"Why?"

"I don't exactly know, but something."

"Hah! I bet they're scared we'd go traveling in the Time Bubble and have some excitement."

"They are not. I guess they just know you'd get bored and wander away from your seats and maybe disturb the adults or upset the electronics or something. But don't worry about it, Butcher. The usher will take care of you."

"Shut up—I'm thinking I'm World Director," the Butcher informed them, contorting his face diabolically.

Hal spoke to the uninjes, pointing to the side of the corridor. Obediently four of them lined up.

But Brute was peering down the corridor toward where it merged into a deeper darkness. His short legs stiffened, his neckless head seemed to retreat even further between his powerful shoulders, his lips writhed back to show his gleaming fangs, and a completely unfamiliar sound issued from his throat. A choked, grating sound. A growl. The other uninjes moved uneasily.

"Do you suppose something's the matter with his circuits?" Joggy whispered. "Maybe he's getting racial memories from the Scands."

"Of course not," Hal said irritably.

"Brute, get over there," the Butcher commanded. Unwillingly, eyes still fixed on the blackness ahead, Brute obeyed.

The three boys started on. Hal and Joggy experienced a vaguely electrical tingling that vanished almost immediately. They looked back. The Butcher had been stopped by an invisible wall.

"I told you you couldn't fool the usher," Hal said.

The Butcher hurled himself forward. The wall gave a little, then bounced him back with equal force.

"I bet it'll be a bum time view anyway," the Butcher said, not giving up, but not trying again. "And I still don't think the usher can tell how old you are. I bet there's an overage teacher spying on you through a hole, and if he doesn't like your looks, he switches on the usher."

But the others had disappeared in the blackness. The Butcher waited and then sat down beside the uninjes. Brute laid his head on his knee and growled faintly down the corridor.

"Take it easy, Brute," the Butcher consoled him. "I don't think Tamerlane was really a Scand of the Navies anyhow."

Two chattering girls hardly bigger than himself stepped through the usher as if it weren't there.

The Butcher grimly slipped out the metal tube and put it to his lips. There were two closely spaced faint *plops* and a large green stain appeared on the bare back of one girl, while purple fluid dripped from the close-cropped hair of the other.

They glared at him and one of them said: "A cub!" But he had his arms folded and wasn't looking at them.

Meanwhile, subordinate ushers had guided Hal and Joggy away from the main entrance to the Time Theater. A sphincter dilated and they found themselves in a small transparent cubicle from which they could watch the show without disturbing the adult audience. They unstrapped their levitators, laid them on the floor, and sat down.

The darkened auditorium was circular. Rising from a low central platform was a huge bubble of light, its lower surface somewhat flattened. The audience was seated in concentric rows around the bubble, their keen and compassionate faces dimly revealed by the pale central glow.

But it was the scene within the bubble that riveted the attention of the boys.

Great brooding trees, the trunks of the nearer ones sliced by the bubble's surface, formed the background. Through the dark, wet foliage appeared glimpses of a murky sky, while from the ceiling of the bubble, a ceaseless rain dripped mournfully. A hooded figure crouched beside a little fire partly shielded by a gnarled trunk. Squatting round about were wiry, blue-eyed men with shoulder-length blond hair and full blond beards. They were clothed in furs and metal-studded leather.

Here and there were scattered weapons and armor—long swords glistening with oil to guard them from rust, crudely painted circular shields, and helmets from which curved the horns of beasts. Back and forth, lean, wolflike dogs paced with restless monotony.

Sometimes the men seemed to speak together, or one would rise to peer down the misty forest vistas, but mostly they were motionless. Only the hooded figure, which they seemed to regard with a mingled wonder and fear, swayed incessantly to the rhythm of some unheard chant.

"The Time Bubble has been brought to rest in one of the barbaric cultures of the Dawn Era," a soft voice explained, so casually that Joggy looked around for the speaker, until Hal nudged him sharply, whispering with barely perceptible embarrassment: "Don't do that, Joggy. It's just the electronic interpreter. It senses our development and hears our questions and then it automats background and answers. But it's no more alive than an adolescer or a kinderobot. Got a billion microtapes, though."

The interpreter continued: "The skin-clad men we are viewing in Time in the Round seem to be a group of warriors of the sort who lived by pillage and rapine. The hooded figure is a most unusual find. We believe it to be that of a sorcerer who pretended to control the forces of nature and see into the future."

Joggy whispered: "How is it that we can't see the audience through the other side of the bubble? We can see through this side, all right."

"The bubble only shines light out," Hal told him hurriedly,

to show he knew some things as well as the interpreter. "Nothing, not even light, can get into the bubble from outside. The audience on the other side of the bubble sees into it just as we do, only they're seeing the other way—for instance, they can't see the fire because the tree is in the way. And instead of seeing us beyond, they see more trees and sky."

Joggy nodded. "You mean that whatever way you look at the bubble, it's a kind of hole through time?"

"That's right." Hal cleared his throat and recited: "The bubble is the locus of an infinite number of one-way holes, all centering around two points in space-time, one now and one then. The bubble looks completely open, but if you tried to step inside, you'd be stopped—and so would an atom beam. It takes more energy than an atom beam just to maintain the bubble, let alone maneuver it."

"I see, I guess," Joggy whispered. "But if the hole works for light, why can't the people inside the bubble step out of it into our world?"

"Why—er—you see, Joggy——"

The interpreter took over. "The holes are one-way for light, but no-way for matter. If one of the individuals inside the bubble walked toward you, he would cross-section and disappear. But to the audience on the opposite side of the bubble it would be obvious that he had walked away along the vista down which they are peering."

As if to provide an example, a figure suddenly materialized on their side of the bubble. The wolflike dogs bared their fangs. For an instant, there was only an eerie, distorted, rapidly growing silhouette, changing from blood-red to black as the boundary of the bubble cross-sectioned the intruding figure. Then they recognized the back of another long-haired warrior and realized that the audience on the other side of the bubble had probably seen him approaching for some time.

He bowed to the hooded figure and handed him a small bag.

"More atavistic cubs, big and little! Hold still, Cynthia," a new voice cut in.

Hal turned and saw that two cold-eyed girls had been ushered into the cubicle. One was wiping her close-cropped hair with one hand while mopping a green stain from her friend's back with the other.

Hal nudged Joggy and whispered: "Butch!"

But Joggy was still hypnotized by the Time Bubble.

"Then how is it, Hal," he asked, "that light comes out of the bubble, if the people don't? What I mean is, if one of the people walks toward us, he shrinks to a red blot and disappears. Why doesn't the light coming our way disappear, too?"

"Well—you see, Joggy, it isn't real light. It's——"

Once more the interpreter helped him out.

"The light that comes from the bubble is an isotope. Like atoms of one element, photons of a single frequency also have isotopes. It's more than a matter of polarization. One of these isotopes of light tends to leak futureward through holes in space-time. Most of the light goes down the vistas visible to the other side of the audience. But one isotope is diverted through the walls of the bubble into the Time Theater. Perhaps, because of the intense darkness of the theater, you haven't realized how dimly lit the scene is. That's because we're getting only a single isotope of the orginal light. Incidentally, no isotopes have been discovered that leak pastward, though attempts are being made to synthesize them."

"Oh, explanations!" murmured one of the newly arrived girls. "The cubs are always angling for them. Apple-polishers!"

"*I* like this show," a familiar voice announced serenely. "They cut anybody yet with those choppers?"

Hal looked down beside him. "Butch! How did you manage to get in?"

"I don't see any blood. Where's the bodies?"

"But how *did* you get in—Butcher?"

The Butcher replied airily: "A red-headed man talked to me and said it certainly was sad for a future dictator not to be able to enjoy scenes of carnage in his youth, so I told him I'd been inside the Time Theater and just come out to get a drink of water and go to the eliminator, but then my sprained ankle had got worse—I kind of tried to get up and fell down again—so he picked me up and carried me right through the usher."

"Butcher, that wasn't honest," Hal said a little worriedly. "You tricked him into thinking you were older and his brain waves blanketed yours, going through the usher. I really *have* heard it's dangerous for you under-fives to be in here."

"The way those cubs beg for babying and get it!" one of the girls commented. "Talk about sex favoritism!" She and her companion withdrew to the far end of the cubicle.

The Butcher grinned at them briefly and concentrated his attention on the scene in the Time Bubble.

"Those big dogs—" he began suddenly. "Brute must have smelled 'em."

"Don't be silly," Hal said. "Smells can't come out of the Time Bubble. Smells haven't any isotopes and—"

"I don't care," the Butcher asserted. "I bet somebody'll figure out someday how to use the bubble for time traveling."

"You can't travel in a point of view," Hal contradicted, "and that's all the bubble is. Besides, some scientists think the bubble isn't real at all, but a—uh—"

"I believe," the interpreter cut in smoothly, "that you're thinking of the theory that the Time Bubble operates by hyper-memory. Some scientists would have us believe that all memory is time traveling and that the basic location of the bubble is not space-time at all, but ever-present eternity. Some of them go so far as to state that it is only a mental inability that prevents the Time Bubble from being used for time traveling—just as it may be a similar disability that keeps a robot with the same or even more scopeful memories from being a real man or animal.

"It is because of this minority theory that under-age individuals and other beings with impulsive mentalities are barred from the Time Theater. But do not be alarmed. Even if the minority theory should prove true—and no evidence for it has ever appeared—there are automatically operating safeguards to protect the audience from any harmful consequences of time traveling (almost certainly impossible, remember) in either direction."

"Sissies!" was the Butcher's comment.

"You're rather young to be here, aren't you?" the interpreter inquired.

The Butcher folded his arms and scowled.

The interpreter hesitated almost humanly, probably snatching through a quarter-million microtapes. "Well, you wouldn't have got in unless a qualified adult had certified you as plus-age. Enjoy yourself."

There was no need for the last injunction. The scene within the bubble had acquired a gripping interest. The shaggy warriors were taking up their swords, gathering about the hooded sorcerer. The hood fell back, revealing a face with hawklike, disturbing eyes that seemed to be looking straight out of the bubble at the future.

"This is getting good," the Butcher said, squirming toward the edge of his seat.

"Stop being an impulsive mentality," Hal warned him a little nervously.

"Hah!"

The sorcerer emptied the small bag on the fire and a thick cloud of smoke puffed toward the ceiling of the bubble. A clawlike hand waved wildly. The sorcerer appeared to be expostulating, commanding. The warriors stared uncomprehendingly, which seemed to exasperate the sorcerer.

"That's right," the Butcher approved loudly. "Sock it to 'em!"

"Butcher!" Hal admonished.

Suddenly the bubble grew very bright, as if the Sun had

just shone forth in the ancient world, though the rain still dripped down.

"A viewing anomaly has occurred," the interpreter announced. "It may be necessary to collapse the Time Bubble for a short period."

In a frenzy, his ragged robes twisting like smoke, the sorcerer rushed at one of the warriors, pushing him backward so that in a moment he must cross-section.

"Attaboy!" the Butcher encouraged.

Then the warrior was standing outside the bubble, blinking toward the shadows, rain dripping from his beard and furs.

"Oh, *boy!*" the Butcher cheered in ecstasy.

"Butcher, you've done it!" Hal said, aghast.

"I sure did," the Butcher agreed blandly, "but that old guy in the bubble helped me. Must take two to work it."

"Keep your seats!" the interpreter said loudly. "We are energizing the safeguards!"

The warriors inside the bubble stared in stupid astonishment after the one who had disappeared from their view. The sorcerer leaped about, pushing them in his direction.

Abrupt light flooded the Time Theater. The warriors who had emerged from the bubble stiffened themselves, baring their teeth.

"The safeguards are now energized," the interpreter said.

A woman in a short golden tunic stood up uncertainly from the front row of the audience.

The first warrior looked her up and down, took one hesitant step forward, then another, then suddenly grabbed her and flung her over his left shoulder, looking around menacingly and swinging his sword in his right hand.

"I repeat, the safeguards have been fully energized! Keep your seats!" the interpreter enjoined.

In the cubicle, Hal and Joggy gasped, the two girls squeaked, but the Butcher yelled a "Hey!" of disapproval, snatched up something from the floor, and darted out through the sphincter.

Here and there in the audience other adults stood up. The emerged warriors formed a ring of swinging swords and questing eyes. Between their legs their wolfish dogs, emerged with them, crouched and snarled. Then the warriors began to fan out.

"There has been an unavoidable delay in energizing the safeguards," the interpreter said. "Please be patient."

At that moment the Butcher entered the main auditorium, brandishing a levitator above his head and striding purposefully down the aisle. At his heels five stocky forms trotted. In a definitely pre-civilization voice, or at least with pre-civilization volume, he bellowed: "Hey, you! You quit that!"

The first warrior looked toward him, gave his left shoulder a shake to quiet his wriggling captive, gave his right shoulder one to supple his sword arm, and waited until the dwarfish challenger came into range. Then his sword swished down in a flashing arc.

Next moment, the Butcher was on his knees and the warrior was staring at him open-mouthed. The sword had rebounded from something invisible an arm's length above the gnome-like creature's head. The warrior backed a step.

The Butcher stayed down, crouching half behind an aisle seat and digging for something in his pocket. But he didn't stay quiet. "Sic 'em, Brute!" he shrilled. "Sic 'em, Darter! Sic 'em, Pinkie and Whitie and Blue!" Then he stopped shouting and raised his hand to his mouth.

Growling quite unmechanically, the five uninjes hurled themselves forward and closed with the warrior's wolflike dogs. At the first encounter, Brute and Pinkie were grabbed by the throats, shaken, and tossed a dozen feet. The warriors snarled approval and advanced. But then Brute and Pinkie raced back eagerly to the fight—and suddenly the face of the leading warrior was drenched with scarlet. He blinked and touched his fingers to it, then looked at his hand in horror.

The Butcher spared a second to repeat his command to the uninjes. But already the battle was going against the larger dogs. The latter had the advantage of weight and could toss the smaller dogs like so many foxes. But their terrible fangs did no damage, and whenever an uninj clamped on a throat, that throat was torn out.

Meanwhile, great bloody stains had appeared on the bodies of all the warriors. They drew back in a knot, looking at each other fearfully. That was when the Butcher got to his feet and strode forward, hand clenching the levitator above his head.

"Get back where you belong, you big jerks! And drop that lady!"

The first warrior pointed toward him and hissed something. Immediately, a half dozen swords were smiting at the Butcher.

"We are working to energize the safeguards," the interpreter said in mechanical panic. "Remain patient and in your seats."

The uninjes leaped into the melee, at first tearing more fur than flesh. Swords caught them and sent them spinning through the air. They came yapping back for more. Brute fixed on the first warrior's ankle. He dropped the woman, stamped unavailingly on the uninj, and let out a screech.

Swords were still rebounding from the invisible shield under which the Butcher crouched, making terrible faces at his attackers. They drew back, looked again at their bloodstains, goggled at the demon dogs. At their leader's screech, they broke and plunged back into the Time Bubble, their leader stumbling limpingly after them. There they wasted no time on their own ragged sorcerer. Their swords rose and fell, and no repulsor field stayed them.

"Brute, come back!" the Butcher yelled.

The gray uninj let go his hold on the leader's ankle and scampered out of the Time Bubble, which swiftly dimmed to its orginal light intensity and then winked out.

For once in their very mature lives, all of the adults in the auditorium began to jabber at each other simultaneously.

"We are sorry, but the anomaly has made it necessary to collapse the Time Bubble," the interpreter said. "There will be no viewing until further announcement. Thank you for your patience."

Hal and Joggy caught up with the Butcher just as Brute jumped into his arms and the woman in gold picked him up and hugged him fiercely. The Butcher started to pull away, then grudgingly submitted.

"Cubs!" came a small cold voice from behind Hal and Joggy. "Always playing hero! Say, what's that awful smell, Cynthia? It must have come from those dirty past men."

Hal and Joggy were shouting at the Butcher, but he wasn't listening to them or to the older voices clamoring about "revised theories of reality" and other important things. He didn't even squirm as Brute licked his cheek and the woman in gold planted a big kiss practically on his mouth.

He smiled dreamily and stroked Brute's muzzle and murmured softly: "We came, we saw, we conquered, didn't we, Brute?"

Help! I Am Dr. Morris Goldpepper

By AVRAM DAVIDSON

Physicists and engineers can't help—only my colleagues can bridge the interstellar cavity to yank me out of my aching plight!

Four of the men, Weinroth, McAllister, Danbourge, and Smith, sat at the table under the cold blue lighting tubes. One of them, Rorke, was in a corner speaking quietly into a telephone, and one, Fadderman, stood staring out the window at the lights of the city. One, Hansen, had yet to arrive.

Fadderman spoke without turning his head. He was the oldest of those present—the Big Seven, as they were often called.

"Lights," he said. "So many lights. Down here." He waved his hand toward the city. "Up there." He gestured toward the sky. "Even with our much-vaunted knowledge, what," he asked, "do we know?" He turned his head. "Perhaps this is too big for us. In the light of the problem, can we really hope to accomplish anything?"

Heavy-set Danbourge frowned grimly. "We have received the suffrage of our fellow scientists, Doctor. We can but try."

Lithe, handsome McAllister, the youngest officer of the Association, nodded. "The problem is certainly not greater than that which faced our late, great colleague, the immortal Morton." He pointed to a picture on the paneled wall. "And we all know what *he* accomplished."

Fadderman went over and took his hand. "Your words fill me with courage."

McAllister flushed with pleasure.

"I am an old man," Fadderman added falteringly. "Forgive my lack of spirit, Doctor." He sat down, sighed, shook his head slowly. Weinroth, burly and red-haired, patted him gently on the back. Natty, silvery-haired little Smith smiled at him consolingly.

A buzzer sounded. Rorke hung up the telephone, flipped a switch on the wall intercom. "Headquarters here," he said crisply.

"Dr. Carl T. Hansen has arrived," a voice informed him.

"Bring him up at once," he directed. "And, Nickerson——"

"Yes, Dr. Rorke?"

"Let no one else into the building. *No* one."

They sat in silence. After a moment or two, they heard the approach of the elevator, heard the doors slide open, slide shut, heard the elevator descend. Heavy, steady footsteps approached; knuckles rapped on the opaque glass door.

Rorke went over to the door, said, "A conscientious and diligent scientist——"

"—must remain a continual student," a deep voice finished the quotation.

Rorke unlocked the door, peered out into the corridor, admitted Hansen, locked the door.

"I would have been here sooner, but another emergency interposed," Hansen said. "A certain political figure—ethics prevent my being more specific—suffered an oral hemorrhage following an altercation with a woman who shall be nameless, but, boy, did she pack a wallop! A so-called *Specialist*, gentlemen, with offices on Park Avenue, had been, as he called it, 'applying pressure' with a gauze pad. I merely used a little Gelfoam as a coagulant agent and the hemorrhage stopped almost at once. When will the public learn, eh, gentlemen?"

Faint smiles played upon the faces of the assembled scientists. Hansen took his seat. Rorke bent down and lifted two tape-recording devices to the table, set them both in motion. The faces of the men became serious, grim.

"This is an emergency session of the Steering Committee of the Executive Committee of the American Dental Association," Rorke said, "called to discuss measures of dealing with the case of Dr. Morris Goldpepper. One tape will be deposited in the vaults of the Chase Manhattan Bank in New York; the other will be similarly secured in the vaults of the Wells Fargo and Union Trust Company Bank in San Francisco. Present at this session are Doctors Rorke, Weinroth and Smith—President, First and Second Vice-presidents, respectively—Fadderman, Past President, McAllister, Public Information, Danbourge, Legal, and Hansen, Policy."

He looked around at the set, tense faces.

"Doctors," he went on, "I think I may well say that humanity is, as of this moment, face to face with a great danger, and it is a bitter jest that it is not to the engineers or the astronomers, not to medicine nor yet to nuclear nor any other kind of physics, that humanity must now look for salvation —but to the members of the dental profession!"

His voice rose. "Yes—to the practitioners of what has become perhaps the least regarded of all the learned sciences! It is indeed ironical. We may at this juncture consider the comments of the now deceased Professor Earnest Hooton, the Harvard anthropologist, who observed with a sorrow which did him credit that his famed University, instead of assisting its Dental School as it ought, treated it—and I quote his exact words—'Like a yellow dog.'" His voice trembled.

McAllister's clean-cut face flushed an angry red. Weinroth growled. Danbourge's fist hit the table and stayed there, clenched. Fadderman gave a soft, broken sigh.

"But enough of this. We are not jealous, nor are we vindictive," President Rorke went on. "We are confident that History, 'with its long tomorrow,' will show how, at this danger-fraught point, the humble and little-thought-of followers of dental science recognized and sized up the situation and stood shoulder to shoulder on the ramparts!"

He wiped his brow with a paper tissue. "And now I will call upon our beloved Past President, Dr. Samuel I. Fadderman, to begin our review of the incredible circumstances which have brought us here tonight. Dr. Fadderman? If you please . . ."

The well-known Elder Statesman of the A.D.A. nodded his head slowly. He made a little cage of his fingers and pursed and then unpursed his lips. At length he spoke in a soft and gentle voice.

"My first comment, brethren, is that I ask for compassion. *Morris Goldpepper is not to blame!*

"Let me tell you a few words about him. Goldpepper the Scientist needs no introduction. Who has not read, for instance, his 'The Bilateral Vertical Stroke and Its Influence on the Pattern of Occlusion' or his 'Treatment, Planning, Assemblage and Cementation of a 14-Unit Fixed Bridge'—to name only two? But I shall speak about Goldpepper the Man. He is forty-six years of age and served with honor in the United States Navy Dental Corps during the Second World War. He has been a widower since shortly after the conclusion of that conflict. Rae—the late Mrs. Goldpepper, may she rest in peace—often used to say, 'Morry, if I go first, promise me you'll marry again,' but he passed it off with a joke; and, as you know, he never did.

"They had one child, a daughter, Suzanne, a very sweet girl, now married to a Dr. Sheldon Fingerhut, D.D.S. I need not tell you, brethren, how proud our colleague was when his only child married this very fine young member of our profession. The Fingerhuts are now located on Unbalupi, one of the Micronesian islands forming part of the United States

Trust Territory, where Dr. Sheldon is teaching dental hygiene, sanitation, and prosthesis to the natives thereof."

Dr. Hansen asked, "Are they aware of—"

"The son-in-law knows something of the matter," the older man said. "He has not seen fit to inform his wife, who is in a delicate condition and expects shortly to be confined. At his suggestion, I have been writing—or, rather, typing—letters purporting to come from her father, on his stationery, with the excuse that he badly singed his fingers on a Bunsen burner while annealing a new-type hinge for dentures and consequently cannot hold his pen." He sipped from a glass of water.

"Despite his great scientific accomplishments," Dr. Fadderman went on, "Morry had an impractical streak in him. Often I used to call on him at his bachelor apartment in the Hotel Davenport on West End Avenue, where he moved following his daughter's marriage, and I would find him immersed in reading matter of an escapist kind—tales of crocodile hunters on the Malay Peninsula, or magazines dealing with interplanetary warfare, or collections of short stories about vampires and werewolves and similar superstitious creations.

" 'Morry,' I said reproachfully, 'what a way to spend your off-hours. Is it worth it? Is it healthy? You would do much better, believe me, to frequent the pool or the handball court at the Y. Or,' I pointed out to him, 'if you want to read, why ignore the rich treasures of literature: Shakespeare, Ruskin, Elbert Hubbard, Edna Ferber, and so on? Why retreat to these immature-type fantasies?' At first he only smiled and quoted the saying, 'Each to his or her own taste.' "

The silence which followed was broken by young Dr. McAllister. "You say," he said, " 'at first.' "

Old Dr. Fadderman snapped out of his reverie. "Yes, yes. But eventually he confessed the truth to me. He withheld nothing."

The assembled dental scientists then learned that the same

Dr. Morris Goldpepper, who had been awarded not once but three successive times the unique honor of the Dr. Alexander Peabody Medal for New Achievements in Dental Prosthesis, was obsessed with the idea that *there was sentient life on other worlds—that it would shortly be possible to reach these other worlds—and that he himself desired to be among those who went.*

" 'Do you realize, Sam?' he asked me," reported Fadderman. " 'Do you realize that, in a very short time, it will no longer be a question of fuel or even of metallurgy? That submarines capable of cruising for weeks and months without surfacing foretell the possibility of traveling through airless space? The chief problem has now come down to finding how to build a takeoff platform capable of withstanding a thrust of several million pounds.' And his eyes glowed."

Dr. Fadderman had inquired, with good-natured sarcasm, how the other man expected this would involve *him.* The answer was as follows: Any interplanetary expedition would find it just as necessary to take along a dentist as to take along a physician, and that he—Dr. Goldpepper—intended to be that dentist!

Dr. Weinroth's hand slapped the table with a bang. "By thunder, I say the man had courage!"

Dr. Rorke looked at him with icy reproof. "I should be obliged," he said stiffly, "if there would be no further emotional outbursts."

Dr. Weinroth's face fell. "I beg the Committee's pardon, Mr. President," he said.

Dr. Rorke nodded graciously, indicated by a gesture of his hand that Dr. Fadderman had permission to continue speaking. The old man took a letter from his pocket and placed it on the table.

"This came to me like a bolt from the blue beyond. It is dated November 8 of last year. Skipping the formal salutation, it reads: 'At last I stand silent upon the peak in Darien' —a literary reference, gentlemen, to Cortez's alleged discovery of the Pacific Ocean; actually it was Balboa—'my great dream is about to be realized. Before long, I shall be back to tell you about it, but just exactly when, I am not able to say. History is being made! Long live Science! Sincerely yours, Morris Goldpepper, D.D.S.'"

He passed the letter around the table.

Dr. Smith asked, "What did you do on receiving this communication, Doctor?"

Dr. Fadderman had at once taken a taxi to West End Avenue. The desk clerk at the hotel courteously informed him that the man he sought had left on a vacation of short but not exactly specified duration. No further information was known. Dr. Fadderman's first thought was that his younger friend had gotten some sort of position with a government project which he was not free to discuss, and his own patriotism and sense of duty naturally prevented him from making inquiries.

"But I began, for the first time," the Elder Statesman of American Dentistry said, "to read up on the subject of space travel. I wondered how a man forty-six years of age could possibly hope to be selected over younger men."

Dr. Danbourge spoke for the first time. "Size," he said. "Every ounce would count in a spaceship and Morris was a pretty little guy."

"But with the heart of a lion," Dr. Weinroth said softly. "Miles and miles and miles of heart."

The other men nodded their agreement to this tribute.

But as time went on and the year drew to its close and he heard no word from his friend, Dr. Fadderman began to worry. Finally, when he received a letter from the Fingerhuts saying that *they* had not been hearing either, he took action.

He realized it was not likely that the Government would have made plans to include a dentist in this supposed project without communicating with the A.D.A. and he inquired of the current President, Dr. Rorke, if he had any knowledge of such a project, or of the whereabouts of the missing man. The answer to both questions was no. But on learning the reasons for Dr. Fadderman's concern, he communicated with Col. Lemuel Coggins, head of the USAF's Dental Corps.

Colonel Coggins informed him that no one of Dr. Goldpepper's name or description was or had been affiliated with any such project, and that, in fact, any such project was still —as he put it—"still on the drawingboard."

Drs. Rorke and Fadderman, great as was their concern, hesitated to report Dr. Goldpepper missing. He had, after all, paid rent on apartment, office, and laboratory, well in advance. He was a mature man, of very considerable intelligence, and one who presumably knew what he was doing.

"It is at this point," said Dr. Danbourge, "that I enter the picture. On the eleventh of January, I had a call from a Dr. Milton Wilson, who has an office on East Nineteenth Street, with a small laboratory adjoining, where he does prosthetic work. He told me, with a good deal of hesitation, that something exceedingly odd had come up, and he asked me if I knew where Dr. Morris Goldpepper was. . . ."

The morning of the eleventh of January, an elderly man with a curious foreign accent came into Dr. Wilson's office, gave the name of Smith, and complained about an upper plate. It did not feel comfortable, Mr. Smith said, and it irritated the roof of his mouth. There was a certain reluctance on his part to allow Dr. Wilson to examine his mouth. This was understandable, because the interior of his mouth was blue. The gums were entirely edentulous, very hard, almost horny. The plate itself——

"Here is the plate," Dr. Danbourge said, placing it on the table. "Dr. Wilson supplied him with another. You will observe the perforations on the upper, or palatal, surface. They had been covered with a thin layer of gum arabic, which naturally soon wore almost entirely off, with the result that the roof of the mouth became irritated. Now this is so very unusual that Dr. Wilson—as soon as his patient, the so-called

Mr. Smith, was gone—broke open the weirdly made plate to find why the perforations had been made. In my capacity as head of the Association's Legal Department," Dr. Danbourge stated, "I have come across some extraordinary occurrences, but nothing like *this*."

This was a small piece of a white, flexible substance, covered with tiny black lines. Danbourge picked up a large magnifying glass.

"You may examine these objects, Doctors," he said, "but it will save your eyesight if I read to you from an enlarged photostatic copy of this last one. The nature of the material, the method of writing, or of reducing the writing to such size —all are unknown to us. It may be something on the order of microfilm. But that is not important. The important thing is the *content* of the writing—the *portent* of the writing.

"Not since Dr. Morton, the young Boston dentist, realized the uses of sulphuric ether as an anesthetic has any member of our noble profession discovered anything of even remotely similar importance; and perhaps not before, either."

He drew his spectacles from their case and began to read aloud.

Despite the fact that our great profession lacks the glamour and public adulation of the practice of medicine, and even the druggists—not having a Hippocratic Oath—can preen themselves on their so-called Oath of Maimonides (though, believe me, the great Maimonides had no more to do with it than Morris Goldpepper, D.D.S.), no one can charge us with not having as high a standard of ethics and professional conduct as physicians and surgeons, M.D. Nor do I hesitate for one single moment to include prostheticians not holding the degree of Doctor of Dental Surgery or Doctor of Dental Medicine, whose work is so vital and essential.

When the records of our civilization are balanced, then— but perhaps not before—the real importance of dental science will be appreciated. Now it is merely valued at the moment of toothache.

It is only with a heavy heart that I undertake deliberately to produce inferior work, and with the confidence that all those to whom the standards of oral surgery and dental prosthetics are dear will understand the very unusual circumstances which have prompted me so to do. And, understanding, will forgive. No one can hold the standards of our profession higher or more sacred than I.

It must be admitted that I was not very amused on a certain occasion when my cousin, Nathaniel Pomerance, introduced me to an engineering contractor with these words, "You two should have a lot in common—you both build bridges," and uttered a foolish laugh. But I venture to say that this was one of the truest words ever spoken in questionable jest.

Humility is one thing, false pride another. Those who know anything of modern dentistry at all know of the Goldpepper Bridge and the Goldpepper Crown. It is I, Dr. Morris Goldpepper, inventor of both, and perfector of the Semi-retractable Clasp which bears my name, who writes these words you see before you. Nothing further should be needful by way of identification. And now to my report.

On the first of November, a day of evil import forever in the personal calendar of the unhappy wretch who writes these lines, not even knowing for sure if they will ever be read—but what else can I do?—shortly after 5 P.M., my laboratory door was knocked on. I found there a curious-looking man of shriveled and weazened appearance. He asked if I was Dr. Morris Goldpepper, "the famous perfector of the Semi-retractable Clasp," and I pleaded guilty to the flattering impeachment.

The man had a foreign-sounding accent, or—I thought—it may be that he had an impediment in his speech. Might he see me, was his next question. I hesitated.

It has happened to me before, and to most other practitioners—a stranger comes and, before you know it, he is slandering some perfectly respectable D.D.S. or D.M.D. The dentist pulled a healthy tooth—the dentist took such and such a huge sum of money for new plates—they don't fit him, he suffers great anguish—he's a poor man, the dentist won't do anything —*et cetera, ad infinitum nauseamque.* In short, a nut, a crank, a crackpot.

But while I was hesitating, the man yawned, did not courteously cover his mouth with his hand, and I observed to my astonishment that the interior of his mouth was an odd shade of blue!

Bemused by this singular departure from normalcy, I allowed him to enter. Then I wondered what to say, since he himself was saying nothing, but he looked around the lab with interest. "State your business" would be too brusque, and "Why is your mouth blue?" would be too gauche. An impasse.

Whilst holding up a large-scale model of the Goldpepper Cap (not yet perfected—will it ever be? Alas, who knows?) this curious individual said, "I know all about you, Dentist Goldpepper. A great scientist, you are. A man of powerful imagination, you are. One who rebels against narrow horizons and yearns to soar to wide and distant worlds, you are."

All I could think of to say was, "And what can I do for *you?*"

It was all so true; every single word he said was true. In my vanity was my downfall. I was tricked like the crow with the cheese in the ancient fable of Aesop.

The man proceeded to tell me, frankly enough, that he was a denizen of another planet. He had *two hearts,* would you believe it? And, consequently, two circulatory systems. Two pulses—one in each arm, one slow, the other fast.

It reminded me of the situation in Philadelphia some years ago when there were two telephone systems—if you had only a Bell phone, you couldn't call anyone who had only a Keystone phone.

The interior of his mouth was blue and so was the inside of his eyelids. He said his world had three moons.

You may imagine my emotions at hearing that my long-felt dream to communicate with otherworldly forms of sentient life was at last realized! And to think that they had singled out *not* the President of the United States, *not* the Director-General of the U.N., but *me,* Morris Goldpepper, D.D.S.! Could human happiness ask for more, was my unspoken question. I laughed softly to myself and I thought, What would my cousin Nathaniel Pomerance say *now?* I was like wax in this extraterrestrial person's hands (he had six distinct and articulate digits on each one), and I easily agreed to say nothing to anyone until the question of diplomatic recognition could be arranged on a higher echelon.

"Non-recognition *has* its advantages, Goldpepper Dental Surgeon," he said with a slight smile. "No passport for your visit, you will need."

Well! A personal invitation to visit Proxima Centauri Gamma, or whatever the planet's name is! But I felt constrained to look this gift-horse just a little closer in the mouth. How is it that they came inviting *me,* not, let us say, Oppenheimer? Well?

"Of his gifts not in need, we are, Surgical Goldpepper. We have passed as far beyond nuclear power as you have beyond wind power. We can span the Universe—*but in dentistry, like children still, we are.* Come and inspect our facilities of your science, Great Goldpepper. If you say, 'This: Yes,' then it will be yes. If you direct, 'This: No,' then it will be no. In respect to the science of dentistry, our Edison and our Columbus, you will be."

I asked when we would leave and he said in eight days. I asked how long the trip would take. For a moment, I was baffled when he said it would take no longer than to walk the equivalent of the length of the lab floor. Then he revealed his meaning to me: matter transmission! Of course. No spaceship needed.

My next emotion was a brief disappointment at not being able to see the blazing stars in black outer space. But, after all, one ought not be greedy at such a time.

I cannot point out too strongly that at no time did I accept or agree to accept any payment or gratuity for this trip. I looked upon it in the same light as the work I have done for various clinics.

"Should I take along books? Equipment? What?" I asked my (so-to-speak) guide.

He shook his head. Only my presence was desired on the first trip. A visit of inspection. Very well.

On the morning of November 8, I wrote a brief note to my old and dear friend, Dr. Samuel Fadderman, the senior mentor of American Dentistry [on hearing these words, the Elder Statesman sobbed softly into his cupped hands], and in the afternoon, so excited and enthralled that I noticed no more of my destination than that it was north of the Washington Market, I accompanied my guide to a business building in the aforesaid area.

He led me into a darkened room. He clicked a switch. There was a humming noise, a feeling first of heaviness, then of weightlessness, and then an odd sort of light came on.

I was no longer on the familiar planet of my birth! I was on an unknown world!

Over my head, the three moons of this far-off globe sailed majestically through a sky wherein I could note unfamiliar constellations. The thought occurred to me that poets on this planet would have to find another rhyme, inasmuch as *moons* (plural form) does not go with *June* (singular form). One satellite was a pale yellow, one was brown, and the third was a creamy pink. Not knowing the names of these lunary orbs in the native tongue, I decided to call them Vanilla, Chocolate, and Strawberry.

Whilst my mind was filled with these droll fancies, I felt a tug at my sleeve, where my guide was holding it. He gestured and I followed.

"Now," I thought to myself, "he will bring me before the President of their Galactic Council, or whatever he is called," and I stood obediently within a circle marked on the surface of the platform whereon we stood.

In a moment, we were matter-transported to an inside room somewhere, and there I gazed about me in stupefaction, not to say astonishment. My eyes discerned the forms of Bunsen burners, Baldor lathes, casting machines and ovens, denture trays, dental stone, plaster, shellac trays, wires of teeth, and all the necessary equipment of a fully equipped dental prosthetic laboratory.

My surprise at the progress made by these people in the science at which they were allegedly still children was soon mitigated by the realization that all the items had been made on Earth.

As I was looking and examining, a door opened and several people entered. Their faces were a pale blue, and I realized suddenly that my guide must be wearing makeup to conceal his orginal complexion. They spoke together in their native dialect; then one of them, with a rod of some kind in his hand, turned to me. He opened his mouth. I perceived his gums were bare.

"Dentical person," he said, "make me teeth."

I turned in some perplexity to my guide. "I understood you to say my first visit would be one of inspection only."

Everyone laughed, and I observed that all were equally toothless.

The man in the chair poked me rudely with his rod or staff. "Talk not! Make teeth!"

Fuming with a well-justified degree of indignation, I protested at such a gross breach of the laws of common hospitality. Then, casting concealment to the winds, these people informed me as follows:

Their race is entirely toothless in the adult stage. They are an older race than ours and are born looking ancient and wrinkled. It is only comparatively recently that they have established contact with Earth, and in order that they should not appear conspicuous, and in order to be able to eat our food, they realized that they must be supplied with artificial teeth.

My so-called guide, false friend, my enticer and/or kidnaper, to give him his due, had gotten fitted at a dentist's in New York and cunningly inquired who was the leading man in the field. Alas for fame! The man answered without a second of hesitation, "That is no other one than Morris Goldpepper, D.D.S., perfector of the Semi-retractable Clasp."

First this unscrupulous extraterrestrial procured the equipment, then he procured *me*.

"Do I understand that you purport that I assist you in a plan to thwart and otherwise circumvent the immigration laws of the United States?" was my inquiry.

The man in the chair poked me with his rod again. "You understand! So now make teeth!"

What a proposition to make to a law-abiding, patriotic American citizen by birth! What a demand to exact of a war veteran, a taxpayer, and one who has been three times on jury duty since 1946 alone (People vs. Garrity, People vs. Vanderdam, and Lipschutz vs. Krazy-Kut Kool Kaps, Inc.)! My whole being revolted. I spoke coldly to them, informing them that the situation was contrary to my conception of dental ethics. But to no avail.

My treacherous dragoman drew a revolver from his pocket. "Our weapons understand, you do not. Primitive Earth weapons, yes. So proceed with manufacture, Imprisoned Goldpepper."

I went hot and cold. Not, I beg of you to understand, with fear, but with humiliation. *Imprisoned Goldpepper!* The phrase, with all the connotations it implied, rang in my ears.

I bowed my head and a phrase from the literary work *Sampson Agonistes* (studied as a student in the College of the City of New York) rang through my mind:

Eyeless in Gaza, grinding corn . . .
Oh, blind, blind, blind, amidst the
blaze of noon. . . .

But even in this hour of mental agony, an agony which has scarcely abated to speak of, I had the first glimmering of the idea which I hope will enable me to warn Earth.

Without a word, but only a scornful glance to show these blue-complected individuals how well I appreciated that their so-called advanced science was a mere veneer over the base metal of their boorishness, I set to work. I made the preliminary impressions and study casts, using an impression tray with oval floor form, the best suited for taking impressions of edentulous ridges.

And so began the days of my slavery.

Confined as I am here, there is neither day nor night, but an unremitting succession of frenum trims, post dams, boxing in, pouring up, festoon carving, fixing sprue channels, and all the innumerable details of dental prosthetic work. No one assists me. No one converses with me, save in brusque barks relevant to the work at hand. My food consists of liqueous and gelatinous substances such as might be expected would form the diet of a toothless race.

Oh, I am sick of the sight of their blue skins, bluer mouths, and horny ridges! I am sick of my serfdom!

I have been given material to keep records and am writing this in expectation of later reducing it in size by the method here employed, and of thereinafter inserting copies between the palatal and occlusual surfaces of the plates. It will be necessary to make such plates imperfect, so that the wearers will be obliged to go to dentists on Earth for repairs, because it is not always practical for them to matterport—in fact, I believe they can only do it on the eighth day of every third month. Naturally, I cannot do this to every plate, for they might become suspicious.

You may well imagine how it goes against my grain to

produce defective work, but I have no other choice. Twice they have brought me fresh dental supplies, which is how I calculate their matterporting cycle. I have my wristwatch with me and thus I am enabled to reckon the passing of time.

What their exact purpose is in going to Earth, I do not know. My growing suspicion is that their much-vaunted superior science is a fraud and that their only superiority lies in the ability to matterport. One curious item may give a clue: They have questioned me regarding the Old Age Assistance programs of the several States. As I have said, they all *look* old.

Can it be that elsewhere on this planet there is imprisoned some poor devil of a terrestrial printer or engraver, toiling under duress to produce forged birth certificates and other means of identification, to the fell purpose of allowing these aliens to live at ease at the financial expense of the already overburdened U. S. taxpayer?

To whom shall I address my plea for help? To the Federal Government? But it has no official or even unofficial knowledge that this otherworldly race exists. The F.B.I.? But does matterporting under false pretenses to another planet constitute kidnaping across State lines?

It seems the only thing I can do is to implore whichever dental practitioner reads these lines to communicate at once with the American Dental Association. I throw myself upon the mercy of my fellow professional men.

Dentists and Dental Prostheticians! Beware of men with blue mouths and horny, edentulous ridges! Do not be deceived by flattery and false promises! Remember the fate of that most miserable of men, Morris Goldpepper, D.D.S., and, in his horrible predicament, help, oh, help him!

A long silence followed the reading of this document. At length it was broken by Dr. Hansen.

"That brave man," he said in a husky voice. "That brave little man."

"Poor Morris," said Dr. Danbourge. "Think of him imprisoned on a far-off planet, slaving like a convict in a salt mine, so to speak, making false teeth for these inhuman aliens, sending these messages to us across the trackless void. It's pitiful, and yet, Doctors, it is also a tribute to the indomitable spirit of Man!"

Dr. Weinroth moved his huge hands. "I'd like to get ahold of just one of those blue bastards," he growled.

Dr. Rorke cleared his throat. All present looked at their President respectfully and eagerly.

"I need hardly tell you, Doctors," he said crisply, "that the A.D.A. is a highly conservative organization. We do not go about things lightly. One such message we might ignore, but there have been eleven reported, all identical with the first. Even eleven such messages we might perhaps not consider, but when they come from a prominent scientist of the stature of Dr. Morris Goldpepper—

"Handwriting experts have pronounced this to be *his* handwriting beyond cavil of a doubt. Here"—he delved into a box—"are the eleven plates in question. Can any of you look at these clean lines and deny that they are the work of the incomparable Goldpepper?"

The six other men looked at the objects, shook their heads.

"Beautiful," murmured Dr. Smith, "even in their broken state. Poems in plastic! M. G. *couldn't* produce bad work if he tried!"

Dr. Rorke continued. "Each report confirmed that the person who brought in the plate had a blue mouth and edentulous ridges, just as the message states. Each blue-mouthed patient exhibited the outward appearance of old age. *And*, gentlemen, of those eleven, no less than *eight* were reported from the State of California. Do you realize what that means? California offers the highest amount of financial assistance to the elderly! Goldpepper's surmise was right!"

Dr. Hansen leaned forward. "In addition, our reports show that five of those eight are leaders in the fight against fluoridation of drinking water! It is my carefully considered belief that there is something in their physical makeup, evolved on another planet, which cannot tolerate fluorine even in minute quantities, because they certainly—being already toothless—wouldn't be concerned with the prevention of decay."

Young Dr. McAllister took the floor. "We have checked with dental supply houses and detail men in the New York metropolitan area and we found that large quantities of prosthetic supplies have been delivered to an otherwise unknown outfit—called the Echs Export Company—located not far north of the Washington Market! There is every reason to believe that this is the place Dr. Goldpepper mentioned. One of our men went there, found present only one man, in appearance an *old* man. Our representative feigned deafness, thus obliging this person to open his mouth and talk loudly. Doctors, he reports that this person *has a blue mouth!*"

There was a deep intake of breath around the table.

Dr. Rorke leaned forward and snapped off the tape recorders. "This next is off the record. It is obvious, Doctors, that no ordinary methods will suffice to settle this case, to ensure the return of our unfortunate colleague, or to secure the withdrawal of these extraterrestrial individuals from our nation and planet. I cannot, of course, officially endorse what might be termed 'strong-arm' methods. At the same time, I feel that our adversaries are not entitled to polite treatment. And obviously the usual channels of law enforcement are completely closed to us.

"Therefore—and remember, no word of this must pass outside our circle—therefore I have communicated something of this matter to Mr. Albert Annapollo, the well-known waterfront figure, who not long ago inaugurated the splendid Longshoremen's Dental Health Plan. Mr. Annapollo is a somewhat rough person, but he is nonetheless a *loyal* American. . . .

"We know now the Achilles heel of these alien creatures. It is fluorine. We know also how to identify them. And I think we may shortly be able to announce results. Meanwhile—" he drew a slip of paper from his pocket—"it is already the first of the month in that quarter when the dental supplies are due to be transported—or matterported, as Dr. Goldpepper terms it—to their distant destination. A large shipment is waiting to be delivered from the warehouses of a certain wholesaler to the premises of the Echs Export Company. I have had copies of this made and wrapped around each three-ounce bottle of Ellenbogen's Denture Stik-Phast. I presume it meets with your approval."

He handed it to Dr. Hansen, who, as the others present nodded in grimly emphatic approval, read it aloud:

"From The American Dental Association, representing over 45,000 registered dentists in the United States and its Territories, to Dr. Morris Goldpepper, wherever you may be: DO NOT DESPAIR! We are intent upon your rescue! We will bend every effort to this end! We shall fight the good fight!

"Have courage, Dr. Morris Goldpepper! You shall return!"

A Wind Is Rising

By FINN O'DONNEVAN

They knew how to survive—but what were the odds on a world where every good hurricane in the Galaxy went when it died!

Outside, a wind was rising. But within the station the two men had other things on their minds. Clayton turned the handle of the water faucet again and waited. Nothing happened.

"Try hitting it," said Nerishev.

Clayton pounded the faucet with his fist. Two drops of water came out. A third drop trembled on the spigot's lip, swayed, and fell. That was all.

"That does it," Clayton said bitterly. "That damned water pipe is blocked again. How much water we got in storage?"

"Four gallons—assuming the tank hasn't sprung another leak," said Nerishev. He stared at the faucet, tapping it with long, nervous fingers. He was a big, pale man with a sparse beard, fragile looking in spite of his size. He didn't look like the type to operate an observation station on a remote and alien planet. But the Advance Exploration Corps had discovered, to its regret, that there was no type to operate a station.

Nerishev was a competent biologist and botanist. Although

chronically nervous, he had surprising reserves of calm. He was the sort of man who needs an occasion to rise to. This, if anything, made him suitable to pioneer a planet like Carella I.

"I suppose somebody should go out and unblock the water pipe," said Nerishev, not looking at Clayton.

"I suppose so," Clayton said, pounding the faucet again. "But it's going to be murder out there. Listen to it!"

Clayton was a short man, bull-necked, red-faced, powerfully constructed. This was his third tour of duty as a planetary observer.

He had tried other jobs in the Advance Exploration Corps, but none suited him. PEP—Primary Extraterrestrial Penetration—faced him with too many unpleasant surprises. It was work for daredevils and madmen. But Base Operations was much too tame and restricting.

He liked the work of a planetary observer, though. His job was to sit tight on a planet newly opened by the PEP boys and checked out by a drone camera crew. All he had to do on this planet was stoically endure discomfort and skillfully keep himself alive. After a year of this, the relief ship would remove him and note his report. On the basis of the report, further action would or would not be taken.

Before each tour of duty, Clayton dutifully promised his wife that this would be the last. After *this* tour, he was going to stay on Earth and work on the little farm he owned. He promised. . . .

But at the end of each rest leave, Clayton journeyed out again, to do the thing for which he was best suited: staying alive through skill and endurance.

But this time, he had had it. He and Nerishev had been eight months on Carella. The relief ship was due in another four months. If he came through alive, he was going to quit for good.

"Just listen to that wind," Nerishev said.

Muffled, distant, it sighed and murmured around the steel hull of the station like a zephyr, a summer breeze.

That was how it sounded to them inside the station, separated from the wind by three inches of steel plus a soundproofing layer.

"It's rising," Clayton said. He walked over to the windspeed indicator. According to the dial, the gentle-sounding wind was blowing at a steady 82 miles an hour.

A light breeze on Carella.

"Man, oh, man!" Clayton said. "I don't want to go out there. Nothing's worth going out there."

"It's your turn," Nerishev pointed out.

"I know. Let me complain a little first, will you? Come on, let's get a forecast from Smanik."

They walked the length of the station, their heels echoing on the steel floor, past compartments filled with food, air supplies, instruments, extra equipment. At the far end of the station was the heavy metal door of the receiving shed. The men slipped on air masks and adjusted the flow.

"Ready?" Clayton asked.

"Ready."

They braced themselves, gripping handholds beside the door. Clayton touched the stud. The door slid away and a gust of wind shrieked in. The men lowered their heads and butted into the wind, entering the receiving shed.

The shed was an extension of the station, some thirty feet long by fifteen feet wide. It was not sealed, like the rest of the structure. The walls were built of openwork steel, with baffles set in. The wind could pass through this arrangement, but slowed down, controlled. A gauge told them it was blowing 34 miles an hour within the shed.

It was a damned nuisance, Clayton thought, having to confer with the natives of Carella in a 34-mile gale. But there was no other way. The Carellans, raised on a planet where the wind never blew less than 70 miles an hour, couldn't stand the "dead air" within the station. Even with the oxygen content cut down to the Carellan norm, the natives couldn't make the adjustment. Within the station, they grew dizzy and apprehensive. Soon they began strangling, like a man in a vacuum.

Thirty-four miles an hour of wind was a fair compromise-point for human and Carellan to meet.

Clayton and Nerishev walked down the shed. In one corner lay what looked like a tangle of dried-out octopi. The tangle stirred and waved two tentacles ceremoniously.

"Good day," said Smanik.

"Good day," Clayton said. "What do you think of the weather?"

"Excellent," said Smanik.

Nerishev tugged at Clayton's sleeve. "What did he say?" he asked, and nodded thoughtfully when Clayton translated it for him. Nerishev lacked Clayton's gift for language. Even after eight months, the Carellan tongue was still an undecipherable series of clicks and whistles to him.

Several more Carellans came up to join the conversation. They all looked like spiders or octopi, with their small centralized body and long, flexible tentacles. This was the optimum survival shape on Carella, and Clayton frequently envied it. He was forced to rely absolutely on the shelter of the station, but the Carellans lived directly in their environment.

Often he had seen a native walking against a tornado-force wind, seven or eight limbs hooked into the ground and pulling, other tentacles reaching out for further grips. He had seen them rolling down the wind like tumbleweed, their tentacles curled around them, wickerwork-basket fashion. He thought of the gay and audacious way they handled their land ships, scudding merrily along on the wind. . . .

Well, he thought, they'd look damned silly on Earth.

"What is the weather going to be like?" he asked Smanik.

The Carellan pondered the question for a while, sniffed the wind, and rubbed two tentacles together.

"The wind may rise a shade more," he said finally. "But it will be nothing serious."

Clayton wondered. *Nothing serious* for a Carellan could

mean disaster for an Earthman. Still, it sounded fairly promising.

He and Nerishev left the receiving shed and closed the door.

"Look," said Nerishev, "if you'd like to wait——"

"Might as well get it over with," Clayton said.

Here, lighted by a single dim overhead bulb, was the smooth, glittering bulk of the Brute. That was the nickname they had given to the vehicle specially constructed for transportation on Carella.

The Brute was armored like a tank and streamlined like a spheric section. It had vision slits of shatterproof glass, thick enough to match the strength of its steel plating. Its center of gravity was low; most of its twelve tons were centered near the ground. The Brute was sealed. Its heavy diesel engine, as well as all necessary openings, were fitted with special dustproof covers. The Brute rested on its six fat tires, looking, in its immovable bulk, like some prehistoric monster.

Clayton got in, put on crash helmet and goggles, and strapped himself into the padded seat. He revved up the engine, listened to it critically, then nodded.

"Okay," he said, "the Brute's ready. Get upstairs and open the garage door."

"Good luck," said Nerishev. He left.

Clayton went over the instrument panel, making sure that all the Brute's special gadgets were in working order. In a moment, he heard Nerishev's voice coming in over the radio.

"I'm opening the door."

"Right."

The heavy door slid back and Clayton drove the Brute outside.

The station had been set up on a wide, empty plain. Mountains would have offered some protection from the wind; but the mountains on Carella were in a constant restless state of building up and breaking down. The plain presented dangers of its own, however. To avert the worst of those dangers, a field of stout steel posts had been planted around the station. The closely packed posts pointed outward, like ancient tank traps, and served the same purpose.

Clayton drove the Brute down one of the narrow, winding channels that led through the field of posts. He emerged, located the pipeline and started along it. On a small screen above his head a white line flashed into view. The line would show any break or obstruction in the pipeline.

A wide, rocky, monotonous desert stretched before him. An occasional low bush came into sight. The wind was directly behind him, blanketed by the sound of the diesel.

He glanced at the windspeed indicator. The wind of Carella was blowing at 92 miles an hour.

He drove steadily along, humming to himself under his breath. From time to time he heard a crash. Pebbles, propelled by the hurricane wind, were cannonading against the Brute. They shattered harmlessly against the thick armor.

"Everything all right?" Nerishev asked over the radio.

"Fine," Clayton said.

In the distance, he saw a Carellan land ship. It was about forty feet long, he judged, and narrow in the beam, skimming rapidly on crude wooden rollers. The ship's sails were made from one of the few leaf-bearing shrubs on the planet.

The Carellans waved their tentacles as they went past. They seemed to be heading toward the station.

Clayton turned his attention back to the pipeline. He was beginning to hear the wind now, above the roar of the diesel. The windspeed indicator showed that the wind had risen to 97 miles an hour.

Somberly he stared through the sand-pocked slit-window. In the far distance were jagged cliffs, seen dimly through the dust-blown air. More pebbles ricocheted off his hull and the sound rang hollowly through his vehicle. He glimpsed another Carellan land ship, then three more. They were tacking stubbornly into the wind.

It struck Clayton that a lot of Carellans were moving toward the station. He signaled to Nerishev on the radio.

"How are you doing?" Nerishev asked.

"I'm close to the spring and no break yet," Clayton reported. "Looks like a lot of Carellans heading your way."

"I know. Six ships are moored in the lee of the shed and more are coming."

"We've never had any trouble with the natives before," Clayton said slowly. "What does this look like?"

"They've brought food with them. It might be a celebration."

"Maybe. Watch yourself."

"Don't worry. You take care and hurry—"

"I've found the break! Speak to you later."

The break showed on the screen, glowing white. Peering out the port, Clayton saw where a boulder had rolled across the pipeline, crushing it, and rolled on.

He brought the truck to a stop on the windward side of the pipe. It was blowing 113 miles an hour. Clayton slid out of the truck, carrying several lengths of pipe, some patches, a blowtorch, and a bag of tools. They were all tied to him and he was secured to the Brute by a strong nylon rope.

Outside, the wind was deafening. It thundered and roared like breaking surf. He adjusted his mask for more oxygen and went to work.

Two hours later, he had completed a fifteen-minute repair job. His clothing was shredded and his air extractor was completely clogged with dust.

He climbed back into the Brute, sealed the port, and lay on the floor, resting. The truck was starting to tremble in the wind gusts. Clayton ignored it.

"Hello? Hello?" Nerishev called over the radio.

Wearily Clayton climbed back into the driver's seat and acknowledged.

"Hurry back now, Clayton! No time to rest! The wind's up to 138! I think a storm is coming!"

A storm on Carella was something Clayton didn't even want to think about. They had experienced only one in eight months. During it, the winds had gone over 160 miles an hour.

He nosed the truck around and started back, driving directly into the wind. At full throttle, he found he was making very little progress. Three miles an hour was all the heavy diesel would do against the pressure of a 138-mile wind.

He stared ahead through the slit-window. The wind, outlined by long streamers of dust and sand, seemed to be coming straight at him, funneled out of an infinitely wide sky to the tiny point of his window. Windborne rocks sailed at him, grew large, immense, and shattered against his window. He couldn't stop himself from ducking each time one came.

The heavy engine was beginning to labor and miss.

"Oh, baby," Clayton breathed, "don't quit now. Not now. Get Papa home. *Then* quit. Please!"

He figured he was about ten miles from the station, which lay directly upwind.

He heard a sound like an avalanche plummeting down a mountainside. It was made by a boulder the size of a house. Too big for the wind to lift, it was rolling at him from windward, digging a furrow in the rocky ground as it came.

Clayton twisted the steering wheel. The engine labored, and with infinite slowness the truck crept out of the boulder's path. Shaking, Clayton watched the boulder bearing down. With one hand he pounded on the instrument panel.

"Move, baby, move!"

Booming hollowly, the boulder rolled past at a good thirty miles an hour.

"Too close," Clayton said to himself. He tried to turn the Brute back into the wind, toward the station. The Brute wouldn't do it.

The diesel labored and whined, trying to turn the big truck into the wind. And the wind, like a solid gray wall, pushed the truck away.

The windspeed indicator stood at 159 miles an hour.

"How are you doing?" Nerishev asked over the radio.

"Just great! Leave me alone, I'm busy."

Clayton set his brakes, unstrapped and raced back to the engine. He adjusted timing and mixture, and hurried back to the controls.

"Hey, Nerishev! That engine's going to conk out!"

It was a full second before Nerishev answered. Then, very calmly, he asked, "What's wrong with it?"

"Sand!" Clayton said. "Particles driven at 159 miles an hour —sand's in the bearings, injectors, everything. I'm going to make all the distance I can."

"And then?"

"Then I'll try to sail her back," Clayton said. "I just hope the mast will take it."

He turned his attention to the controls. At windspeeds like this, the truck had to be handled like a ship at sea. Clayton picked up speed with the wind on his quarter, then came about and slammed into the wind.

The Brute made it this time and crossed over onto the other tack.

It was the best he could do, Clayton decided. His windward distance would have to be made by tacking. He edged toward the eye of the wind. But at full throttle, the diesel couldn't bring him much closer than forty degrees.

For an hour the Brute forged ahead, tacking back and forth across the wind, covering three miles in order to make two. Miraculously the engine kept on running. Clayton blessed the manufacturer and begged the diesel to hold out a little while longer.

Through a blinding screen of sand, he saw another Carellan land ship. It was reefed down and heeled precariously over. But it forged steadily to windward and soon outdistanced him.

Lucky natives, Clayton thought—165 miles of wind was a sailing breeze to them!

The station, a gray half-sphere, came into sight ahead.

"I'm going to make it!" Clayton shouted. "Break out the rum, Nerishev, old man! Papa's getting drunk tonight!"

The diesel chose that moment to break down for good. Clayton swore violently as he set the brakes. What lousy luck! If the wind were behind him, he could roll in. But, of course, it had to be in front.

"What are you going to do now?" Nerishev asked.

"I'm going to sit here," Clayton said. "When the wind calms down to a hurricane, I'm going to walk home."

The Brute's twelve-ton mass was shaking and rattling in the wind blasts.

"You know," Clayton said, "I'm going to retire after this tour."

"That so? You really mean it?"

"Absolutely. I own a farm in Maryland, with frontage on Chesapeake Bay. You know what I'm going to do?"

"What?"

"I'm going to raise oysters. You see, the oyster— Hold it."

The station seemed to be drifting slowly upwind, away from him. Clayton rubbed his eyes, wondering if he were going crazy. Then he realized that in spite of its brakes, in spite of its streamlining, the truck was being pushed downwind, away from the station.

Angrily he shoved a button on his switchboard, releasing the port and starboard anchors. He heard the solid clunk of the anchors hitting the ground, heard the steel cables scrape and rattle. He let out a hundred and seventy feet of steel line, then set the winch brakes. The truck was holding again.

"I dropped the anchors," Clayton said.

"Are they holding?"

"So far." Clayton lighted a cigarette and leaned back in his padded chair. Every muscle in his body ached from tension. His eyelids were twitching from watching the wind lines converging on him. He closed his eyes and tried to relax.

The sound of the wind cut through the truck's steel plating.

The wind howled and moaned, tugging at the truck, trying to find a hold on the smooth surface. At 169 miles an hour, the ventilator baffles blew out. He would be blinded, Clayton thought, if he weren't wearing sealed goggles, choked if he weren't breathing canned air. Dust swirled, thick and electric, within the Brute's cabin.

Pebbles, flung with the velocity of rifle bullets, splattered against the hull. They were striking harder now. He wondered how much more force they'd need before they started piercing the armor plating.

At times like this, Clayton found it hard to maintain a common-sense attitude. He was painfully aware of the vulnerability of human flesh, appalled at the possibilities for violence in the Universe. What was he doing out here? Man's place was in the calm, still air of Earth. If he ever got back . . .

"Are you all right?" Nerishev asked.

"Making out just great," Clayton said wearily. "How are things at the station?"

"Not so good. The whole structure's starting sympathetic vibration. Enough wind for long enough and the foundations could shatter."

"And they want to put a fuel station here!" Clayton said.

"Well, you know the problem. This is the only solid planet between Angarsa III and the South Ridge Belt. All the rest are gas giants."

"They better build their station in space."

"The cost—"

"Hell, man, it'll cost less to build another planet than to try to maintain a fuel base on this one!" Clayton spat out a mouthful of dust. "I just want to get on that relief ship. How many natives at the station now?"

"About fifteen, in the shed."

"Any sign of violence?"

"No, but they're acting funny."

"How so?"

"I don't know," said Nerishev. "I just don't like it."

"Stay out of the shed, huh? You can't speak the language, anyhow, and I want you in one piece when I come back." He hesitated. "If I come back."

"You'll be fine," Nerishev said.

"Sure I will. I—oh, Lord!"

"What's it? What's wrong?"

"Boulder coming down! Talk to you later!"

Clayton turned his attention to the boulder, a rapidly growing black speck to windward. It was heading directly toward his anchored and immobilized truck. He glanced at the windspeed indicator. Impossible—174 miles an hour! And yet, he reminded himself, winds in the stratospheric jet stream on Earth blow at 200 miles an hour.

The boulder, large as a house, still growing as it approached, was rolling directly his way.

"Swerve! Turn!" Clayton bellowed at the boulder, pounding the instrument panel with his fist.

The boulder was coming at him, straight as a ruler line, rolling right down the wind.

With a yell of agony Clayton touched a button, releasing both anchors at the cable end. There was no time to winch them in, even assuming the winch could take the strain. Still the boulder grew.

Clayton released his brakes.

The Brute, shoved by a wind of 178 miles an hour, began to pick up speed. Within seconds he was traveling at 38 miles an hour, staring through his rear-vision mirror at the boulder overtaking him.

As the boulder rolled up, Clayton twisted the steering wheel hard to the left. The truck tilted over precariously, swerved, fishtailed on the hard ground, and tried to turn itself over. He fought the wheel, trying to bring the Brute back to equilibrium. He thought: *I'm probably the first man who ever jibed a twelve-ton truck!*

The boulder, looking like a whole city block, roared past.

The heavy truck teetered for a moment, then came to rest on its six wheels.

"Clayton! What happened? Are you all right?"

"Fine," Clayton gasped. "But I had to slip the cables. I'm running downwind."

"Can you turn?"

"Almost knocked her over, trying to."

"How far can you run?"

Clayton stared ahead. In the distance he could make out the dramatic black cliffs that rimmed the plain.

"I got about fifteen miles to go before I pile into the cliffs. Not much time, at the speed I'm traveling." He locked his brakes. The tires began to scream and the brake linings smoked furiously. But the wind, at 183 miles an hour, didn't even notice the difference. His speed over the ground had picked up to 44 miles an hour.

"Try sailing her out!" Nerishev said.

"She won't take it."

"Try, man! What else can you do? The wind's hit 185 here. The whole station's shaking! Boulders are tearing up the whole post defense. I'm afraid some boulders are going to get through and flatten—"

"Stow it," Clayton said. "I got troubles of my own."

"I don't know if the station will stand! Clayton, listen to me. Try the—"

The radio suddenly and dismayingly went dead.

Clayton banged it a few times, then gave up. His speed over the ground had reached 49 miles an hour. The cliffs were already looming large before him.

"So all right," Clayton said. "Here we go." He released his last anchor, a small emergency job. At its full length of 250 feet of steel cable, it slowed him to 30 miles an hour. The anchor was breaking and ripping through the ground like a jet-propelled plow.

Clayton then turned on the sail mechanism. This had been installed by the Earth engineers upon much the same theory that has small ocean-going motorboats carry a small mast and auxiliary sail. The sails are insurance, in case the engine fails. On Carella, a man could never walk home from a stranded vehicle. He had to come in under power.

The mast, a short, powerful steel pillar, extruded itself through a gasketed hole in the roof. Magnetic shrouds and stays snapped into place, supporting it. From the mast fluttered a sail made of link-woven metal. For a mainsheet, Clayton had a three-part flexible-steel cable, working through a winch.

The sail was only a few square feet in area. It could drive a twelve-ton monster with its brakes locked and an anchor out on 250 feet of line.

Easily—with the wind blowing 185 miles an hour.

Clayton winched in the mainsheet and turned, taking the wind on the quarter. But a quartering course wasn't good enough. He winched the sail in still more and turned further into the wind.

With the super-hurricane on his beam, the ponderous truck heeled over, lifting one entire side into the air. Quickly Clayton released a few feet of mainsheet. The metal-link sail screamed and chattered as the wind whipped it.

Driving now with just the sail's leading edge, Clayton was able to keep the truck on its feet and make good a course to windward.

Through the rear-vision mirror, he could see the black, jagged cliffs behind him. They were his lee shore, his coast of wrecks. But he was sailing out of the trap. Foot by foot, he was pulling away.

"That's my baby!" Clayton shouted to the battling Brute.

His sense of victory snapped almost at once, for he heard an ear-splitting clang and something whizzed past his head. At 187 miles an hour, pebbles were piercing his armor plating. He was undergoing the Carellan equivalent of a machine-gun barrage. The wind shrieked through the holes, trying to batter him out of his seat.

Desperately he clung to the steering wheel. He could hear the sail wrenching. It was made out of the toughest flexible alloys available, but it wasn't going to hold up for long. The short, thick mast, supported by six heavy cables, was whipping like a fishing rod.

His brake linings were worn out, and his speed over the ground came up to 57 miles an hour.

He was too tired to think. He steered, his hands locked to the wheel, his slitted eyes glaring ahead into the storm.

The sail ripped with a scream. The tatters flogged for a moment, then brought the mast down. Wind gusts were approaching 190 miles an hour.

The wind now was driving him back toward the cliffs. At 192 miles an hour of wind, the Brute was lifted bodily, thrown for a dozen yards, slammed back on its wheels. A front tire blew under the pressure, then two rear ones. Clayton put his head on his arms and waited for the end.

Suddenly the Brute stopped short. Clayton was flung forward. His safety belt checked him for a moment, then snapped. He banged against the instrument panel and fell back, dazed and bleeding.

He lay on the floor, half conscious, trying to figure out what had happened. Slowly he pulled himself back into the seat, foggily aware that he hadn't broken any limbs. His stomach was one great bruise. His mouth was bleeding.

At last, looking through the rear-vision mirror, he saw what had happened. The emergency anchor, trailing at 250 feet of steel cable, had caught in a deep outcropping of rock. A fouled anchor had brought him up short, less than half a mile from the cliffs. He was saved—

For the moment, at least.

But the wind hadn't given up yet. The 193-mile-an-hour wind bellowed, lifted the truck bodily, slammed it down, lifted it again, slammed it down. The steel cable hummed like a guitar string. Clayton wrapped his arms and legs around the seat. He couldn't hold on much longer. And if he let go, the madly leaping Brute would smear him over the walls like toothpaste——

If the cable didn't part first and send him hurtling into the cliffs.

He held on. At the top of one swing, he caught a glimpse of the windspeed indicator. The sight of it sickened him. He was through, finished, done for. How could he be expected to hold on through the force of a 187-mile-an-hour wind? It was too much.

It was—187 miles an hour? That meant that the wind was dropping!

He could hardly believe it at first. But slowly, steadily, the dial hand crept down. At 160 miles an hour, the truck stopped slamming and lay passively at the end of its anchor line. At 153, the wind veered—a sure sign that the blow was nearly over.

When it had dropped to 142 miles an hour, Clayton allowed himself the luxury of passing out.

Carellan natives came out for him later in the day. Skillfully they maneuvered two big land ships up to the Brute, fastened on their long vines—which tested out stronger than steel—and towed the derelict truck back to the station.

They brought him into the receiving shed and Nerishev carried him into the station's dead air.

"You didn't break anything except a couple of teeth," said Nerishev. "But there isn't an unbruised inch on you."

"We came through it," Clayton said.

"Just. Our boulder defense is completely flattened. The station took two direct hits from boulders and barely contained them. I've checked the foundations; they're badly strained. Another blow like that——"

"—and we'd make out somehow. Us Earth lads, we come through! That was the worst in eight months. Four months more and the relief ship comes! Buck up, Nerishev. Come with me."

"Where are we going?"

"I want to talk to that damned Smanik!"

They came into the shed. It was filled to overflowing with Carellans. Outside, in the lee of the station, several dozen land ships were moored.

"Smanik!" Clayton called. "What's going on here?"

"It is the Festival of Summer," Smanik said. "Our great yearly holiday."

"Hm. What about that blow? What did you think of it?"

"I would classify it as a moderate gale," said Smanik. "Nothing dangerous, but somewhat unpleasant for sailing."

"Unpleasant! I hope you get your forecasts a little more accurate in the future."

"One cannot always outguess the weather," Smanik said. "It is regrettable that my last forecast should be wrong."

"Your *last?* How come? What's the matter?"

"These people," Smanik said, gesturing around him, "are my entire tribe, the Seremai. We have celebrated the Festival of Summer. Now summer is ended and we must go away."

"Where to?"

"To the caverns in the far west. They are two weeks' sail from here. We will go into the caverns and live there for three months. In that way, we will find safety."

Clayton had a sudden sinking feeling in his stomach. "Safety from what, Smanik?"

"I told you. Summer is over. We need safety now from the winds—the powerful storm winds of winter."

"What is it?" Nerishev said.

"In a moment." Clayton thought very quickly of the super-hurricane he had just passed through, which Smanik had classified as a moderate and harmless gale. He thought of their immobility, the ruined Brute, the strained foundations of the station, the wrecked boulder barrier, the relief ship four months away. "We could go with you in the land ships, Smanik, and take refuge in the caverns with you—be protected from the—"

"Of course," said Smanik hospitably.

"No, we couldn't," Clayton answered himself, his sinking feeling even lower than during the storm. "We'd need extra oxygen, our own food, a water supply—"

"What is it?" Nerishev repeated impatiently. "What the devil did he say to make you look like that?"

"He says the *really* big winds are just coming," Clayton replied.

The two men stared at each other.

Outside, a wind was rising.

Ideas Die Hard

By ISAAC ASIMOV

The technical problem had been solved long ago, but now the ultimate question had to be answered—could men be sent to do Man's job?

They strapped them in against the acceleration of take-off, surrounded their cleverly designed seats with fluid, and fortified their bodies with drugs.

Then, when the time came that the straps might be unhooked, they were left with little more space than before.

The single light garment each wore gave an illusion of freedom, but only an illusion. They might move their arms freely, but their legs just to a limited extent. Only one at a time could be completely straightened, not both at once.

They could shift position into a half recline to the right or left, but they could not leave their seats. The seats were all there were. They could eat, sleep, take care of all their bodily needs in a barely adequate way while sitting there, and they had to sit there.

What it amounted to was that for a week (slightly more, actually) they were condemned to a tomb. At the moment, it didn't matter that the tomb was surrounded by all of space.

Acceleration was over and done with. They had begun the

silent, even swoop through the space that separated Earth and Moon and there was a great horror upon them.

Bruce G. Davis, Jr., said hollowly, "What do we talk about?"

Marvin Oldbury said, "I don't know." There was silence again.

They were not friends. Until recently they had never even met. But they were imprisoned together. Each had volunteered. Each had met the requirements. They were single, intelligent, and in good health.

Moreover, each had undergone extensive psychotherapy for months beforehand.

And the great advice of the psych-boys had been—*talk!*

"Talk continuously, if necessary," they had said. "Don't let yourself start feeling alone."

Oldbury said, "How do they know?" He was the taller and larger of the two, strong and square-faced. There was a tuft of hair just over the bridge of his nose that made a period between two dark eyebrows.

Davis was sandy-haired and freckled, with a pugnacious grin and the beginnings of shadows beneath his eyes. It might be those shadows that seemed to fill his eyes with foreboding.

He said, "How do who know?"

"The psychs. They say talk. How do they know it will do any good?"

"What do they care?" asked Davis sharply. "It's an experiment. If it doesn't work, they'll tell the next pair: 'Don't say a word.' "

Oldbury stretched out his arms and the fingers touched the great semisphere of information devices that surrounded them. He could move the controls, handle the air-conditioning equipment, tweak the plastic tubes out of which they could suck the bland nutrient mixture, nudge the waste-disposal unit, and brush the dials that controlled the viewscope.

All was bathed in the mild glow of the lights which were

fed by electricity from the solar batteries exposed on the hull of the ship to sunlight that never failed.

Thank heaven, he thought, for the spin that had been given the vessel. It produced a centrifugal force that pressed him down in his seat with the feel of weight. Without that touch of gravity to make it seem like Earth, it could not have been borne.

Still, they might have made space within the ship, space that they could spare from the needs of equipment and use for the tight in-packing of two men.

He put the thought into words and said, "They might have allowed for more room."

"Why?" asked Davis.

"So we could stand up."

Davis grunted. It was really all the answer that could be made.

Oldbury said, "Why did you volunteer?"

"You should have asked me that before we left. I knew then. I was going to be one of the first men around the Moon and back. I was going to be a big hero at twenty-five. Columbus and I, you know." He turned his head from side to side restlessly, then sucked a moment or two at the water tube. He said, "But just the same, I've wanted to back out for two months. Each night I went to bed sweating, swearing I would resign in the morning."

"But you didn't."

"No, I didn't. Because I couldn't. Because I was too yellow to admit I was yellow. Even when they were strapping me into this seat, I was all set to shout: 'No! Get someone else!' I couldn't, not even then."

Oldbury smiled without lightness. "I wasn't even going to tell them. I wrote a note saying I couldn't make it. I was going to mail it and disappear into the desert. Know where the note is now?"

"Where?"

"In my shirt pocket. Right here."

Davis said, "Doesn't matter. When we come back, we'll be heroes—big, famous, trembling heroes."

Lars Nilsson was a pale man with sad eyes and with prominent knuckles on his thin fingers. He had been civilian-in-charge of Project Deep Space for three years. He had enjoyed the job, all of it, even the tension and the failures—until now. Until the moment when two men had finally been strapped into place within the machine.

He said, "I feel like a vivisectionist, somehow."

Dr. Godfrey Mayer, who headed the psychology group, looked pained. "Men have to be risked as well as ships. We've done what we could in the way of preparation and of safeguarding them as far as is humanly possible. After all, these men are volunteers."

Nilsson said colorlessly, "I know that." The fact did not really comfort him.

Staring at the controls, Oldbury wondered when, if ever, any of the dials would turn danger-red, when a warning ring would sound.

They had been assured that, in all likelihood, this would not happen, but each had been thoroughly trained in the exact manner of adjustment, manually, of each control.

And with reason. Automation had advanced to the point where the ship was a self-regulating organism, as self-regulating, almost, as a living thing. Yet three times, unmanned ships, almost as complicated as this one they were entombed in, had been sent out to follow a course boomeranging about the Moon, and three times, the ships had not returned.

Furthermore, each time the information devices relaying data back to Earth had failed before even the Moon's orbit had been reached on the forward journey.

Public opinion was impatient and the men working on Project Deep Space voted not to wait on the success of an unmanned vehicle before risking human beings. It was decided that a manned vehicle was needed so that manual correction could be introduced to compensate for the small, cumulative failure of the imperfect automation.

A crew of two men—they feared for the sanity of one man alone.

Oldbury said, "Davis! Hey, Davis!"

Davis stirred out of a withdrawn silence. "What?"

"Let's see what Earth looks like."

"Why?" Davis wanted to know.

"Why not? We're out here. Let's enjoy the view, at least."

He leaned back. The viewscope was an example of automation. The impingement of short-wave radiation blanked it out. The Sun could not be viewed under any circumstances. Other than that, the viewscope oriented itself toward the brightest source of illumination in space, compensating, as it did so, for any proper motion of the ship, as the engineers had explained offhandedly. Little photoelectric cells located at four sides of the ship whirled restlessly, scanning the sky. And if the brightest light source was not wanted, there was always the manual control.

Davis closed contact and the 'scope was alive with light. He put out the room's artificial lights and the view in the 'scope grew brighter against the contrast of darkness.

It wasn't a globe, of course, with continents on it. What they saw was a hazy mixture of white and blue-green filling the screen.

The dial that measured distance from Earth, by determining the value of the gravitational constant, put them just under thirty thousand miles away.

Davis said, "I'll get the edge." He reached out to adjust the sights and the view lurched.

A curve of black swept in across the 'scope. There were no stars in it.

Oldbury said, "It's the night shadow."

The view moved jerkily back. Blackness advanced from the other side and was curved more sharply and in the opposite sense. This time, the darkness showed the hard points of stars.

Oldbury swallowed. "I wish I were back there," he said solemnly.

Davis said, "At least we can see the Earth is round."

"Isn't that a discovery?"

Davis seemed immediately stung at the manner in which Oldbury tossed off his remark. He said, "Yes, it is a discovery, if you put it that way. Only a small percentage of the Earth's population has ever been convinced the Earth was round." He put on ship's lights, scowling, and doused the 'scope.

"Not since 1500," said Oldbury.

"If you consider the New Guinea tribes, there were flat-world believers even in 1950. And there were religious sects in America as late as the 1930s who believed the Earth was flat. They offered prizes for anyone who could prove it was round. Ideas die hard!"

"Crackpots," Oldbury grunted.

Davis grew warmer. He said, "Can *you* prove it's round? I mean except for the fact that you see it is right now?"

"You're being ridiculous."

"Am I? Or were you just taking your fourth-grade teacher's word as gospel? What proofs were you given? That the Earth's shadow on the Moon during a lunar eclipse is round and that only a sphere can cast a round shadow? That's plain nonsense! A circular disk can cast a round shadow. So can an egg or any shape, however irregular, with one circular projection. Would you point out that men have traveled around the Earth? They might just be circling the central point of a flat Earth at a fixed distance. It would have the same effect. Do ships appear top-first on the horizon? Optical illusion, for all you know. There are queerer ones."

"Foucault's pendulum," said Oldbury briefly. He was taken aback at the other man's intensity.

Davis said, "You mean a pendulum staying in one plane and that plane revolving as Earth moves under it at a rate depending on the latitude of the place where the experiment is being performed. Sure! *If* a pendulum keeps to one plane. *If* the theories involved are correct. How does that satisfy the man in the street, who's no physicist, unless he's just willing to take the word of the physicists on faith? I tell you what! There was no satisfactory proof that the Earth was round till rockets flew high enough to take pictures of enough of the planet to show the curvature."

"Nuts," said Oldbury. "The geography of Argentina would be all distorted if the Earth were flat with the North Pole as the center. Any other center would distort the geography of some other portion. The skin of the Earth just would not have the shape it has if it weren't pretty nearly spherical. You can't refute that."

Davis fell silent for a moment, then said sulkily, "What the devil are we arguing for, anyway? The hell with it."

Seeing Earth and talking about it, even just about its roundness, had driven Oldbury into a sharp nostalgia. He began to talk of home in a low voice. He talked about his youth in Trenton, New Jersey, and brought up anecdotes about his family that were so trivial that he had not thought of them in years, laughing at things that were scarcely funny and feeling the sting of childish pain he had thought healed over years before.

At one point, Oldbury slipped off into shallow sleep, then woke with a start and was plunged in confusion at finding himself in a cold, blue-tinged light. Instinctively he made to rise to his feet and sank back with a groan as his elbow struck metal hard.

The 'scope was aglow again. The blue-tinged light that had startled him at the moment of waking was reflected from Earth.

The curve of Earth's rim was noticeably sharper now. They were 50,000 miles away.

Davis had turned at the other's sudden futile movement and said pugnaciously, "Earth's roundness is no test. After all, Man could crawl over its surface and see its shape by its geography, as you said. But there are other places where we act as though we know and with less justification."

Oldbury rubbed his twinging elbow and said, "All right, all right."

Davis was not to be placated. "There's Earth. Look at it. How old is it?"

Oldbury said cautiously, "A few billion years, I suppose."

"You *suppose?* What right have you to suppose? Why not a few thousand years? Your great-grandfather probably believed Earth was six thousand years old, dating from Genesis 1. I know mine did. What makes you so sure they're wrong?"

"There's a good deal of geological evidence involved."

"The time it takes for the ocean to grow as salt as it is? The time it takes to lay down a thickness of sedimentary rock? The time it takes to form a quantity of lead in uranium ore?"

Oldbury leaned back in his seat and was watching the Earth with a kind of detachment. He scarcely heard Davis. A little more and they would see all of it in the 'scope. Already, with the planetary curve against space visible at one end of the 'scope, the night-shadow was about to encroach on the other.

The night-shadow did not change its position, of course. The Earth revolved, but to the men aboard ship it remained fat with light.

"Well?" demanded Davis.

"What?" said Oldbury, startled.

"What about your damned geological evidence?"

"Oh. Well, there's uranium decay."

"I mentioned it. You're a fool. Do you know that?"

Oldbury counted ten to himself before replying, "I don't think so."

"Then listen. Suppose the Earth had come into existence some six thousand years ago just as the Bible describes it. Why couldn't it have been created then with a certain amount of lead already existing in the uranium? If the uranium could be created, why not the lead with it? Why not create the ocean as salt as it is and the sedimentary rocks as thick as they are? Why not create the fossils exactly as they exist?"

"In other words, why not create the Earth complete with internal evidence proving that it is several billion years old?"

"That's right," said Davis, "why not?"

"Let me ask the opposite question. Why?"

"I don't care why. I'm just trying to show you that all the so-called proofs of Earth's age don't necessarily disprove Earth's creation six thousand years ago."

Oldbury said, "I suppose you consider it all to be intended as a kind of game—a scientific puzzle to test mankind's ingenuity, or exercise his mind—a mental jungle gym on his intellectual crib."

"You think you're being funny, Oldbury, but actually what's so damned impossible about it? It might be just that. You can't prove it isn't."

"I'm not trying to prove anything."

"No, you're satisfied to take things as they're handed to you. That's why I said you were a fool. *If* we could go back in time and see for ourselves, then that would be another matter. If we could go back in time before 4004 B.C. and see predynastic Egypt, or earlier still and bag a saber-toothed—"

"Or a tyrannosaur."

"Or a tyrannosaur, yes. Until we can do that, we can only speculate and there's nothing to say where speculation is correct and where it isn't. All science is based on faith in the original premises and in faith on the validity of deduction and induction."

"There's no crime in that."

"There *is* crime!" said Davis vehemently. "You come to believe, and once you come to believe, you shut the doors of your mind. You've got your idea and you won't replace it with another. Galileo found out how hard ideas can die."

"Columbus, too," Oldbury put in drowsily. Staring at the

blue-tinged Earth with the slow whirling changes of the cloud formations had an almost hypnotic effect.

Davis seized on his comment with an obvious glee. "Columbus! I suppose you think he maintained the Earth was round when everyone else thought it was flat."

"More or less."

"That's the result of listening to your fourth-grade teacher, who listened to *her* fourth-grade teacher, and so on. Any intelligent and educated man in Columbus's time would have been willing to concede that the Earth was round. The point at issue was the *size* of the Earth."

"Is that a fact?"

"Absolutely. Columbus followed the maps of an Italian geographer which had the Earth about 15,000 miles in circumference, with the eastern edge of Asia about three or four thousand miles from Europe. The geographers at the court of King John of Portugal insisted that this was wrong, that the Earth was about 25,000 miles in circumference, that the eastern edge of Asia was about 12,000 miles west of the western edge of Europe, and that King John had better keep on trying for the route around Africa. The Portuguese geographers were, of course, a hundred per cent right and Columbus was a hundred per cent wrong. The Portuguese did reach India and Columbus never did."

Oldbury said, "He discovered America just the same. You can't deny that fact."

"That had nothing to do with his ideas. It was strictly accidental. He was such an intellectual fraud that when his actual voyage showed his map was wrong, he falsified his log rather than change his ideas. *His* ideas died hard—they never died till he did, in fact. And so do yours. I could talk myself blue in the face and leave you still convinced that Columbus was a great man because he thought the Earth was round when everyone else said it was flat."

"Have it your way," mumbled Oldbury. He was caught in lassitude and in the memory of the chicken soup his mother made when he was a child. She used barley. He remembered the smell of the kitchen on Saturday morning—French-toast morning—and the look of the streets after an afternoon of rain and the——

Lars Nilsson had the transcripts before him, with the more significant portions marked off on the tape by the psychologists.

He said, "Are we still receiving them clearly?"

He was assured that the receiving devices were working perfectly.

"I wish there were some way to avoid listening to their conversations without their knowledge," he said. "I suppose that's foolish of me."

Godfrey Mayer saw no point in denying the other's diagnosis. "It is," he agreed. "Quite foolish. Look at it as merely additional information necessary to the study of human reaction to space. When we were testing human response to high-g acceleration, did you feel embarrassed to be caught looking at the recording of their blood-pressure variations?"

"What do you make of Davis and his odd theories? He worries me."

Mayer shook his head. "We don't know what we ought to be worried about as yet. Davis is working off aggressions against the science that has placed him in the position he finds himself in."

"That's your theory?"

"It's one theory. Expressing the aggressions may be a good thing. It may keep him stable. And then again, it may go too far. It's too soon to tell. It may be that Oldbury is the one who's in greater danger. He's growing passive."

"Do you suppose, Mayer, that we may find that Man just isn't suited for space? Any man?"

"If we could build ships that would carry a hundred men in an Earthlike environment, we'd have no trouble. As long as we build ships like this one"—he jerked a thumb over his shoulder in a vague directional gesture—"we may have a great deal of trouble."

Nilsson felt vaguely dissatisfied. He said, "Well, they're in their third day now and still safe so far."

"We're in the third day now," said Davis harshly. "We're better than halfway there."

"Umm. I had a cousin who owned a lumberyard. Cousin Raymond. I used to visit him sometimes on the way home from school," Oldbury reminisced.

Unaccountably his line of thought was interrupted by the fleeting memory of Longfellow's *The Village Blacksmith*, and then he remembered that it contained a phrase about "the children coming home from school" and wondered how many people among those who rattled off so glibly, "Under the spreading chestnut tree, the village smithy stood" knew that the "smithy" was not the smith but the shop in which the smith worked.

He asked, "What was I saying?"

"I don't know," retorted Davis irritably. "*I* said we're more than halfway there and we haven't looked at the Moon yet."

"Let's look at the Moon, then."

"All right, *you* adjust the 'scope. I've done it long enough. Damn it, I've got blisters on my rump." He moved jerkily in the enclosing confines of the bucket seat, as though to get a slightly new section of rear end in contact with cushioned metal. "I don't know that it's such a blasted fine idea to spin the damned ship and have gravity press us down. Floating a little would take the weight off and be relaxing."

"There's no room to float," sighed Oldbury, "and if we were in free fall, you'd be complaining of nausea."

Oldbury was working the controls of the 'scope as he spoke. Stars moved past the line of vision.

It wasn't difficult. The engineers back home in Trenton—no, in New Mexico, really; on Earth, anyway—the engineers had schooled them carefully. Get it almost right. Get it pointed away from Earth, one hundred and eighty degrees.

Once it is nearly right, then let the light meters take over. The Moon would be the brightest object in the vicinity and it would be centered in unstable equilibrium. It would take a few seconds for the meters to scan the rest of the sky and switch the 'scope back to Earth, but in those few seconds, switch back to manuals and there, you have it.

The Moon was crescent. It would have to be in opposite phase to Earth as long as the ship sped along a course that was almost on the line connecting the two worlds.

But the crescent was a bloated one, as if it were part of a cheap calendar illustration. Oldbury thought there should be two heads, leaning toward one another, short straight hair against longer waved hair, silhouetted against the Moon. Except that it would have to be a full Moon.

Davis snorted. "It's there, at any rate."

"Did you expect it wouldn't be?"

"I don't expect anything in space. Anything yes or anything no. No one's been in space, so no one knows. But at least I see the Moon."

"You see it from Earth, if it comes to that."

"Don't be so sure what you see from Earth. For all anyone can tell from Earth, the Moon is only a yellow painted patch on a blue background with a shade that's drawn back and forth across it by clockwork."

"And stars and planets also run by clockwork?"

"Same as they are in a planetarium. Why not? And a telescope shows more stars painted on—"

"With a built-in red shift?"

"Why not?" challenged Davis. "Only we're halfway to the Moon and it looks bigger and maybe we'll find it exists. I'll reserve judgment on the other planets and the stars."

Oldbury looked at the Moon and sighed. In a few days they would be edging around it, moving past and over the hidden side.

He said, "I never did believe the story about the man in

the Moon. I never saw him. What I saw was the face of a woman—two eyes, rather lopsided, but very sad. I could see the full Moon from my bedroom window and she always made *me* feel sad, yet friendly, too. When clouds drifted past, it was the Moon—*she*—that always seemed to be moving, not the clouds, but still she didn't go away from the window. And you could see her through the clouds, even though you could never see the Sun through clouds, not even through little clouds, and it was so much brighter. Why is that, Dad—uh —Davis?"

Davis said, "What's wrong with your voice?"

"Nothing's wrong with my voice."

"You're squeaking."

Oldbury, with an effort of will, forced his voice an octave lower. "I'm *not* squeaking!"

He stared at the small clocks in the dashboard, two of them. It wasn't the first time. One of them gave the time by Mountain Standard, and in that he wasn't interested. It was the other, the one that measured the number of hours elapsed in flight, that caught at him periodically. It said sixty-four and a fraction, and in red, working backward, were the hours remaining before they were to land on Earth again. The red was marked off now at one hundred forty-four and a fraction.

Oldbury was sorry that the time left to go was recorded. He would have liked to work it out for himself. Back in Trenton he used to count the hours to summer vacation, working it out painfully in his head during geography lesson —always geography lesson, somehow—so many days, then so many hours. He would write the result in tiny numbers in his exercise book. Each day the number would grow smaller. Half the excitement of approaching summer vacation was in watching those numbers grow smaller.

But now the numbers grew smaller by themselves as the sweep second-hand went round and round, slicing time by minutes, paper-thin sections of time like corned beef peeling off in the big slicer in the delicatessen.

Davis's voice impinged on his ear suddenly: "Nothing seems to be going wrong so far."

Oldbury said confidently, "Nothing will go wrong."

"What makes you so sure?"

"Because the numbers just get smaller."

"Huh? How's that again?"

For a moment Oldbury was confused. He said, "Nothing."

It was dim in the ship in the light of the crescent Moon only. He dipped into sleep again, skin-diving fashion, half conscious of the real Moon and half dreaming of a full Moon at a window with a sad woman-face, being driven motionlessly by the wind.

"Two hundred thousand miles," said Davis. "That's almost eighty-five per cent of the way there."

The lighted portion of the Moon was speckled and pimpled and its horns had outgrown the screen. Mare Crisium was a dark oval, distorted by the slanting view, but large enough to put a fist into.

"And nothing wrong," Davis went on. "Not one little red light on a single instrument dial."

"Good," said Oldbury.

"Good?" Davis looked about to stare at Oldbury and his eyes were squinting in suspicion. "In every previous try, nothing went wrong till they got out this far, so it's not good *yet.*"

"I don't think anything will go wrong."

"I think it will. Earth isn't supposed to know."

"Isn't supposed to know what?"

Davis laughed and Oldbury looked at him wearily. He felt queerly frightened at the other's gathering monomania. Davis was not a bit like the father Oldbury remembered so queerly (only he remembered him younger than he was now, with all his hair and a sound heart).

Davis's profile was sharp in the moonlight. He said, "There

may be a lot in space we're not supposed to know. There are a billion light-years ahead of us. Only, for all we know, there's a solid black wall instead, just on the other side of the Moon, with stars painted on it and planets moving all squint-eyed so that smart cockerels on Earth can figure out all sorts of fancy orbits and theories of gravitation out of it."

"A game to test our minds?" said Oldbury. His memory brought that out of Davis's previous remarks—or were they his own?—with something of a wrench. This whole business with the ship seemed distant.

"Why not?"

"It's all right," Oldbury soothed anxiously. "It's all right so far. Some day, you'll see, it will be all right all the way out."

"Then why do every one of the recording devices go wrong past two hundred thousand miles? Why? Answer me that!"

"We're here this time. We'll adjust them."

Davis said, "No, we won't."

A sharp memory of a story he had encountered in early teenhood stirred Oldbury into excitement. "You know, I once read a book about the Moon. The Martians had set up a base on the other side of the Moon. We could never see them, you see. They were hidden, but they could observe us——"

"How?" asked Davis sourly. "There was two thousand miles' thickness of Moon between Earth and the other side."

"No. Let me start from the beginning." Oldbury heard his voice go squeaky again, but he didn't mind. He wanted to get out of his seat so he could jump up and down because just remembering the story made him feel good, but for some reason he couldn't. "You see, it was in the future, and what Earth didn't know was——"

"Will you shut up?"

Oldbury's voice cut off at the interruption. He felt hurt, stifled. Then he said, subdued, "You *said* Earth isn't supposed to know and that's why the instruments went off and the only new thing we're going to see is the other side of the Moon and if the Martians——"

"*Will* you let up with your stupid Martians?"

Oldbury fell silent. He was very resentful against Davis. Just because Davis was grown up didn't make it all right for him to holler like that.

His eyes drifted back to the clock. Summer vacation was only one hundred and ten hours away.

They were falling toward the Moon now. Free fall. Speeding down at cataclysmic velocity. Moon's gravity was weak, but they had fallen from a great height. And now, finally, the view on the Moon began to shift and, very slowly, new craters were coming into view.

Of course, they would miss the Moon and their speed would sweep them safely around. They would move across half the Moon's surface, across three thousand miles of it in one hour; then back they would hurl to meet the Earth once more.

But Oldbury sadly missed the familiar face in the Moon. There was no face this close, only ragged surface. He felt his eyes brimming as he watched morosely.

And then, suddenly, the small cramped room within the ship was full of loud buzzing and half the dials on the panel before them clamored into the red of disorder.

Oldbury cowered back, but Davis howled in what seemed almost triumph. "I told you! Everything's going wrong!"

He worked at the manuals uselessly. "No information will get back. Secrets! Secrets!"

But Oldbury still looked at the Moon. It was terribly close and now the surface was moving quickly. They were starting the swing in earnest and Oldbury's scream was high-pitched. "Look! Lookathat!" His pointing finger was stiff with terror.

Davis looked up and said, "Oh, God! Oh, God——" over and over again, until finally the 'scope blanked out and the dials governing it showed red.

Lars Nilsson could not really go paler than he was, but his hands trembled as they clenched into fists.

"Again! It's a damned jinx. For ten years, the automation hasn't held out. Not on the unmanned flights. Not on this. Who's responsible?"

There was no use trying to fix responsibility. No one was responsible, as Nilsson admitted with a groan almost at once. It was just that at the crucial moment—once again—things had failed.

"We've got to pull them through this somehow," he said, knowing that the outcome was questionable now.

Still, what could be done was being put into operation.

Davis said, "You saw that, too, didn't you?"

"I'm scared," whimpered Oldbury.

"You *saw* it. You saw the hidden side of the Moon as we went past and you saw *there wasn't any!* Good Lord, just sticks, just big beams holding up six million square miles of canvas. I swear it, *canvas!*"

He laughed wildly till he choked into breathlessness.

Then he said hoarsely, "For a million years mankind has been looking at the biggest false front ever dreamed of. Lovers spooned under a world-size stretch of canvas and called it Moon. The stars are painted; they must be. If we could only get out far enough, we could scrape some off and carry them home. Oh, it's funny." He was laughing again.

Oldbury wanted to ask why the grownup was laughing. He could only manage a "Why—why—" because the other's laughter was so wild that it froze the words into thick fright in his throat.

Davis said, "Why? How the devil should I know why? Why does Television City build false-front houses by the streetful for its shows? Maybe we're a show, and the two of us have stumbled way out here where the gimcrack scenery is set up instead of being on stage-center where we're supposed to be. Mankind isn't supposed to know about the scenery, either. That's why the information devices always go wrong past two hundred thousand miles. Of course, *we* saw it."

He looked crookedly at the big man beside him. "You know why it didn't matter if we saw it?"

Oldbury stared back out of his tear-stained face. "No. Why?"

Davis said, "Because it *doesn't* matter if we see it. If we get back to Earth and say that the Moon is canvas propped up by wood, they'd kill us. Or maybe lock us up in a madhouse for life if they felt kindhearted. That's why we won't say a word about this."

His voice suddenly deepened with menace. "You understand? Not a word!"

"I want my mother," whined Oldbury plaintively.

"Do you *understand?* We keep quiet. It's our only chance to be treated as sane. Let someone else come out and find out the truth and be slaughtered for it. Swear you'll keep quiet! Cross your heart and hope to die if you tell them!"

Davis was breathing harshly as he raised a threatening arm.

Oldbury shrank back as far as his prison-seat would let him. "Don't hit me. Don't!"

But Davis, past himself with fury, cried, "There's only one safe way," and struck at the cowering figure, and again, and again—

Godfrey Mayer sat at Oldbury's bedside and said, "Is it all clear to you?" Oldbury had been under observation for the better part of a month now.

Lars Nilsson sat at the other end of the room, listening and watching. He remembered Oldbury as he had appeared before he had climbed into the ship. The face was still square, but the cheeks had fallen inward and the strength was gone from it.

Oldbury's voice was steady, but half a whisper. "It wasn't a ship at all. We weren't in space."

"Now we're not just *saying* that. We *showed* you the ship and the controls that handled the *images* of the Earth and the Moon. You *saw* it."

"Yes. I know."

Mayer went on quietly, matter-of-factly, "It was a dry run, a complete duplication of conditions to test how men would hold out. Naturally, you and Davis couldn't be told this or the test would mean nothing. If things didn't work out, we could stop it at any time. We could learn by experience and make changes, try again with a new pair."

He had explained this over and over again. Oldbury had to be made to understand if he was ever to learn to live a useful life again.

"Has a new pair been tried yet?" asked Oldbury wistfully.

"Not yet. They will be. There are some changes to be made."

"I failed."

"We learned a great deal, so the experiment was a success in its way. Now listen—the controls of the ship were designed to go wrong when they did in order to test your reaction to emergency conditions after several days of travel strain. The breakdown was timed for the simulated swing about the Moon, which we were going to switch about so that you could see it from a new angle on the return trip. You weren't intended to see the other side and so we didn't build the other side. Call it economy. This test alone cost fifty million dollars and it's not easy to get appropriations."

Nilsson added bitterly, "Except that the shut-off switch on the 'scope didn't shut off in time. A valve caught. You saw the unfinished back of the Moon and we had to stop the ship to prevent——"

"That's it," interrupted Mayer. "Now repeat it, Oldbury. Repeat everything."

They walked down the corridor thoughtfully. Nilsson said, "He seemed almost himself today. Don't you think so?"

"There's improvement," Mayer acknowledged. "A great deal. But he's not through with therapy by any means."

Nilsson asked, "Any hope with Davis?"

Mayer shook his head slowly. "That's a different case. He's completely withdrawn. Won't talk. And that deprives us of any handle with which to reach him. We've tried aldosterone, ergot therapy, counter-electroencephalography, and so on. No good. He thinks if he talks, we'll put him in an institution or kill him. You couldn't ask for a more developed paranoia."

"Have you told him we *know?*"

"If we do, we'll bring on a homicidal seizure again and we may not be as lucky as we were in saving Oldbury. I rather think he's incurable. Sometimes, when the Moon is in the sky, the orderly tells me, Davis stares up at it and mutters, 'Canvas,' to himself."

Nilsson said soberly, "It reminds me of what Davis himself said in the early part of the trip. Ideas die hard. They do, don't they?"

"It's the tragedy of the world. Only——" Mayer hesitated.

"Only what?"

"Our unmanned rockets, three of them—the information devices on each stopped transmitting just before the boomerang swing and not one returned. Sometimes I just wonder——"

"*Shut up!*" said Nilsson fiercely.

Dead Ringer

By LESTER DEL REY

There was nothing, especially on Earth, which could set him free—the truth least of all!

Dane Phillips slouched in the window seat, watching the morning crowds on their way to work and carefully avoiding any attempt to read Jordan's old face as the editor skimmed through the notes. He had learned to make his tall, bony body seem all loose-jointed relaxation, no matter what he felt. But the oversized hands in his pockets were clenched so tightly that the nails were cutting into his palms.

Every tick of the old-fashioned clock sent a throb racing through his brain. Every rustle of the pages seemed to release a fresh shot of adrenalin into his blood stream. *This time,* his mind was pleading. *It has to be right this time.* . . .

Jordan finished his reading and shoved the folder back. He reached for his pipe, sighed, and then nodded slowly. "A nice job of researching, Phillips. And it might make a good feature for the Sunday section, at that."

It took a second to realize that the words meant acceptance, for Phillips had prepared himself too thoroughly against another failure. Now he felt the tautened muscles release, so quickly that he would have fallen if he hadn't been braced against the seat.

He groped in his mind, hunting for words, and finding none. There was only the hot, sudden flame of unbelieving hope. And then an almost blinding exultation.

Jordan didn't seem to notice his silence. The editor made a neat pile of the notes, nodding again. "Sure. I like it. We've been short of shock stuff lately and the readers go for it when we can get a fresh angle. But naturally you'd have to leave out all that nonsense on Blanding. Hell, the man's just buried, and his relatives and friends——"

"But that's the proof!" Phillips stared at the editor, trying to penetrate through the haze of hope that had somehow grown chilled and unreal. His thoughts were abruptly disorganized and out of his control. Only the urgency remained. "It's the key evidence. And we've got to move fast! I don't know how long it takes, but even one more day may be too late!"

Jordan nearly dropped the pipe from his lips as he jerked upright to peer sharply at the younger man. "Are you crazy? Do you seriously expect me to get an order to exhume him now? What would it get us, other than lawsuits? Even if we could get the order without cause—which we can't!"

Then the pipe did fall as he gaped open-mouthed. "My God, you believe all that stuff. You expected us to publish it *straight!*"

"No," Dane said thickly. The hope was gone now, as if it had never existed, leaving a numb emptiness where nothing mattered. "No, I guess I didn't really expect anything. But I believe the facts. Why shouldn't I?"

He reached for the papers with hands he could hardly control and began stuffing them back into the folder. All the careful documentation, the fingerprints—smudged, perhaps, in some cases, but still evidence enough for anyone but a fool——

"Phillips?" Jordan said questioningly to himself, and then his voice was taking on a new edge. "Phillips! Wait a minute, I've got it now! *Dane* Phillips, not *Arthur!* Two years on the

Trib. Then you turned up on the *Register* in Seattle? Phillip Dean, or some such name there."

"Yeah," Dane agreed. There was no use in denying anything now. "Yeah, Dane Arthur Phillips. So I suppose I'm through here?"

Jordan nodded again and there was a faint look of fear in his expression. "You can pick up your pay on the way out. And make it quick, before I change my mind and call the boys in white!"

It could have been worse. It had been worse before. And there was enough in the pay envelope to buy what he needed—a flash camera, a little folding shovel from one of the surplus houses, and a bottle of good scotch. It would be dark enough for him to taxi out to Oakhaven Cemetery, where Blanding had been buried.

It wouldn't change the minds of the fools, of course. Even if he could drag back what he might find, without the change being completed, they wouldn't accept the evidence. He'd been crazy to think anything could change their minds. And they called *him* a fanatic! If the facts he'd dug up in ten years of hunting wouldn't convince them, nothing would. And yet he had to see for himself, before it was too late!

He picked a cheap hotel at random and checked in under an assumed name. He couldn't go back to his room while there was a chance that Jordan still might try to turn him in. There wouldn't be time for Sylvia's detectives to bother him, probably, but there was the ever-present danger that one of the aliens might intercept the message.

He shivered. He'd been risking that for ten years, yet the likelihood was still a horror to him. The uncertainty made it harder to take than any human-devised torture could be. There was no way of guessing what an alien might do to anyone who discovered that all men were not human—that some were . . . zombies.

There was the classic syllogism: *All men are mortal; I am*

a man; therefore, I am mortal. But not Blanding—or Corporal Harding.

It was Harding's "death" that had started it all during the fighting on Guadalcanal. A grenade had come flying into the foxhole where Dane and Harding had felt reasonably safe. The concussion had knocked Dane out, possibly saving his life when the enemy thought he was dead. He'd come to in the daylight to see Harding lying there, mangled and twisted, with his throat torn. There was blood on Dane's uniform, obviously spattered from the dead man. It hadn't been a mistake or delusion; Harding had been dead.

It had taken Dane two days of crawling and hiding to get back to his group, too exhausted to report Harding's death. He'd slept for twenty hours. And when he awoke, Harding had been standing beside him, with a whole throat and a fresh uniform, grinning and kidding him for running off and leaving a stunned friend behind.

It was no ringer, but Harding himself, complete to the smallest personal memories and personality traits.

The pressures of war probably saved Dane's sanity while he learned to face the facts. All men are mortal; Harding is not mortal; therefore, Harding is not a man! Nor was Harding alone—Dane found enough evidence to know there were others.

The *Tribune* morgue yielded even more data. A man had faced seven firing squads and walked away. Another survived over a dozen attacks by professional killers. Fingerprints turned up mysteriously "copied" from those of men long dead. Some of the aliens seemed to heal almost instantly; others took days. Some operated completely alone; some seemed to have joined with others. But they were legion.

Lack of a clearer pattern of attack made him consider the possibility of human mutation, but such tissue was too wildly different, and the invasion had begun long before atomics or X-rays. He gave up trying to understand their alien motivations. It was enough that they existed in secret, slowly growing in numbers while mankind was unaware of them.

When his proof was complete and irrefutable, he took it to his editor—to be fired, politely but coldly. Other editors were less polite. But he went on doggedly trying and failing. What else could he do? Somehow, he had to find the few people who could recognize facts and warn them. The aliens would get him, of course, when the story broke, but a warned humanity could cope with them. *Ye shall know the truth, and the truth shall make you free.*

Then he met Sylvia by accident after losing his fifth job—a girl who had inherited a fortune big enough to spread his message in paid ads across the country. They were married before he found she was hardheaded about her money. She demanded a full explanation for every cent beyond his allowance. In the end, she got the explanation. And while he was trying to cash the check she gave him, she visited Dr. Buehl, to come back with a squad of quiet, refined strong-arm boys who made sure Dane reached Buehl's "rest home" safely.

Hydrotherapy . . . Buehl as the kindly firm father image . . . analysis . . . hypnosis that stripped every secret from him, including his worst childhood nightmare.

His father had committed a violent, bloody suicide after one of the many quarrels with Dane's mother. Dane had found the body.

Two nights after the funeral, he had dreamed of his father's face, horror-filled, at the window. He knew now that it was a normal nightmare, caused by being forced to look at the face in the coffin, but the shock had lasted for years. It had bothered him again, after his discovery of the aliens, until a thorough check had proved without doubt that his father had been fully human, with a human, if tempestuous, childhood behind him.

Dr. Buehl was delighted.

"You see, Dane? You *know* it was a nightmare, but you don't really believe it even now. Your father was an alien monster to you—no adult is quite human to a child. And that literal-minded self, your subconscious, saw him after he died. So there are alien monsters who return from death. Then you come to from a concussion. Harding is sprawled out unconscious, covered with blood—probably your blood, since you say he wasn't wounded, later.

"But after seeing your father, you can't associate blood with yourself—you see it as a horrible wound on Harding. When he turns out to be alive, you're still in partial shock, with your subconscious dominant. And that has the answer already. There are monsters who come back from the dead! An exaggerated reaction, but nothing really abnormal. We'll have you out of here in no time."

No non-directive psychiatry for Buehl. The man beamed paternally, chuckling as he added what he must have considered the clincher. "Anyhow, even zombies can't stand fire, Dane, so you can stop worrying about Harding. I checked up on him. He was burned to a crisp in a hotel fire two months ago."

It was logical enough to shake Dane's faith, until he came across Milo Blanding's picture in a magazine article on society in St. Louis. According to the item, Milo was a cousin of *the* Blandings, whose father had vanished in Chile as a young man, and who had just rejoined the family. The picture was of Harding!

An alien could have gotten away by simply committing suicide and being carried from the rest home, but Dane had to do it the hard way, watching his chance and using commando tactics on a guard who had come to accept him as a harmless nut.

In St. Louis, he'd used the "Purloined Letter" technique to hide—going back to newspaper work and using almost his real name. It had seemed to work, too. But he'd been less lucky about Harding-Blanding. The man had been in Europe on some kind of tour until his return only this last week.

Dane had seen him just once then—but long enough to be sure it was Harding—before he died again.

This time, it was in a drunken auto accident that seemed to be none of his fault, but left his body a mangled wreck.

It was almost dark when Dane dismissed the taxi at the false address, a mile from the entrance to the cemetery. He watched it turn back down the road, then picked up the valise with his camera and folding shovel. He shivered as he moved reluctantly ahead. War had proved that he would never be a brave man and the old fears of darkness and graveyards were still strong in him. But he had to know what the coffin contained now, if it wasn't already too late.

It represented the missing link in his picture of the aliens. What happened to them during the period of regrowth? Did they revert to their natural form? Were they at all conscious while the body reshaped itself into wholeness? Dane had puzzled over it night after night, with no answer.

Nor could he figure how they could escape from the grave. Perhaps a man could force his way out of some of the coffins he had inspected. The soil would still be soft and loose in the grave and a lot of the coffins and the boxes around them were strong in appearance only. A determined creature that could exist without much air for long enough might make it. But there were other caskets that couldn't be cracked, at least without the aid of outside help.

What happened when a creature that could survive even the poison of embalming fluids and the draining of all the blood woke up in such a coffin? Dane's mind skitted from it, as always, and then came back to it reluctantly.

There were still accounts of corpses turned up with the nails and hair grown long in the grave. Could normal tissues stand the current tricks of the morticians to have life enough for such growth? The possibility was absurd. Those cases had to be aliens—ones who hadn't escaped. Even they must die eventually in such a case—after weeks and months! It took time for hair to grow.

And there were stories of corpses that had apparently

fought and twisted in their coffins still. What was it like for an alien then, going slowly mad while it waited for true death? How long did madness take?

He shivered again, but went steadily on while the cemetery fence appeared in the distance. He'd seen Blanding's coffin —and the big, solid metal casket around it that couldn't be cracked by any amount of effort and strength. He was sure the creature was still there, unless it had a confederate. But that wouldn't matter. An empty coffin would also be proof.

Dane avoided the main gate, unsure about whether there would be a watchman or not. A hundred feet away, there was a tree near the ornamental spikes of the iron fence. He threw his bag over and began shinnying up. It was difficult, but he made it finally, dropping onto the soft grass beyond. There was the trace of the Moon at times through the clouds, but it hadn't betrayed him, and there had been no alarm wire along the top of the fence.

He moved from shadow to shadow, his hair prickling along the base of his neck. Locating the right grave in the darkness was harder than he had expected, even with an occasional brief use of the small flashlight. But at last he found the marker that was serving until the regular monument could arrive.

His hands were sweating so much that it was hard to use the small shovel, but the digging of foxholes had given him experience and the ground was still soft from the grave-diggers' work. He stopped once, as the Moon came out briefly. Again, a sound in the darkness above left him hovering and sick in the hole. But it must have been only some animal.

He uncovered the top of the casket with hands already blistering.

Then he cursed as he realized the catches were near the bottom, making his work even harder.

He reached them at last, fumbling them open. The metal top of the casket seemed to be a dome of solid lead, and he had no room to maneuver, but it began swinging up reluctantly, until he could feel the polished wood of the coffin.

Dane reached for the lid with hands he could barely control. Fear was thick in his throat now. What could an alien do to a man who discovered it? Would it be Harding there—or some monstrous thing still changing? How long did it take a revived monster to go mad when it found no way to escape?

He gripped the shovel in one hand, working at the lid with the other. Now, abruptly, his nerves steadied, as they had done whenever he was in real battle. He swung the lid up and began groping for the camera.

His hand went into the silk-lined interior and found nothing! He was too late. Either Harding had gotten out somehow before the final ceremony or a confederate had already been here. The coffin was empty.

There were no warning sounds this time—only hands that slipped under his arms and across his mouth, lifting him easily from the grave. A match flared briefly and he was looking into the face of Buehl's chief strong-arm man.

"Hello, Mr. Phillips. Promise to be quiet and we'll release you. Okay?" At Dane's sickened nod, he gestured to the others. "Let him go. And, Tom, better get that filled in. We don't want any trouble from this."

Surprise came from the grave a moment later. "Hey, Burke, there's no corpse here!"

Burke's words killed any hopes Dane had at once. "So what? Ever hear of cremation? Lots of people use a regular coffin for the ashes."

"He wasn't cremated," Dane told him. "You can check up on that." But he knew it was useless.

"Sure, Mr. Phillips. We'll do that." The tone was one reserved for humoring madmen. Burke turned, gesturing. "Better come along, Mr. Phillips. Your wife and Dr. Buehl are waiting at the hotel."

The gate was open now, but there was no sign of a watchman; if one worked here, Sylvia's money would have taken care of that, of course. Dane went along quietly, sitting in the rubble of his hopes while the big car purred through the morning and on down Lindell Boulevard toward the hotel. Once he shivered, and Burke dug out hot brandied coffee. They had thought of everything, including a coat to cover his dirt-soiled clothes as they took him up the elevator to where Buehl and Sylvia were waiting for him.

She had been crying, obviously, but there were no tears or recriminations when she came over to kiss him. Funny, she must still love him—as he'd learned to his surprise he loved her. Under different circumstances . . .

"So you found me?" he asked needlessly of Buehl. He was operating on purely automatic habits now, the reaction from the night and his failure numbing him emotionally. "Jordan got in touch with you?"

Buehl smiled back at him. "We knew where you were all along, Dane. But as long as you acted normal, we hoped it might be better than the home. Too bad we couldn't stop you before you got all mixed up in this."

"So I suppose I'm committed to your booby-hatch again?"

Buehl nodded, refusing to resent the term. "I'm afraid so, Dane—for a while, anyhow. You'll find your clothes in that room. Why don't you clean up a little? Take a hot bath, maybe. You'll feel better."

Dane went in, surprised when no guards followed him. But they had thought of everything. What looked like a screen on the window had been recently installed and it was strong enough to prevent his escape. Blessed are the poor, for they shall be poorly guarded!

He was turning on the shower when he heard the sound of voices coming through the door. He left the water running and came back to listen. Sylvia was speaking.

"—seems so logical, so completely rational."

"It makes him a dangerous person," Buehl answered, and there was no false warmth in his voice now. "Sylvia, you've got to admit it to yourself. All the reason and analysis in the world won't convince him he's wrong. This time we'll have to use shock treatment. Burn over those memories, fade them out. It's the only possible course."

There was a pause and then a sigh. "I suppose you're right."

Dane didn't wait to hear more. He drew back, while his mind fought to accept the hideous reality. Shock treatment! The works, if what he knew of psychiatry was correct. Enough of it to erase his memories—a part of himself. It wasn't therapy Buehl was considering; it couldn't be.

It was the answer of an alien that had a human in its hands —one who knew too much!

He might have guessed. What better place for an alien than in the guise of a psychiatrist? Where else was there the chance for all the refined, modern torture needed to burn out a man's mind? Dane had spent ten years in fear of being discovered by them—and now Buehl had him.

Sylvia? He couldn't be sure. Probably she was human. It wouldn't make any difference. There was nothing he could do through her. Either she was part of the game or she really thought him mad.

Dane tried the window again, but it was hopeless. There would be no escape this time. Buehl couldn't risk it. The shock treatment—or whatever Buehl would use under the name of shock treatment—would begin at once. It would be easy to slip, to use an overdose of something, to make sure Dane was killed. Or there were ways of making sure it didn't matter. They could leave him alive, but take his mind away.

In alien hands, human psychiatry could do worse than all the medieval torture chambers!

The sickness grew in his stomach as he considered the worst that could happen. Death he could accept, if he had to. He could even face the chance of torture by itself, as he had accepted the danger while trying to have his facts published. But to have his mind taken from him, a step at a time—to watch his personality, his ego, rotted away under him—and to know that he would wind up as a drooling idiot . . .

He made his decision, almost as quickly as he had come to realize what Buehl must be.

There was a razor in the medicine chest. It was a safety razor, of course, but the blade was sharp and it would be big enough. There was no time for careful planning. One of the guards might come in at any moment if they thought he was taking too long.

Some fear came back as he leaned over the wash basin, staring at his throat, fingering the suddenly murderous blade. But the pain wouldn't last long—a lot less than there would be under shock treatment, and less pain. He'd read enough to feel sure of that.

Twice he braced himself and failed at the last second. His mind flashed out in wild schemes, fighting against what it knew had to be done.

The world still had to be warned! If he could escape, somehow . . . if he could still find a way. . . . He couldn't quit, no matter how impossible things looked.

But he knew better. There was nothing one man could do against the aliens in this world they had taken over. He'd never had a chance. Man had been chained already by carefully developed ridicule against superstition, by carefully indoctrinated gobbledegook about insanity, persecution complexes, and all the rest.

For a second, Dane even considered the possibility that he was insane. But he knew it was only a blind effort to cling to life. There had been no insanity in him when he'd groped for evidence in the coffin and found it empty!

He leaned over the wash basin, his eyes focused on his throat, and his hand came down and around, carrying the razor blade through a lethal semicircle.

Dane Phillips watched fear give place to sickness on his face as the pain lanced through him and the blood spurted.

He watched horror creep up to replace the sickness while the bleeding stopped and the gash began closing.

By the time he recognized his expression as the same one he'd seen on his father's face at the window so long ago, the wound was completely healed.

The Haunted Corpse

By FREDERIK POHL

With Horn's invention, we had the world by the tail, by God . . . or was that our own tail?

Well, we moved in pretty promptly. This Van Pelt turned up at the Pentagon on a Thursday, and by the following Monday, I had a task force of a hundred and thirty-five men with full supply bivouacked around the old man's establishment.

He didn't like it. I rather expected he wouldn't. He came storming out of the big house as the trucks came in. "Get out of here! Go on, get out! This is private property and you're trespassing. I won't have it, do you hear me? Get out!"

I stepped out of the jeep and gave him a soft salute. "Colonel Windermere, sir. My orders are to establish a security cordon around your laboratories. Here you are, sir—your copy of the orders."

He scowled and fussed and finally snatched the orders out of my hand. Well, they were signed by General Follansbee himself, so there wasn't much argument. I stood by politely, prepared to make matters as painless for him as I could. I don't hold with antagonizing civilians unnecessarily. But he evidently didn't want it to be painless.

"Van Pelt!" he bellowed. "Why, that rotten, decrepit, back-stabbing monster of a——"

I listened attentively. He was very good. What he was saying in essence was that he felt his former associate, Van Pelt, had had no right to report to the Pentagon that there was potential military applicability in the Horn Effect. Of course, it was the trimmings with which he stated his complaint that made it so effective.

I finally had to interrupt him. "Dr. Horn, the general asked me to give you his personal assurance that we will not in any way interfere with your work here. It is only a matter of security. I'm sure you understand the importance of security, sir."

"Security! Now listen here, Lieutenant, I won't tolerate——"

"Colonel, sir. Lieutenant Colonel Windermere."

"Colonel, general, lieutenant, what the hell do I care? Listen to me! The Horn Effect is my personal property, not yours, not Van Pelt's, not the government's, not anybody's but mine! I was working in personality dissociation before you were born and——"

"*Security, sir!*" I made it crackle.

He looked at me pop-eyed and I nodded toward my driver. "He isn't cleared, Dr. Horn," I explained. "All right, O'Hare. You're dismissed."

Sergeant O'Hare saluted from behind the wheel and took off.

I said soothingly: "Now, Dr. Horn, I want you to know that I'm here to help you. If there's anything you want, just ask; I'll get it. Even if you want to go into town, that can be arranged. Of course, you'd better give us twenty-four-hours' notice so we can arrange a route and——"

He said briefly: "Young man, go to the devil." And he turned and stalked into the big house. I watched him and I remember thinking that, for a lean old goat of eighty or eighty-five, he had a lot of spirit.

I went about my business and Dr. Horn picked up the phone in his house and demanded the Pentagon to protest our being here. When he finally realized he was talking to our intercept monitor, and that no calls would go out on his line without authorization from me, he yelled up another storm.

But naturally that wasn't going to get him anywhere. Not when General Follansbee himself had signed the orders.

About oh-eight-hundred the next morning, I ran a surprise full-scale inspection and simulated infiltration to keep the detachment on its toes. It all checked out perfectly. I had detailed Sergeant O'Hare to try to sneak in from the marshland south of the old man's place, and he was spotted fifty yards from the perimeter. When he reported to me, he was covered with mud and shaking.

"Those trigger-happy ba—those guards, sir, nearly blew my head off. If the officer of the day hadn't happened by, I think they would of done it, only he recognized me."

"All right, Sergeant." I dismissed him and went in to breakfast. The wire-stringing detail had worked all night and we were now surrounded with triple-strand electrified barbwire, with an outer line of barbwire chevaux-de-frise. There were guard towers every fifty yards and at the corners, and a construction detail was clearing the brush for an additional twenty yards outside the wire. I thought briefly of bulldozing a jeep-path in the cleared area for permanent rotating patrols, but it didn't really seem necessary.

I was rather hungry and a little sleepy—that wire-stringing detail had made quite a lot of noise. But on the whole, I was pleased, if a little irritable.

The O.D. phoned in for instructions while I was breakfasting; Van Pelt had arrived from town and the O.D. wouldn't let him in without my approval. I authorized it, and in a moment Van Pelt turned up in my private mess, looking simultaneously worried and jubilant.

"How'd he take it, Colonel?" he asked. "Is he—I mean is he sore?"

"Very."

"Oh." Van Pelt quivered slightly, then shrugged. "Well, you're here, so I guess he won't try anything." He looked hungrily at my buckwheat cakes and sausages. "I, uh, didn't get a chance to have breakfast on the way down——"

"Be my guest, Dr. Van Pelt." I ordered another place set and extra portions of everything. He ate it all—God knows how. Looking at him, you'd think he could march two hundred miles on the stored fat he already had. He wasn't much over five-six, perhaps five-seven, and I'd guess two hundred and eighty pounds bone-dry. He was about as unlike Dr. Horn as you could imagine.

I wondered how they had got along, working together—but I already knew the answer. They got along badly, else Van Pelt never would have gone running to the Pentagon. I tried to keep an open mind about that, of course. I mean General Follansbee thought it was important to national defense, and so on——

But I couldn't help thinking how I would feel if some junior went over my head in that way. Military discipline is one thing, and civilian affairs, as I understand it, are something else, but all the same——

Anyway, he had done it and here we were. Not much like a fighting command for me, but orders are orders.

At fourteen hundred, I paid a call on Dr. Horn.

He looked up as the clerk-typist corporal and I came in. He didn't say anything, just stood up and pointed to the door.

I said: "Good afternoon, Dr. Horn. If this is an inconvenient time for you to make your daily progress report, just say the word. I'm here to help you, you know. Would from twelve to thirteen hundred every day be more satisfactory? Or in the morning?"

"Every *day?*"

"That's right, sir. Perhaps you didn't notice Paragraph Eight of my orders. General Follansbee's instructions were to——"

He interrupted me with a disrespectful comment on General Follansbee, but I pretended not to hear. Besides, he might have been right.

I said: "As a starter, sir, perhaps you'll be good enough to show us around the laboratories. I think you'll find that Corporal McCabe will be able to take your words down at normal speed."

"Take *what* words down?"

"Your progress report, sir. What you've accomplished in the past twenty-four hours. Only this time, of course, we'd better have a fill-in on everything to date."

He roared: "*No!* I *won't!* I absolutely will *not!*"

I was prepared for that. I let him roar. When he was through roaring, I put it to him very simply. I said: "That's the way it's going to be."

He stuttered and gagged. "Why, you stinking little two-bit Army—— Listen, what's the idea——"

He stopped and looked at me, frowning. I was glad that he stopped, since in the confidential section of my orders—the paragraphs I didn't show Dr. Horn, as he was not cleared for access to such material—there had been a paragraph which was relevant here.

Van Pelt had told the general that Horn's health was not good. Apoplexy, I believe—I am not very familiar with medical terms. At any rate, Van Pelt, while being de-briefed by the general's Intelligence section, had reported that the old man might drop dead at any minute. Well, he looked it, at least when he was mad. I certainly didn't want him to drop dead before I had made a proper Situation Analysis, for which I needed his report.

Horn sat down. He said, with rusty craft: "You're going to stick to what you say?"

"Yes, sir."

"Then," he said, with a pathetic, senile cunning, "I suppose I must reconcile myself to the situation. Exactly what is it you want, Lieutenant?"

"The report, sir."

He nodded briefly. "Just so."

Ah-ha, I thought—to myself, of course—this will prove interesting. Do you suppose he will try to win my confidence so he can phone his Congressman? Or merely get me to turn my back so he can clobber me over the head?

"Yes, yes, the report. Just so," he said, staring thoughtfully at a machine of some kind. It rather resembled an SCR-784, the Mark XII model, the one that has something to do with radar, or radio, something electronic. I leave that sort of thing to the Signal Corpsmen, naturally. I have my job and they have theirs. "Just so," he repeated. "Well, I shall have to do as you wish. Observe," he said, rising, "my polycloid quasitron. As you see——"

There was a strangling noise from Corporal McCabe. I looked at him; he was in difficulties.

"Sir," I interrupted the doctor, "will you spell that, please?"

He chuckled rather grimly. "Just so. P-o-l-y-c-l-o-i-d q-u-a-s-i-t-r-o-n. Well, Lieutenant, you're familiar with the various potentiometric studies of the brain which—— Perhaps I should begin further back. The brain, you must realize, is essentially an electrical device. Potentiometer studies have shown——"

Every thirty to fifty seconds he glanced at me, and turned his head half to one side, and waited. And I said, "I see," and he said, "Just so," and he went on. Corporal McCabe was in acute distress, of course, but I rather enjoyed the exposition; it was restful. One learns to make these things restful, you see. One doesn't spend as much time as I have in staff meetings without learning a few lessons in survival tactics.

When he had entirely finished (McCabe was groaning softly to himself), I summed it all up for him.

"In other words, sir, you've perfected a method of electronically killing a man without touching him."

For some reason, that rocked Dr. Horn.

He stared at me. "Electronically," he said after a moment. "Killing. A man. Without. Touching. Him."

"That's what I said, sir," I agreed.

"Just so, just so." He cleared his throat and took a deep breath. "Lieutenant, will you tell me one thing? What in the sweet name of heaven did I say that gave you that particular stupid notion?"

I could hardly believe my ears. "Why—why, that's what the general said, Dr. Horn! And he talked to Van Pelt, you realize."

I wondered: Was that his little trick? Was he trying to pretend the weapon wouldn't work?

He raved for twenty-five seconds about Van Pelt. Then he checked himself and looked thoughtful again.

"No," he said. "No, it can't be Van Pelt. That idiot general of yours must be off his rocker."

I said formally: "Dr. Horn, do you state that your, ah—" I glanced at McCabe; he whispered the name—"your polycloid quasitron does not, through electronic means, deprive a person of life at a distance?"

He scowled like a maniac. It was almost as if something were physically hurting him. With an effort, he conceded: "Oh—yes. Yes, perhaps. Would you say a locomotive oxidizes coal into impure silicaceous aggregates? It does, you know—they call them ashes. Well, then, you could say that's what the quasitron does."

"Well, then!"

He said, still painfully: "All right. Just so. Yes, I see what you mean. No doubt that explains why you're here. I had wondered, I confess. You feel this is a weapon."

"Of course, sir."

"Ah."

He sat down and took out a fat, stickily black pipe and began to fill it. He said cheerfully: "We understand each other then. My machine renders humans into corpses. A chipped flint will also do that—*Pithecanthropus erectus* discovered that quite independently some time ago—but no matter, that is the aspect which interests you. Very good."

He lit the pipe. "I mention," he added, puffing, "that my quasitron does something no chipped flint can do. It removes that thing which possesses only a negative definition from the human body, the quantity that we will term x, which, added to the body, produces a man, subtracted from it, leaves a corpse. You don't care about this."

He had me going for a moment, I admit. I said briskly: "Sir, I'm afraid I don't understand you."

"You're bloody well told you don't understand me!" he howled. "We're all corpses, don't you understand? Corpses inhabited by ghosts! And there's only one man in the world who can separate the two without destroying them and that's me. And there's only one way in the world to do it and that's with my quasitron! Lieutenant, you're a stupid, pigheaded man! I——"

Well, enough was enough.

"Good afternoon, sir," I said politely, though I knew he couldn't hear what I said with his own voice drowning me out. I nodded to Corporal McCabe. He closed his notebook with a snap, jumped to open the door for me, and the two of us left.

There was no reason to stay, do you see? I already had all the material for my Situation Analysis.

Just the same, I got Van Pelt into my private quarters that evening. I wanted to see if I could make an assessment of the old man's sanity.

"He's perfectly sane, Colonel Windermere. Perfectly!" Van Pelt's jowls were shaking. "He's dangerous—very dangerous. Particularly dangerous to me. I mean, of course, if I hadn't had your promise of complete protection. Of course. But dangerous. I—"

He paused, glancing at the sideboard where the bowl of fruit (I always take fruit after the evening meal) still reposed. He coughed. "Colonel, I wonder if—"

"Help yourself," I told him.

"Thank you, thank you! My, but that looks good! Honestly, Colonel Windermere, I feel that an apple is almost Nature's rarest treat. Well, pears, yes. I must say that pears—"

I said: "Dr. Van Pelt, excuse me. I want the straight dope on Horn. What's this ghost business?"

He looked at me blankly, crunching. "Ghost business?" He took another bite. Crunch, crunch, "My goodness, Colonel—" crunch, crunch—"Colonel Windermere, I don't know—Oh, the *ghost* business!" Crunch. "Oh, that. Why, that's just Dr. Horn's way of putting it. You know his manner. You see, there is a difference between a living man and a dead man, and that difference is what Dr. Horn whimsically terms a 'ghost.'" He chuckled, tossed the core into my wastebasket, and took another apple. "Call it life, plus intelligence, plus soul, if there is such a word in your lexicon, Colonel. Dr. Horn merely sums them up and terms the total 'ghost.'"

I pressed him closely. "This machine is a—a ghost conjurer?"

"No, no!" he cried, nearly losing his temper. "Colonel, don't permit yourself to be fooled. Dr. Horn is an arrogant, unprincipled man, but he is not an ass or a faker. Forget the term 'ghost,' since it distresses you. Think of—think of—"

He searched for words, shrugged. "Think merely of the difference between being alive and being dead. It is that difference that Dr. Horn's machine works on. Life, intelligence —electrical phenomena, you understand? And Dr. Horn drains them from the body, stores them—can, if he wishes, replace them, or even put them in another body." He nodded, beamed at me, bit into the second apple. Crunch, crunch, crunch.

Well, sir!

When I had got rid of him, I sat, trying to control my temper, for some time.

This strange old man had a machine that could take a mind right out of a body—yes, and put it in another body!

Confound them, why hadn't they said so instead of beating around the bush?

Naturally, I didn't believe it until I saw it—and then I saw it. The next morning, at my request, Dr. Horn put a hen and a cocker spaniel into what he called his polycloid quasitron and exchanged them.

Then I believed. I saw the hen trying to wag its tail and the spaniel, whimpering, its snout bruised, endeavoring to peck corn.

Corporal McCabe's eyes were popping out of his head. He started to write something, glanced at me, shook his head slowly and sat staring into space.

Well, time for him later. I said: "You can do it, Dr. Horn. You can take a hen and put it into a cocker spaniel and vice versa."

He nodded, too stiff-necked to show his gratification. "Just so, Lieutenant."

"And—and you can do it with people, too?"

"Oh, indeed I can! Indeed I can!" He scowled. "These ridiculous laws governing the conduct of institutions! I've tried, I swear I've tried, to be permitted to conduct a simple exchange. A man dying of terminal cancer, you see, and a feeble-minded youth. Why not? Put the sound mind in the sound body and let the decayed parts rot together! But will they let me?"

"I see. Then you've never done it."

"Never." He looked at me, his old eyes gleaming. "But now you're here, Lieutenant. A military man. Very brave, eh? All I've needed is a volunteer. That coward Van Pelt refused, my gardener refused, everyone has refused! But you——"

"Negative, sir!" Confound the man's arrogance! "I am not a

lieutenant. I am a field-grade officer! I don't imagine you appreciate the investment our service has in me!"

"But, Lieutenant, the importance——"

"Negative, sir!"

The man's stupidity amazed me. Me, a lieutenant colonel! What would it do to my 201 file? What about my time in grade? The Pentagon would rock, literally rock!

I said, trying to be calm: "You don't understand military matters, Dr. Horn. I assure you, if there is a need for volunteers, we will find them for you. Believe me, sir, we are here to help! Why, one of our enlisted men will be pleased—proud, sir!—to offer his services in this——Corporal McCabe! Come back here!"

But it was too late. Moaning, he had fled the room.

I turned to Dr. Horn, a little embarrassed. "Well, sir, we understand these things—a shock to the boy, of course. But I'll find you a volunteer. Trust me."

The man was as pleased as a fourth-year cadet in June Week, but he still wouldn't show it. Stiffly, he said: "Just so, Lieutenant—Major, I mean. Or Captain. Tomorrow will do splendidly."

Tomorrow! That wonderful day! For I saw Dr. Horn do just as he had promised and I—I alone among them all—I saw what it meant. A weapon? Nonsense, it was much, much more than that!

There was the matter of finding volunteers. Trust me for that, as I had told Dr. Horn.

There was the latrine orderly in Able Company—AWOL, and when I explained to him what a court-martial would do, he volunteered with blinding speed. Didn't even ask what he was volunteering for.

We needed two. My executive officer, I am proud to say, volunteered to be the second. A courageous man, typical of the very best leadership type.

We arrived in Dr. Horn's laboratory. The men were strapped in place and anesthetized—at my request; I wanted to maintain security, so naturally I couldn't let them know what was happening. Just before he went under, the exec whispered, "Sir—no Korea?"

"I promise, Captain," I said solemnly, and before his eyes I ripped up the transfer recommendation I had written the night before. He went to sleep happy.

Biz, buzz, crackle. I don't understand these scientific things, but when the electric sparks had stopped flashing and the whiny, drony sounds had died away, Dr. Horn gave them each a shot of something, one at a time.

The latrine orderly opened his eyes. I stepped before him. "Name, rank, and serial number!"

"Sir," he said crisply, "Lefferts, Robert T., Captain, A.U.S., Serial Number 0-3339615!"

Good heavens! But I made sure with a test question: "Where is it you don't want to be transferred?"

"Why—why, Korea, sir. Please, sir, not there! I'll volunteer for your test. I'll——"

I nodded to Dr. Horn and another needle put him back to sleep.

Then the body that was my exec. The body opened its eyes. "Cunnel, suh! I changin' my mind. I'll take the guardhouse, suh, only——"

"At ease!" I commanded, and nodded to Dr. Horn.

There was no doubt about it. "You really did it."

He nodded. "Just so, Lieutenant. I really did."

As he switched them back again, I began to realize what it all meant.

In my office, I got on the phone.

"Crash priority!" I ordered. "The Pentagon! General Follansbee, priority and classified. Ask him to stand by for scrambler!"

I slapped the field phone into its case. A weapon? A weapon was nothing by comparison. We had the world by the tail. I confess I was floating on a cloud of pure joy. I saw my eagles within my grasp, perhaps, in a year or less, my first star—there was nothing the Army would deny the officer who could give them what I could offer.

A rattle and a crash, and Van Pelt thumped into my room, his face smeared, one hand clutching a melting chocolate bar. "Colonel Windermere!" he gasped. "You let Horn make his test! But that's all he's been waiting for! He——"

It was unbearable. "O'Hare!" I roared. Sergeant O'Hare appeared, looking uncomfortable. "How dare you let this man in here without my permission? Don't you realize I'm making a classified scrambler call to the *Pentagon?*"

O'Hare said weakly: "Sir, he——"

"Get him out of here!"

"Yessir!" The fat little man kicked up a fuss, but O'Hare was much bigger than he. Just the same, Van Pelt gave him a tussle. He was yelling something, all upset, but my call to the Pentagon came through and I frankly didn't listen.

"General Follansbee? Windermere here, sir. Please scramble!" I slapped the button that scrambled the call from my end. In a moment I heard the general's voice come through in clear, but anyone tapping in on the scrambled circuit would hear nothing but electronic garbage.

I gave him a quick, concise account of what I had seen. He was irritated at first—disappointed. I had thought he would be.

"Change them around, Windermere?" he complained in a high-pitched voice. "Why, what's the use of changing them around? Do you see any strategic value in that? Might confuse them a little, I suppose—if we could get a couple of the enemy commanders. But is that all there is to it? I was looking for something bigger, Windermere, something of more immediate military advantage. That Van Pelt must learn not to waste the time of high Army officers!"

"General Follansbee, may I point out something? Suppose—suppose, sir, that someone way up top should visit the States. Suppose, for instance, that we surrounded him, him and his whole entourage. Switched them all. Put our own men in their bodies. You see?"

He was thinking I was insane; you could tell it. "Colonel Windermere, what in the world are you talking about?"

"It would work, sir," I said persuasively. "Believe me, I've seen it. But suppose we couldn't do that. What about a hostile U.N. envoy, eh? Get him, put one of G-2's operatives inside his body. Do you follow me, sir? No question about whose Intelligence would get the facts in a case like that, is there, sir? Or—maybe we wouldn't want to do anything like that in peacetime, but what about in war? Take a couple of their prisoners, sir, put our own men in their bodies. Exchange the prisoners!"

Well, I went on and I won't say I convinced him of anything. But by the time he hung up, he was thinking pretty hard.

And I had an appointment to see him in the Pentagon the following day. Once I was on the spot, I knew I was in, for he wouldn't take the responsibility of passing up a thing like this alone. He'd call a staff meeting, and somewhere on the staff, somebody would understand.

I could feel the stars on my shoulders already. . . .

"What is it, O'Hare?" I demanded.

I was becoming very irritated with the man. He was sticking his head in the door, looking very worried. Well, that was reasonable; I was quite close to giving him something to worry about.

"Sir, it's that Van Pelt." He swallowed and looked a little foolish. "I—I don't know if he's nuts or what, sir, but he says —he says that Dr. Horn wants to live forever! He says all Horn was waiting for was to make a test on a human being. I don't know what he's talking about, but he says that now that you've given Horn his test, sir, Horn's going to grab the first man he sees and, uh, steal his body. Does that make sense, sir?"

Did it make *sense?*

I shoved him out of the way, stopping only to grab my side arm.

It made all the sense in the world.

It was just what you'd expect of a man like Horn—he'd take an invention like this and use it to steal other people's bodies, to prolong his own nearly senile existence in a younger body!

And if that happened, what would become of my general's star?

Oh, I knew just the way Horn's mind would work. Steal a body; smash the machine; get away. Could we trace him? Impossible—there was no test in the world, no fingerprints, no eye-retina charts, no blood-type classifications that could distinguish John Smith from Horn inhabiting John Smith.

It was the obvious thing to do; it had occurred to me at once.

Van Pelt had gone blundering in, conquering his cowardice. His objective was to try to stop Horn, I supposed, but what was the effect of his mad rush into the laboratory? Why, to furnish Horn with a body!

And if one was not enough, there would be others, for there were the men of my own detachment, standing guard, going about their duties; it would not be impossible for Horn to lure one inside. He would not wait. No, for the chance that his own body would wear out on him in a moment, any moment, was very great—old, worn, and now subject to the pounding of a new hope and excitement, it might collapse at the lightest touch, like the bombed-out hulk of a barracks.

So I hurried—into the building, through the long dark halls, into the room where the big polycloid quasitron stood——

And I tripped over a human body, stumbled, fell, the gun spinning out of my hand. I scrambled to my hands and knees, touching the body—still warm, but not very warm. Dr. Horn! His castoff cocoon, abandoned!

And before me capered and screeched the figure that once had been Van Pelt, holding a weapon.

"Too late!" he cried. "Too late, Colonel Windermere!"

Van Pelt! But it was not Van Pelt that lived in that fat, soft corpse today, I knew, for the Horn-in-Van Pelt held a gun of his own in one hand and in the other a bar of metal. And with it he was bashing, bashing the polycloid quasitron! Bam, and showers of sparks flew from it; crash, and it began to glow, sag, melt.

And he had the gun. It was a very difficult situation.

But not hopeless. For we were not alone.

Next to my fallen gun lay another body. Not dead, this one; unconscious. It was Corporal McCabe, struck down with a blow to the head.

"Stop!" I cried, getting to my knees. Horn-Van Pelt turned to stare at me. "Stop, don't wreck the machine! More depends on it than you can possibly realize, Dr. Horn. It isn't only a matter of your life—trust me for that, Dr. Horn. I shall see that you have bodies, fine bodies, to hold your mind as long as you want it. But think of the safety of our country! And think of your sacred duty to science!" I appealed, thinking of my general's stars.

Corporal McCabe twitched and stirred.

I stood up. Horn's carrier, Van Pelt, dropped his iron bar in alarm, switched the gun to his right hand, stared at me. Good! Better at me than at McCabe.

I said: "You must not destroy the machine, Dr. Horn! We need it."

"But it is destroyed already," the little fat figure said stupidly, gesturing. "And I am not Dr.——"

Splat.

McCabe's bullet caught him at the base of the skull. The brain that had evicted Van Pelt to house a Horn now housed no one; the blubbery little figure was dead.

And I was raging!

"You fool, you idiot, you unutterable ass!" I screamed at McCabe. "Why did you kill him? Wing him, yes; injure him, break his leg, shoot the gun out of his hand. But now he's dead and the machine is gone!"

And so, sadly, were my general's stars.

The corporal was looking at me with a most peculiar expression.

I got hold of myself. A life's dream was gone, but there was no help for it now. Maybe the engineers could tinker and discover and rebuild—but, glancing at the wreck of the polycloid quasitron, I knew that was a dream.

I took a deep breath.

"All right, McCabe," I said crisply. "Report to your quarters. I'll talk to you later on. Right now, I must phone the Pentagon and try to account for your blundering in this matter!"

McCabe patted the gun fondly, put it on the floor, and left. I reported manfully to the general, stood at attention while he chewed me out, and had just hung up when the phone rang and I heard McCabe's voice at the other end.

"What is it, Corporal?" I demanded, annoyed. "I'm busy!"

"I just called in to report that I haven't found quarters yet, but I will soon—very far away, Lieutenant."

"Dr. Horn!" I gasped.

"Just so, Lieutenant," he said and chuckled as he hung up.

The Model of a Judge

By WILLIAM MORRISON

Should a former outlaw become a judge—even if he need only pass sentence on a layer cake?

Ronar was reformed, if that was the right word, but he could see that they didn't trust him. Uneasiness spoke in their awkward hurried motions when they came near him; fear looked out of their eyes. He had to reassure himself that all this would pass. In time they'd learn to regard him as one of themselves and cease to recall what he had once been. For the time being, however, they still remembered. And so did he.

Mrs. Claymore, of the Presiding Committee, was babbling, "Oh, Mrs. Silver, it's so good of you to come. Have you entered the contest?"

"Not really," said Mrs. Silver with a modest laugh. "Of course I don't expect to win against so many fine women who are taking part. But I just thought I'd enter to—to keep things interesting."

"That was very kind of you. But don't talk about not winning. I still remember some of the dishes you served for dinner at your home that time George and I paid you a visit. Mmmm—they were really delicious."

Mrs. Silver uttered another little laugh. "Just ordinary recipes. I'm so glad you liked them, though."

"I certainly did. And I'm sure the judge will like your cake, too."

"The judge? Don't you usually have a committee?"

He could hear every word. They had no idea how sharp his sense of hearing was, and he had no desire to disconcert them further by letting them know. He could hear every conversation taking place in ordinary tones in the large reception room. When he concentrated he could make out the whispers. At this point he had to concentrate, for Mrs. Claymore leaned over and breathed into her friend's attentive ear.

"My dear, haven't you heard? We've had such trouble with that committee—there were such charges of favoritism! It was really awful."

"Really? But how did you find a judge then?"

"Don't look now—no, I'll tell you what to do. Pretend I said something funny, and throw your head back and laugh. Take a quick glance at him while you do. He's sitting up there alone, on the platform."

Mrs. Silver laughed gracefully as directed, and her eyes swept the platform. She became so excited, she almost forgot to whisper.

"Why, he's——"

"Shhh. Lower your voice, my dear."

"Why—he isn't human!"

"He's supposed to be—now. But, of course, that's a matter of opinion!"

"But who on Earth thought of making him judge?"

"No one on Earth. Professor Halder, who lives over on that big asteroid the other side of yours, heard of the troubles we had, and came up with the suggestion. At first it seemed absurd——"

"It certainly seems absurd to me!" agreed Mrs. Silver.

"It was the only thing we could do. There was no one else we could trust."

"But what does he know about cakes?"

"My dear, he has the most exquisite sense of taste!"

"I still don't understand."

"It's superhuman. Before we adopted Professor Halder's suggestion, we gave him a few tests. The results simply left us gasping. We could mix all sorts of spices—the most delicate, most exotic herbs from Venus or Mars, and the strongest, coarsest flavors from Earth or one of the plant-growing asteroids—and he could tell us everything we had added, and exactly how much."

"I find that hard to believe, Matilda."

"Isn't it? It's honestly incredible. If I hadn't seen him do it myself, I wouldn't have believed it."

"But he doesn't have human preferences. Wasn't he—wasn't he——"

"Carnivorous? Oh, yes. They say he was the most vicious creature imaginable. Let an animal come within a mile of him, and he'd scent it and be after it in a flash. He and the others of his kind made the moon he came from uninhabitable for any other kind of intelligent life. Come to think of it, it may have been the very moon we're on now!"

"Really?"

"Either this, or some other moon of Saturn's. We had to do something about it. We didn't want to kill them off, naturally; that would have been the easiest way, but so uncivilized! Finally, our scientists came up with the suggestion for psychological reforming. Professor Halder told us how difficult it all was, but it seems to have worked. In his case, at least."

Mrs. Silver stole another glance. "Did it? I don't notice any one going near him."

"Oh, we don't like to tempt fate, Clara. But if there were

really any danger, I'm sure the psychologists would never have let him out of their clutches."

"I hope not. But psychologists take the most reckless risks sometimes—with other people's lives!"

"Well, there's one psychologist who's risking his own life —and his own wife, too. You know Dr. Cabanis, don't you?"

"Only by sight. Isn't his wife that stuck-up thing?"

"That's the one. Dr. Cabanis is the man who had actual charge of reforming him. And he's going to be here. His wife is entering a cake."

"Don't tell me that she really expects to win!"

"She bakes well, my dear. Let's give the she-devil her due. How on Earth an intelligent man like Dr. Cabanis can stand her, I don't know, but, after all, he's the psychologist, not I, and he could probably explain it better than I could."

Ronar disengaged his attention.

So Dr. Cabanis was here. He looked around, but the psychologist was not in sight. He would probably arrive later.

The thought stirred a strange mixture of emotions. Some of the most painful moments of his life were associated with the presence of Dr. Cabanis. His early life, the life of a predatory carnivore, had been an unthinkingly happy one. He supposed that he could call his present life a happy one too, if you weren't overly particular how you defined the term. But that period in between!

That had been, to say the least, painful. Those long sessions with Dr. Cabanis had stirred him to the depths of a soul he hadn't known he possessed. The electric shocks and the druggings he hadn't minded so much. But the gradual reshaping of his entire psyche, the period of basic instruction, in which he had been taught to hate his old life so greatly that he could no longer go back to it even if the way were open, and the conditioning for a new and useful life with human beings—that was torture of the purest kind.

If he had known what was ahead of him, he wouldn't have

gone through it at all. He'd have fought until he dropped, as so many of the others like him did. Still, now that it was over, he supposed that the results were worth the pain. He had a position that was more important than it seemed at first glance. He exercised control over a good part of the food supply intended for the outer planets, and his word was trusted implicitly. Let him condemn an intended shipment, and cancellation followed automatically, without the formality of confirmation by laboratory tests. He was greatly admired. And feared.

They had other feelings about him too. He overheard one whisper that surprised him. "My dear, I think he's really handsome."

"But, Charlotte, how can you say that about someone who isn't even human!"

"He looks more human than many human beings do. And his clothes fit him beautifully. I wonder—does he have a tail?"

"Not that I know of."

"Oh." There was disappointment in the sound. "He looks like a pirate."

"He was a kind of wolf, they tell me. You'd never guess, to see him, that he ran on all fours, would you?"

"Of course not. He's so straight and dignified."

"It just shows you what psychology can do."

"Psychology, and a series of operations, dear ladies," he thought sarcastically. "Without them I wouldn't be able to stand so nice and straight with the help of all the psychologists in this pretty little solar system of ours."

From behind a potted Martian nut-cactus came two low voices—not whispers this time. And there was several octaves' difference in pitch between them. One male, one female.

The man said, "Don't be worried, sweetheart. I'll match your cooking and baking against anybody's."

There was a curious sound, between a click and a hiss. What human beings called a kiss, he thought. Between the sexes, usually an indication of affection or passion. Sometimes, especially within the ranks of the female sex, a formality behind which warfare could be waged.

The girl said tremulously, "But these women have so much experience. They've cooked and baked for years."

"Haven't you, for your own family?"

"Yes, but that isn't the same thing. I had to learn from a cookbook. And I had no one with experience to stand over me and teach me."

"You've learned faster that way than you'd have done with some of these old hens standing at your elbow and giving you directions. You cook *too* well. I'll be fat in no time."

"Your mother doesn't think so. And your brother said something about a bride's biscuits——"

"The older the joke, the better Charles likes it. Don't let it worry you." He kissed her again. "Have confidence in yourself, dear. You're going to win."

"Oh, Gregory, it's awfully nice of you to say so, but really I feel so unsure of myself."

"If only the judge were human and took a look at you, nobody else would stand a chance. Have I told you within the last five minutes that you're beautiful?"

Ronar disengaged his attention again. He found human love-making as repulsive as most human food.

He picked up a few more whispers. And then Dr. Cabanis came in.

The good doctor looked around, smiled, greeted several ladies of his acquaintance as if he were witnessing a private strip tease of their souls, and then came directly up to the platform. "How are you, Ronar?"

"Fine, Doctor. Are you here to keep an eye on me?"

"I hardly think that's necessary. I have an interest in the results of the judging. My wife has baked a cake."

"I had no idea that cake-baking was so popular a human avocation."

"Anything that requires skill is sure to become popular among us. By the way, Ronar, I hope you don't feel hurt."

"Hurt, Doctor? What do you mean?"

"Come now, you understand me well enough. These people still don't trust you. I can tell by the way they keep their distance."

"I can take human frailty into account, Doctor. Frailty, and lack of opportunity. These men and women haven't had the opportunity for extensive psychological treatment that I've had. I don't expect too much of them."

"You've scored a point there, Ronar."

"Isn't there something that can be done for them, Doctor? Some treatment that it would be legal to give them?"

"It would have to be voluntary. You see, Ronar, you were considered only an animal, and treatment was necessary to save your life. But these people are supposed to have rights. One of their rights is to be left alone with their infirmities. Besides, none of them are seriously ill. They hurt no one."

For a second Ronar had a human temptation. It was on the tip of his tongue to say, "Your wife too, Doctor? People wonder how you stand her." But he resisted it. He had resisted more serious temptations.

A gong sounded gently but pervasively. Dr. Cabanis said, "I hope you have no resentment against me at this stage of the game, Ronar. I'd hate to have my wife lose the prize because the judge was prejudiced."

"Have no fear, Doctor. I take professional pride in my work. I will choose only the best."

"Of course, the fact that the cakes are numbered and not signed with the names of their creators will make things simpler."

"That would matter with human judges. It does not affect me."

Another gong sounded, more loudly this time. Gradually the conversation stopped. A man in a full dress suit, with yellow stripes down the sides of his shorts, and tails hanging both front and rear, climbed up on the platform. His eyes shone with a greeting so warm that the fear was almost completely hidden. "How are you, Ronar? Glad to see you."

"I'm fine, Senator. And you?"

"Couldn't be better. Have a cigar."

"No, thank you. I don't smoke."

"That's right, you don't. Besides, I'd be wasting the cigar. You don't vote!" He laughed heartily.

"I understand that they're passing a special law to let—people—like me vote at the next election."

"I'm for it, Ronar, I'm for it. You can count on me."

The chairman came up on the platform, a stout and dignified woman who smiled at both Ronar and the Senator, and shook hands with both without showing signs of distaste for either. The assembled competitors and spectators took seats.

The chairman cleared her throat. "Ladies and gentlemen, let us open this meeting by singing the *Hymn of All Planets.*"

They all rose, Ronar with them. His voice wasn't too well adapted to singing, but neither, it seemed, were most of the human voices. And, at least, he knew all the words.

The chairman proceeded to greet the gathering formally, in the name of the Presiding Committee.

Then she introduced Senator Whitten. She referred archly to the fact that the Senator had long since reached the age of indiscretion and had so far escaped marriage. He was an enemy of the female sex, but they'd let him speak to them anyway.

Senator Whitten just as archly took up the challenge. He had escaped more by good luck—if you could call it good—than by good management. But he was sure that if he had ever had the fortune to encounter some of the beautiful ladies here this fine day, and to taste the products of their splendid cooking and baking, he would have been a lost man. He would long since have committed polygamy.

Senator Whitten then launched into a paean of praise for the ancient art of preparing food.

Ronar's attention wandered. So did that of a good part of

the audience. His ears picked up another conversation, this time whispered between a man and a woman in the front row.

The man said, "I should have put your name on it, instead of mine."

"That would have been silly. All my friends know that I can't bake. And it would look so strange if I won."

"It'll look stranger if I win. I can imagine what the boys in the shop will say."

"Oh, the boys in the shop are stupid. What's so unmanly in being able to cook and bake?"

"I'm not anxious for the news to get around."

"Some of the best chefs have been men."

"I'm not a chef."

"Stop worrying." There was exasperation in the force of her whisper. "You won't win anyway."

"I don't know. Sheila—"

"What?"

"If I win, will you explain to everybody how manly I really am? Will you be my character witness?"

She repressed a giggle.

"If you won't help me, I'll have to go around giving proof myself."

"Shh, someone will hear you."

Senator Whitten went on and on.

Ronar thought back to the time when he had wandered over the surface of this, his native satellite. He no longer had the old desires, the old appetites. Only the faintest of ghosts still persisted, ghosts with no power to do harm. But he could remember the old feeling of pleasure, the delight of sinking his teeth into an animal he had brought down himself, the savage joy of gulping the tasty flesh. He didn't eat raw meat any more; he didn't eat meat at all. He had been conditioned against it. He was now half vegetarian, half synthetarian. His meals were nourishing, healthful, and a part of his life he would rather not think about.

He took no real pleasure in the tasting of the cakes and other delicacies that born human beings favored. His sense of taste had remained keen only to the advantage of others. To himself it was a tantalizing mockery.

Senator Whitten's voice came to a sudden stop. There was applause. The Senator sat down; the chairman stood up. The time for the judging had arrived.

They set out the cakes—more than a hundred of them, topped by icings of all colors and all flavors. The chairman introduced Ronar and lauded both his impartiality and the keenness of his sense of taste.

They had a judging card ready. Slowly Ronar began to go down the line.

They might just as well have signed each cake with its maker's name. As he lifted a portion of each to his mouth, he could hear the quick intake of breath from the woman who had baked it, could catch the whispered warning from her companion. There were few secrets they could keep from him.

At first they all watched intently. When he had reached the fifth cake, however, a hand went up in the audience. "Madam Chairman!"

"Please, ladies, let us not interrupt the judging."

"But I don't think the judging is right. Mr. Ronar tastes hardly more than a crumb of each!"

"A minimum of three crumbs," Ronar corrected her. "One from the body of the cake, one from the icing, and an additional crumb from each filling between layers."

"But you can't judge a cake that way! You have to eat it, take a whole mouthful——"

"Please, madam, permit me to explain. A crumb is all I need. I can analyze the contents of the cake sufficiently well from that. Let me take, for instance, Cake Number 4, made from an excellent recipe, well baked. Martian granis flour, goover eggs, tingan-flavored salt, a trace of Venusian orange spice, synthetic shortening of the best quality. The icing is excellent, made with rare dipentose sugars which give it a delightful flavor. Unfortunately, however, the cake will not win first prize."

An anguished cry rose from the audience. "Why?"

"Through no fault of your own, dear lady. The purberries used in making the filling were not freshly picked. They have the characteristic flavor of refrigeration."

"The manager of the store swore to me that they were fresh! Oh, I'll kill him, I'll murder him——"

She broke down in a flood of tears.

Ronar said to the lady who had protested, "I trust, madam, that you will now have slightly greater confidence in my judgment."

She blushed and subsided.

Ronar went on with the testing. Ninety percent of the cakes he was able to discard at once, from some fault in the raw materials used or in the method of baking. Eleven cakes survived the first elimination contest.

He went over them again, more slowly this time. When he had completed the second round of tests, only three were left. Number 17 belonged to Mrs. Cabanis. Number 43 had been made by the man who argued with his wife. Number 64 was the product of the young bride, whom he had still not seen.

Ronar paused. "My sense of taste is somewhat fatigued. I shall have to ask for a short recess before proceeding further."

There was a sigh from the audience. The tension was not released, it was merely relaxed for a short interval.

Ronar said to the chairman, "I should like a few moments of fresh air. That will restore me. Do you mind?"

"Of course not, Mr. Ronar."

He went outside. Seen through the thin layer of air which surrounded the group of buildings, and the plastic bubble which kept the air from escaping into space, the stars were brilliant and peaceful. The Sun, far away, was like a father star who was too kind to obliterate his children. Strange, he thought, to recall that this was his native satellite. A few years ago it had been a different world. As for himself, he could live just as well outside the bubble as in it, as well in rarefied air as in dense. Suppose he were to tear a hole in the plastic——

Forbidden thoughts. He checked himself, and concentrated on the three cakes and the three contestants.

"You aren't supposed to let personal feelings interfere. You aren't even supposed to know who baked those cakes. But you know, all right. And you can't keep personal feelings from influencing your judgment.

"Any one of the cakes is good enough to win. Choose whichever you please, and no one will have a right to criticize. To which are you going to award the prize?

"Number 17? Mrs. Cabanis is, as one of the other women has so aptly termed her, a bitch on wheels. If she wins, she'll be insufferable. And she'll probably make her husband suffer. Not that he doesn't deserve it. Still, he thought he was doing me a favor. Will I be doing him a favor if I have his wife win?

"Number 64, now, is insufferable in her own right. That loving conversation with her husband would probably disgust even human ears. On the other hand, there is this to be said for her winning, it will make the other women furious. To think that a young snip, just married, without real experience in homemaking, should walk away with a prize of this kind!

"Ah, but if the idea is to burn them up, why not give the prize to Number 43? They'd be ready to drop dead with chagrin. To think that a mere man should beat them at their own specialty! They'd never be able to hold their heads up again. The man wouldn't feel too happy about it, either. Yes, if it's a matter of getting back at these humans for the things they've done to me, if it's a question of showing them what I really think of them, Number 43 should get it.

"On the other hand, I'm supposed to be a model of fairness.

That's why I got the job in the first place. Remember, Ronar? Come on, let's go in and try tasting them again. Eat a mouthful of each cake, much as you hate the stuff. Choose the best on its merits."

They were babbling when he walked in, but the babbling stopped quickly. The chairman said, "Are we ready, Mr. Ronar?"

"All ready."

The three cakes were placed before him. Slowly he took a mouthful of Number 17. Slowly he chewed it and swallowed it. Number 43 followed, then Number 64.

After the third mouthful, he stood lost in thought. One was practically as good as another. He could still choose which he pleased.

The assemblage had quieted down. Only the people most concerned whispered nervously.

Mrs. Cabanis, to her psychologist husband: "If I don't win, it'll be your fault. I'll pay you back for this."

The good doctor's fault? Yes, you could figure it that way if you wanted to. If not for Dr. Cabanis, Ronar wouldn't be the judge. If Ronar weren't the judge, Mrs. C. would win, she thought. Hence it was all her husband's fault. Q.E.D.

The male baker to his wife: "If he gives the prize to me, I'll brain him. I should never have entered this."

"It's too late to worry now."

"I could yell 'Fire,'" he whispered hopefully. "I could create a panic that would empty the hall. And then I'd destroy my cake."

"Don't be foolish. And stop whispering."

The young post-honeymooning husband: "You're going to win, dear; I can feel it in my bones."

"Oh, Greg, please don't try to fool me. I've resigned myself to losing."

"You won't lose."

"I'm afraid. Put your arm around me, Greg. Hold me tight. Will you still love me if I lose?"

"Mmmm." He kissed her shoulder. "You know, I didn't fall in love with you for your cooking, sweetheart. You don't have to bake any cakes for me. You're good enough to eat yourself."

"He's right," thought Ronar, as he stared at her. "The man's right. Not in the way he means, but he's right." And suddenly, for one second of decision, Ronar's entire past seemed to flash through his mind.

The young bride never knew why she won first prize.

Man in the Jar

By DAMON KNIGHT

Vane did not indiscriminately bottle live people—he had to have a sound business reason!

The hotel room on the planet Meng was small and crowded. Blue-tinged sunlight from the window fell on a soiled gray carpet, a massive sandbox dotted with cigarette butts, a clutter of bottles. One corner of the room was piled high with baggage and curios. The occupant, a Mr. R. C. Vane of Earth, was sitting near the door: a man about fifty, clean-shaven, with bristling iron-gray hair. He was soberly, murderously drunk.

There was a tap on the door and the bellhop slipped in —a native, tall and brown, with greenish black hair cut too long in the back. He looked about nineteen. He had one green eye and one blue.

"Set it there," said Vane.

The bellhop put his tray down. "Yes, sir." He took the unopened bottle of Ten Star off the tray, and the ice bucket, and the seltzer bottle, crowding them in carefully among the things already on the table. Then he put the empty bottles and the ice bucket back on the tray. His hands were big and knob-jointed; he seemed too long and wide-shouldered for his tight green uniform.

"So this is Meng City," said Vane, watching the bellhop.

Vane was sitting erect and unrumpled in his chair, with his striped moth-wing jacket on and his string tie tied. He might have been sober, except for the deliberate way he spoke and the redness of his eyes.

"Yes, sir," said the bellhop, straightening up with the tray in his hands. "This your first time here, sir?"

"I came through two weeks ago," Vane told him. "I did not like it then and I do not like it now. Also, I do not like this room."

"Management is sorry if you don't like the room, sir. Very good view from this room."

"It's dirty and small," said Vane, "but it doesn't matter. I'm checking out this afternoon. Leaving on the afternoon rocket. I wasted two weeks upcountry, investigating Marack stories. Nothing to it—just native talk. Miserable little planet." He sniffed, eying the bellhop. "What's your name, boy?"

"Jimmy Rocksha, sir."

"Well, Jimmy Rocks, look at that pile of stuff." Tourist goods, scarves and tapestries, rugs, blankets and other things were heaped over the piled suitcases. It looked like an explosion in a curio shop. "There's about forty pounds of it I have no room for, not counting that knocked-down jar. Any suggestions?"

The bellhop thought about it slowly. "Sir, if I might suggest, you could put the scarves and things inside the jar. I think they'll fit."

Vane said grudgingly, "That might work. You know how to put those jars together?"

"I don't know, sir."

"Well, let's see you try. Go on, don't stand there." Vane swirled his warm, flat drink.

The bellhop set his tray down again and crossed the room. A big bundle of gray pottery pieces, tied together with twine, had been stowed on top of Vane's wardrobe trunk, a little above the bellhop's head. Rocksha carefully removed his shoes and climbed on a chair. His brown feet were bare and clean. He lifted the bundle without effort, got down, set the bundle on the floor, and put his shoes back on.

Vane took a long swallow of his lukewarm highball, finishing it. He closed his eyes while he drank and nodded over the glass for a moment afterward, as if listening to something whispering inside him.

"All right," he said, getting up, "let us see."

The bellhop loosened the twine. There were six long, thick, curving pieces, shaped a little like giant shoehorns. Then there were two round ones. One was bigger; that was the bottom. The other had a handle; that was the lid. The bellhop began to separate the pieces carefully, laying them out on the carpet.

"Watch out how you touch those together," Vane grunted, coming up behind him. "I wouldn't know how to get them apart again."

"Yes, sir."

"That's an antique I got upcountry. They used to be used for storing grain and oil. The natives claim the Maracks had the secret of making them stick the way they do. Ever heard that?"

"Upcountry boys tell a lot of fine stories, sir," said the bellhop. He had the six long pieces arranged, well separated, in a kind of petal pattern around the big flat piece. They took up most of the free space; the jar would be chest-high if it could be assembled.

Standing up, the bellhop took two of the long curved pieces and carefully brought the edges closer together. They seemed to jump the last fraction of an inch, like magnets, and merged into one smooth piece. Peering, Vane could barely make out the join.

In the same way, the bellhop added another piece to the first two. Now he had half the jar assembled. Carefully, he lowered this half jar toward the edge of the big flat piece.

The pieces clicked together. The bellhop stooped for another side piece.

"Hold on a minute," said Vane suddenly. "Got an idea. Instead of putting that thing all together, then trying to stuff things into it, load the things in, *then* put the rest of the sides on."

"Yes, sir." The bellhop laid the piece of crockery down again and picked up some light blankets, which he dropped on the bottom of the jar.

"Not that way, dummy," said Vane impatiently. "Get *in* there—pack them down tight."

The bellhop hesitated. "Yes, sir." He stepped delicately over the remaining unassembled pieces and knelt on the bottom of the jar, rolling the blankets and pressing them snugly in.

Behind him, Vane moved on tiptoe, putting two long pieces silently together—*tic!*—then a third—*tic!*—and then as he lifted them, *tic, clack!* the sides melted into the bottom and the top. The jar was complete.

The bellhop was inside.

Vane breathed hard through flared nostrils. He took a cigar out of a green lizard pocket case, cut it with a lapel knife, and lit it. Exhaling smoke, he leaned over and looked down into the jar.

Except for a moan of surprise when the jar closed, the bellhop had not made a sound. Looking down, Vane saw his brown face looking up.

"Let me out of this jar, please, sir," said the bellhop.

"Can't do that," Vane said. "They didn't tell me how, upcountry."

The bellhop moistened his lips. "Upcountry, they use a kind of tree grease. It creeps between the pieces and they fall apart."

"They didn't give me anything like that," said Vane indifferently.

"Then please, sir, you break this jar and let me come out."

Vane picked a bit of tobacco off his tongue. He looked at it curiously and then flicked it away. "I spotted you in the lobby the minute I came in this morning. Tall and thin. Too strong for a native. One green eye, one blue. Two weeks I spent upcountry, looking—and there you were in the lobby."

"Sir?"

"You're a Marack," said Vane flatly.

The bellhop did not answer for a moment. "But, sir," he said incredulously, "Maracks are *legends,* sir. Nobody believes that any more. There are no Maracks."

"You lifted that jar down like nothing," said Vane, "though it took two boys to put it up there. You've got the hollow temples. You've got the long jaw and the hunched shoulders." Frowning, he took a billfold out of his pocket and took out a yellowed card. He showed it to the bellhop. "Look at that picture. I hope," he added, "it won't upset you. Might be a relative of yours."

It was a faded photograph of a skeleton in a glass case. There was something disturbing about the skeleton. It was too long and thin; the shoulders seemed hunched and the skull was narrow and hollow-templed. Under it the printing said: ABORIGINE OF NEW CLEVELAND, MENG (SIGMA LYRA II) and in smaller letters: NEWBOLD ANTHROPOLOGICAL MUSEUM, TEN EYCK, QUEENSLAND, N. T. COURTESY OF ESTATE OF WALTER B. SOONG.

"Found it between the pages of a book two hundred years old," said Vane, carefully putting it back. "It was mailed as a postcard to an ancestor of mine. A year later I happened to be on Nova Terra. Now get this—the museum is still there, but that skeleton is not! They deny it ever was there. Curator seemed to think it was a fake. None of the native races on Meng have skeletons like that, he said."

"Must be a fake, sir," the bellhop agreed.

"I will tell you what I did next," Vane went on. "I read all the contemporary accounts I could find of frontier days on this planet. A couple of centuries ago nobody on Meng thought the Maracks were legends. They looked enough like the natives to pass, but they had certain special powers. They could turn one thing into another. They could influence your mind, if you weren't on your guard against them. I next read all the export records back to a couple of centuries ago. Also the geological charts in Planetary Survey. I discovered something. It just happens that there is no source of natural diamonds anywhere on Meng."

"No, sir?" asked the bellhop nervously.

"Not one. No diamonds and no place where they ever could have been mined. But until two hundred years ago, Meng exported one billion stellors' worth of flawless diamonds every year. I ask, where did they come from? And why did they stop?"

"I don't know, sir."

"The Maracks made them," Vane said bluntly. "For a trader named Soong and his family. They died. After that, no more diamonds from Meng."

He opened a suitcase, rummaged inside it a moment, and took out two objects. One was a narrow oval bundle of something wrapped in stiff yellow plant fibers; the other was a shiny gray-black lump half the size of his fist.

"Do you know what this is?" Vane asked, holding up the oval bundle.

"No, sir."

"Air weed, they call it upcountry. One of the old men had this one buried under his hut, along with the jar. *And* this." He held up the black lump. "Nothing special about it, would you say? Just a piece of graphite, probably from the old mine at Badlong. But graphite is pure carbon. And so is a diamond."

He put both objects carefully down on the nearby table and wiped his hands. The graphite had left black smudges on them.

"Think about it," he said. "You've got exactly one hour, till three o'clock." Delicately, he tapped his cigar over the mouth of the jar. A few flakes of powdery ash floated down on the bellhop's upturned face.

Vane went back to his chair. He moved deliberately and a little stiffly, but did not stagger. He peeled the foil off the bottle of Ten Star. He poured himself a substantial drink, added ice, splashed a little seltzer in. He took a long, slow swallow.

"Sir," said the bellhop finally, "you know I can't make any diamonds out of black rock. What's going to happen when it comes three o'clock and that rock is still just a piece of rock?"

"I think," Vane answered, "I will just take the wrappings off that air weed and drop it in the jar with you. Air weed, I am told, will expand to hundreds of times its volume in air. When it fills the jar to the brim, I will put the lid on. And when we're crossing that causeway to the spaceport, I think you may get tipped off the packrat into the bay. The bottom is deep silt, they tell me."

He took another long, unhurried swallow.

"Think about it," he said, staring at the jar with red eyes.

Within the jar it was cool and dim. The bellhop had enough room to sit fairly comfortably with his legs crossed, or else he could kneel, but then his face came right up to the mouth of the jar. The opening was too small for his head. He could not straighten up any farther or put his legs out. The bellhop was afraid and was sweating in his tight uniform. He was only nineteen and nothing like this had ever happened to him before.

The clink of ice came from across the room. The bellhop said, "Sir?"

The chair springs whined and, after a moment, the Earthman's face appeared over the mouth of the jar. His chin was dimpled. There were gray hairs in his nostrils and a few gray and black bristles in the creases of loose skin around his jaw. His red eyes were hooded and small. He looked down into the bellhop's face without speaking.

"Sir," the bellhop said earnestly, "do you know how much they pay me here at this hotel?"

"No."

"Twelve stellors a week, sir, and my meals. If I could make diamonds, sir, why would I be working here?"

Vane's expression did not change. "Ask me a hard one. Soong had to sweat you Maracks to get a billion stellors a year. There used to be thousands of you on this continent alone, but now there are so few that you can disappear among the natives. The diamonds took too much out of you. You're close to extinction now. And you're all scared. You've gone underground. You've still got your powers, but you don't dare use them—unless there's no other way to keep your secret. You were lords of this planet once, but you'd rather stay alive. Of course, all this is merely guesswork."

"Yes, sir," said the bellhop despairingly.

The house phone rang. Vane crossed the room and thumbed the key down, watching the bellhop from the corner of his eye. "What is it?" he said, flat-voiced.

"Mr. Vane," said the voice of the desk clerk, "if I may ask, did the refreshments you ordered arrive?"

"The bottle came," Vane answered. "Why?"

The bellhop was listening, balling his fists on his knees. Sweat stood out on his brown forehead.

"Oh, nothing really, Mr. Vane, only the boy did not come back. He is usually very reliable, Mr. Vane. But excuse me for troubling you."

"No trouble," said Vane stonily, and turned the phone off.

He came back to the jar. He swayed a little, rocking back and forth from heels to toes. In one hand he had the highball glass; with the other he was playing with the little osmiridium knife that hung by an expanding chain from his lapel.

After a while, he said, "Why didn't you call for help?"

The bellhop did not answer. Vane went on softly, "Those hotel phones will pick up a voice across the room. I know that. So why were you quiet?"

The bellhop said unhappily, "If I did yell, sir, they would find me in this jar."

"What of it?"

The bellhop grimaced. "There's some other people that still believe in Maracks, sir. I have to be careful about my eyes. They would know there could only be the one reason why you would treat me like this."

Vane studied him for a moment. "And you'd take a chance on the air weed, and the bay, just to keep anyone from finding out?"

"It's a long time since we had any Marack hunts on this planet, sir."

Vane snorted softly. He glanced up at the wall clock. "Forty minutes," he said, and went back to his chair by the door.

The room was silent except for the faint whir of the clock. After a while Vane moved to the writing desk. He put a printed customs declaration form in the machine and began tapping keys slowly, muttering over the complicated Interstellar symbols.

"Sir," said the bellhop quietly, "you know you can't kill a biped person and just get away. This is not like the bad old times."

Vane grunted, tapping keys. "Think not?" He took a sip from his highball and set it down again.

"Even if they find out you have mistreated the headman upcountry, sir, they will be very severe."

"They won't find out," Vane said. "Not from him."

"Sir, even if I could make you your diamond, it would only be worth a few thousand stellors. That is nothing to a man like you."

Vane paused and half turned. "Flawless, that weight, it would be worth a hundred thousand. But I'm not going to sell it." He turned back to the machine, finished a line, and started to tap out another.

"No, sir?"

"No. I'm going to keep it." Vane's eyes half closed; his fingers poised motionless on the keys. He seemed to come to himself with a start, hit another key, and rolled the paper out of the machine. He picked up an envelope and rose, looking over the paper in his hand.

"Just to keep it, sir, and look at it now and then?" the bellhop asked softly. Sweat was running down into his eyes, but he kept his fists motionless on his knees.

"That's it," said Vane, with the same faraway look.

He folded the paper slowly and put it into the envelope as he walked toward the message chute near the door. At the last moment he checked himself, snapped the paper open again, and stared at it. A slow flush came to his cheeks.

Crumpling the paper slowly in his hands, he said, "That almost worked."

He tore the paper across deliberately, and then again, and again, before he threw the pieces away.

"Just one symbol in the wrong box," he said, "but it was the right wrong symbol. I'll tell you where you made your mistake, though, boy." He came closer.

"I don't understand," said the bellhop.

"You thought if you could get me to thinking about that diamond, my mind would wander. It did—but I knew what was happening. Here's where you made your mistake: *I don't give a damn about that diamond.*"

"Sir?" asked the bellhop in bewilderment.

"A stellor to you is a new pair of pants. A stellor to me, or a thousand stellors, is just raw material for business deals. That's what counts. I'd offer you money, but you explained yourself why you can't be bought—you could make diamonds and be rich, but you don't dare. That's why I have to use this method."

"Sir, I don't know what you mean."

"You know, all right. You're getting a little dangerous now, aren't you? You're cornered and the time's running out. So you took a little risk." He stooped, picked up one of the scraps of paper, unfolded it and smoothed it out. "Right here, in the box where the loyalty oath to the Archon is supposed to go, I wrote the symbol for 'pig.' If I sent that down, the thought police would be up here in fifteen minutes."

He balled up the paper again, into an even smaller wad, and dropped it on the carpet.

"Think you can make me forget to pick that up again and burn it before I leave?" he asked amiably. "Try."

The bellhop swallowed hard. "Sir, you did that *yourself*. You made a slip of the finger."

Vane smiled at him for the first time and walked away.

The bellhop put his back against the wall of the jar and pushed with all his strength against the opposite side. He pushed until the muscles of his back stood out in knotted ropes. The pottery walls were as solid as rock.

He was sweating more than ever. He relaxed, breathing hard; he rested his head on his knees and tried to think. The bellhop had heard of ruthless Earthmen, but he had never seen one.

He straightened up. "Sir, are you still there?"

The chair creaked and Vane came over, glass in hand.

"Sir," said the bellhop earnestly, "if I can prove to you that I'm really not a Marack, will you let me go? I mean you'll have to let me go then, won't you?"

"Why, certainly," Vane said agreeably. "Go ahead and prove it."

"Well, sir, haven't you heard other things about the Maracks—some other manner of test?"

Vane looked thoughtful; he put his chin down on his chest and his eyes filmed over.

"About what they can or can't do?" the bellhop suggested. "If I tell you, sir, you might think I made it up."

"Wait a minute."

Vane was swaying slightly, back and forth, his eyes half closed. His string tie was still perfectly tied, his striped moth-wing jacket immaculate. He said, "I remember something.

The Marack hunters used this a good deal, I understand. Maracks can't stand liquor. It poisons them."

"You're positive about that, sir?" the bellhop said eagerly.

"Of course I'm positive."

"All right then, sir!"

Vane nodded and went to the table to get the bottle of Ten Star. It was still two-thirds full. He came back with it and said, "Open your mouth."

The bellhop opened his mouth wide and shut his eyes. The liquor hit his teeth and the back of his mouth in one solid splash; it poured down both cheeks and some of it ran up his nose. He choked and strangled. The liquor burned all the way down his throat and windpipe; tears blinded him; he couldn't breathe.

When the paroxysm was over, he gasped, "Sir—sir, that wasn't a fair test. You shouldn't have poured it on me like that. Give me a little bit, in a glass."

"Now I want to be fair. We'll try it again." Vane found an empty glass, poured two fingers of brandy into it and came back. "Easy does it," he said, and trickled a little into the bellhop's mouth.

The bellhop swallowed, his head swimming in brandy fumes.

"Once more," said Vane, and poured again.

The bellhop swallowed. The liquor was gathering in a ball of heat inside him.

"Again."

He swallowed.

Vane stood back. The bellhop opened his eyes and looked blissfully up at him. "You see, sir? No poison. I drank it and I'm not dead!"

"H'm," said Vane with an interested expression. "Well, imagine that. Maracks *can* drink liquor."

The bellhop's victorious smile slowly faded. "Sir, please don't joke with me."

"If you think it's a joke——"

"Sir, you *promised.*"

"I said yes—if you could prove to me that you are not a Marack. Go ahead, prove it. Here's another little test for you, incidentally. An anatomist I know looked at that skeleton and told me it was so constricted at the shoulders that a Marack can't lift his hand higher than his head. All right, begin by telling me why you stood on a chair to get my bundle down—or better yet, just put your arm out the neck of that jar."

There was a silence. Vane took another cigar out of the green lizard case, cut it with the little osmiridium knife, and lit it without taking his eyes off the bellhop.

"Now you're getting dangerous again," he said with enjoyment. "You're thinking it over. This begins to get interesting. You're wondering how you can kill me from inside that jar, without using your Marack powers. Go on, think about it."

He breathed smoke, leaning toward the jar. "You've got fifteen minutes."

Working without haste, Vane rolled up all the blankets and other souvenirs and strapped them into bundles. He removed some toilet articles from the dresser and packed them away in his grip. He took a last look around the room, saw the paper scraps on the floor, and picked up the tiny pellet he had made of one of them. He showed it to the bellhop with a grin, then dropped it into the ash-receiver and burned it. He sat down comfortably in the chair near the door.

"Five minutes," he said.

"Four minutes," he said.

"Three minutes."

"Two minutes."

"All right," said the bellhop.

"Yes?" Vane got up and stood over the jar.

"I'll do it—I'll make the diamond."

"Ahh?" said Vane, half questioningly. He picked up the lump of graphite and held it out.

"I don't need to touch it," the bellhop said listlessly. "Just put it down on the table. It will take about a minute."

"Umm," said Vane, watching him keenly. The bellhop was crouched in the jar, eyes closed; all Vane could see of him was the glossy green-black top of his head.

"If you just hadn't had that air weed," the bellhop said sullenly, his voice muffled.

Vane laughed. "I didn't need the air weed. I could have taken care of you in a dozen ways. This knife—" he held it up —"has a molecular-vibration blade. Turn it on, it'll cut through anything, like cheese. I could have minced you up and floated you down the drain."

The bellhop's face turned up, pale and wide-eyed.

"No time for that now, though," Vane said. "It would have to be the air weed."

"Is that how you're going to get me loose, afterward?" the bellhop asked. "Cut the jar with that knife?"

"Mm? Oh, certainly," said Vane, watching the graphite lump. Was there a change in its appearance or not?

"I'm disappointed, in a way," he said abstractedly. "I thought you'd give me a fight. You Maracks are overrated, I suppose."

"It's all done," said the bellhop. "Take it, please, and let me out."

Vane's eyes narrowed. "It doesn't look done, to me."

"It only looks black on the outside, sir. Just rub it off."

Vane did not move.

"Go ahead, sir," said the bellhop urgently. "Pick it up and see."

"You're a little too eager," Vane said.

He took a fountain pen out of his pocket and used it to prod the graphite gingerly. Nothing happened; the lump moved freely across the tabletop. Vane touched it briefly with one finger, then picked it up in his hand.

"No tricks?" he said quizzically.

He felt the lump, weighed it, put it down again. There were black graphite smears in his palm.

Vane opened his lapel knife and cut the graphite lump down the middle. It fell into two shiny black pieces.

"Graphite," said Vane, and with an angry gesture, he stuck the knife blade into the table.

He turned to the bellhop, dusting off his hands. "I don't get you," he said, prodding the oval bundle of the air weed experimentally. He picked it up. "All you did was stall. Disappointing."

The dry wrappings came apart in his hands. Between the fibers, a dirty-white bulge began to show.

Vane lifted the package to drop it into the jar and saw that the bellhop's scared face filled the opening. While he hesitated briefly, the gray-white floss of the air weed foamed slowly out over the back of his hand. Vane felt a constriction and instinctively tried to drop the bundle. He couldn't. The growing, billowing floss was sticky—it stuck to his hand, then his sleeve. It grew, slowly, but with a horrifying steadiness.

Gray-faced, Vane whipped his arm around, trying to shake off the weed. Like thick lather, the floss spattered downward but did not separate. A glob of it hit his trouser leg and clung. Another, swelling, dripped down to the carpet. His whole right arm and side were covered deep under a mound of white. The floss had now stopped growing and seemed to be stiffening.

The bellhop began to rock himself back and forth inside the jar. The jar tipped and fell back. The bellhop rocked harder. The jar was inching its way across the carpet.

After a few moments, the bellhop paused to put his face up and see which way he was going. Vane, held fast by the weed, was leaning toward the table, straining hard, reaching with his one free hand toward the knife he had put there. The carpet bulged after him, but too much furniture was holding it.

The bellhop lowered his head and rocked the jar again, harder. When he looked up, Vane's eyes were closed tight, his face red with effort. He was extended as far as he could reach across the table, but his fingers were still clawing air an inch short of the knife. The bellhop rocked hard. The jar inched forward, came to rest solidly against the table, pinning Vane's arm against it by the flaring sleeve.

The bellhop relaxed and looked up. Feeling himself caught, the Earthman had stopped struggling and was looking down. He tugged, but could not pull the sleeve free.

"Stalemate," said Vane heavily. He showed his teeth to the bellhop. "Close, but no prize. I can't get at you. You can't hurt me."

The bellhop's head bowed as if in assent. But then his long arm came snaking up out of the jar. His fingers closed around the deadly little knife.

"A Marack *can* lift his arm higher than his head," he said.

Volpla

By WYMAN GUIN

The only kind of gag worth pulling, I always maintained, was a cosmic one—till I learned the Cosmos has a really nasty sense of humor!

There were three of them. Dozens of limp little mutants that would have sent an academic zoologist into hysterics lay there in the metabolic accelerator. But there were three of *them.* My heart took a great bound.

I heard my daughter's running feet in the animal rooms and her roller skates banging at her side. I closed the accelerator and walked across to the laboratory door. She twisted the knob violently, trying to hit a combination that would work.

I unlocked the door, held it against her pushing and slipped out so that, for all her peering, she could see nothing. I looked down on her tolerantly.

"Can't adjust your skates?" I asked again.

"Daddy, I've tried and tried and I just can't turn this old key tight enough."

I continued to look down on her.

"Well, Dad-dee, I can't!"

"Tightly enough."

"What?"

"You can't turn this old key tightly enough."

"That's what I *say*-yud."

"All right, wench. Sit on this chair."

I got down and shoved one saddle shoe into a skate. It fitted perfectly. I strapped her ankle and pretended to use the key to tighten the clamp.

Volplas at last. Three of them. Yet I had always been so sure I could create them that I had been calling them volplas for ten years. No, twelve. I glanced across the animal room to where old Nijinsky thrust his graying head from a cage. I had called them volplas since the day old Nijinsky's elongated arms and his cousin's lateral skin folds had given me the idea of a flying mutant.

When Nijinsky saw me looking at him, he started a little tarantella about his cage. I smiled with nostalgia when the fifth fingers of his hands, four times as long as the others, uncurled as he spun about the cage.

I turned to the fitting of my daughter's other skate.

"Daddy?"

"Yes?"

"Mother says you are eccentric. Is that true?"

"I'll speak to her about it."

"Don't you *know?*"

"Do you understand the word?"

"No."

I lifted her out of the chair and stood her on her skates. "Tell your mother that I retaliate. I say *she* is beautiful."

She skated awkwardly between the rows of cages from which mutants with brown fur and blue fur, too much and too little fur, enormously long and ridiculously short arms, stared at her with simian, canine, or rodent faces. At the door to the outside, she turned perilously and waved.

Again in the laboratory, I entered the metabolic accelerator and withdrew the intravenous needles from my first volplas. I carried their limp little forms out to a mattress in the lab, two girls and a boy. The accelerator had forced them almost to adulthood in less than a month. It would be several hours before they would begin to move, to learn to feed and play, perhaps to learn to fly.

Meanwhile, it was clear that here was no war of dominant mutations. Modulating alleles had smoothed the freakish into a beautiful pattern. These were no monsters blasted by the dosage of radiation into crippled structures. They were lovely, perfect little creatures.

My wife tried the door, too, but more subtly, as if casually touching the knob while calling.

"Lunch, dear."

"Be right there."

She peeked too, as she had for fifteen years, but I blocked her view when I slipped out.

"Come on, you old hermit. I have a buffet on the terrace."

"Our daughter says I'm eccentric. Wonder how the devil she found out."

"From me, of course."

"But you love me just the same."

"I adore you." She stretched on tiptoe and put her arms over my shoulders and kissed me.

My wife did indeed have a delicious-looking buffet ready on the terrace. The maid was just setting down a warmer filled with hot hamburgers. I gave the maid a pinch and said, "Hello, baby."

My wife looked at me with a puzzled smile. "What on earth's got into you?"

The maid beat it into the house.

I flipped a hamburger and a slice of onion onto a plate and picked up the ketchup and said, "I've reached the dangerous age."

"Oh, good heavens!"

I dowsed ketchup over the hamburger, threw the onion on and closed it. I opened a bottle of beer and guzzled from it, blew out my breath, and looked across the rolling hills and oak woods of our ranch to where the Pacific shimmered. I thought: All this and three volplas, too.

I wiped the back of my hand across my mouth and said aloud, "Yes, sir, the dangerous age. And, lady, I'm going to have fun."

My wife sighed patiently.

I walked over and put the arm that held the beer bottle around her shoulder and chucked her chin up with my other hand. The golden sun danced in her blue eyes. I watched that light in her beautiful eyes and said, "But you're the only one I'm dangerous about."

I kissed her until I heard roller skates coming across the terrace from one direction and a horse galloping toward the terrace from the other direction.

"You have lovely lips," I whispered.

"Thanks. Yours deserve the Good Housekeeping Seal of Approval, too."

Our son reared the new palamino I had just bought him for his fourteenth birthday and yelled down, "Unhand that maiden, Burrhead, or I'll give you lead poisoning."

I laughed and picked up my plate and sat down in a chair. My wife brought me a bowl of salad and I munched the hamburger and watched the boy unsaddle the horse and slap it away to the pasture.

I thought, "By God, wouldn't he have a fit if he knew what I have back there in that lab! Wouldn't they all!"

The boy carried the saddle up onto the terrace and dropped it. "Mom, I'd like a swim before I eat." He started undressing.

"You *look* as though a little water might help," she agreed, sitting down next to me with her plate.

The girl was yanking off her skates. "And I want one."

"All right. But go in the house and put on your swim suit."

"Oh, *Mother*. Why?"

"Because, dear, I said so."

The boy had already raced across the terrace and jack-knifed into the pool. The cool sound of the dive sent the girl scurrying for her suit.

I looked at my wife. "What's the idea?"

"She's going to be a young woman soon."

"Is that any reason for wearing clothes? Look at him. He's a young *man* sooner than already."

"Well, if you feel that way about it, they'll both have to start wearing clothes."

I gulped the last of my hamburger and washed it down with the beer. "This place is going to hell," I complained. "The old man isn't allowed to pinch the maid and the kids can't go naked." I leaned toward her and smacked her cheek. "But the food and the old woman are still the best."

"Say, what goes with you? You've been grinning like a happy ape ever since you came out of the lab."

"I told you——"

"Oh, not that again! You were dangerous at any age."

I stood up and put my plate aside and bent over her. "Just the same, I'm going to have a new kind of fun."

She reached up and grabbed my ear. She narrowed her eyes and put a mock grimness on her lips.

"It's a joke," I assured her. "I'm going to play a tremendous joke on the whole world. I've only had the feeling once before in a small way, but I've always . . ."

She twisted my ear and narrowed her eyes even more. "Like?"

"Well, when my old man was pumping his first fortune out of some oil wells in Oklahoma, we lived down there. Outside this little town, I found a litter of flat stones that had young blacksnakes under each slab. I filled a pail with them and took them into town and dumped them on the walk in front of the movie just as Theda Bara's matinee let out. The best part was that no one had seen me do it. They just couldn't understand how so many snakes got there. I learned how great it can be to stand around quietly and watch people encounter the surprise that you have prepared for them."

She let go of my ear. "Is that the kind of fun you're going to have?"

"Yep."

She shook her head. "Did I say you are *eccentric?*"

I grinned. "Forgive me if I eat and run, dear. Something in the lab can't wait."

The fact was that I had something more in the lab than I had bargained for. I had aimed only at a gliding mammal a little more efficient than the Dusky Glider of Australia, a marsupial. Even in the basically mutating colony, there had been a decidedly simian appearance in recent years, a long shift from the garbage-dump rats I had started with. But my first volplas were shockingly humanoid.

They were also much faster than had been their predecessors in organizing their nervous activity after the slumberous explosion of growth in the metabolic accelerator. When I returned to the lab, they were already moving about on the mattress and the male was trying to stand.

He was a little the larger and stood twenty-eight inches high. Except for the face, chest, and belly, they were covered with a soft, almost golden down. Where it was bare of this golden fur, the skin was pink. On their heads and across the shoulders of the male stood a shock of fur as soft as chinchilla. The faces were appealingly humanoid, except that the eyes were large and nocturnal. The cranium was in the same proportion to the body as it is in the human.

When the male spread his arms, the span was forty-eight inches. I held his arms out and tried to tease the spars open. They were not new. The spars had been common to the basic colony for years and were the result of serial mutations effecting those greatly elongated fifth fingers that had first appeared in Nijinsky. No longer jointed like a finger, the spar turned backward sharply and ran alongside the wrist almost to the elbow. Powerful wrist muscles could snap it outward and forward. Suddenly, as I teased the male volpla, this happened.

The spars added nine inches on each side to his span. As they swept out and forward, the lateral skin that had, till now, hung in resting folds was tightened in a golden plane that stretched from the tip of the spar to his wrist and continued four inches wide down his legs to where it anchored at the little toe.

This was by far the most impressive plane that had appeared till now. It was a true gliding plane, perhaps even a soaring one. I felt a thrill run along my back.

By four o'clock that afternoon, I was feeding them solid food and, with the spars closed, they were holding little cups and drinking water from them in a most humanlike way. They were active, curious, playful, and decidedly amorous.

Their humanoid qualities were increasingly apparent. There was a lumbar curvature and buttocks. The shoulder girdle and pectoral muscles were heavy and out of proportion, of course, yet the females had only one pair of breasts. The chin and jaw were humanlike instead of simian and the dental equipment was appropriate to this structure. What this portended was brought home to me with a shock.

I was kneeling on the mattress cuffing and roughing the male as one might a puppy dog, when one of the females playfully climbed up my back. I reached around and brought her over my shoulder and sat her down. I stroked the soft fur on her head and said, "Hello, pretty one. Hello."

The male watched me, grinning.

He said, " 'Ello, 'ello."

As I walked into the kitchen, giddy with this enormous joke, my wife said, "Guy and Em are flying up for dinner. That rocket of Guy's they launched in the desert yesterday was a success. It pulled Guy up to Cloud Nine and he wants to celebrate."

I danced a little jig the way old Nijinsky might do it. "Oh, great! Oh, wonderful! Good old Guy! Everybody's a success. It's great. It's wonderful. Success on success!"

I danced into the kitchen table and tipped over a basket of green corn. The maid promptly left the kitchen for some other place.

My wife just stared at me. "Have you been drinking the lab alcohol?"

"I've been drinking the nectar of the gods. My Hera, you're properly married to Zeus. I've my own little Greeks descended from Icarus."

She pretended a hopeless sag of her pretty shoulders. "Wouldn't you just settle for a worldly martini?"

"I will, yes. But first a divine kiss."

I sipped at my martini and lounged in a terrace chair watching the golden evening slant across the beautiful hills of our ranch. I dreamed. I would invent a euphonious set of words to match the Basic English vocabulary and teach it to them as their language. They would have their own crafts and live in small tree houses.

I would teach them legends: that they had come from the stars, that they had subsequently watched the first red men and then the first white men enter these hills.

When they were able to take care of themselves, I would turn them loose. There would be volpla colonies all up and down the Coast before anyone suspected. One day, somebody would see a volpla. The newspapers would laugh.

Then someone authoritative would find a colony and observe them. He would conclude: "I am convinced that they have a language and speak it intelligently."

The government would issue denials. Reporters would "expose the truth" and ask, "Where have these aliens come from?" The government would reluctantly admit the facts. Linguists would observe at close quarters and learn the simple volpla language. Then would come the legends.

Volpla wisdom would become a cult—and of all forms of comedy, cults, I think, are the funniest.

"Darling, are you listening to me?" my wife asked with impatient patience.

"What? Sure. Certainly."

"You didn't hear a word. You just sit there and grin into space." She got up and poured me another martini. "Here, maybe this will sober you up."

I pointed. "That's probably Guy and Em."

A copter sidled over the ridge, then came just above the oak woods toward us. Guy set it gently on the landing square and we walked down to meet them.

I helped Em out and hugged her. Guy jumped out, asking, "Do you have your TV set on?"

"No," I answered. "Should I?"

"It's almost time for the broadcast. I was afraid we would miss it."

"What broadcast?"

"From the rocket."

"Rocket?"

"For heaven's sake, darling," my wife complained, "I told you about Guy's rocket being a success. The papers are full of it. So are the broadcasts."

As we stepped up on the terrace, she turned to Guy and Em. "He's out of contact today. Thinks he's Zeus."

I asked our son to wheel a TV set out onto the terrace while I made martinis for our friends. Then we sat down and drank the cocktails and the kids had fruit juice and we watched the broadcast Guy had tuned in.

Some joker from Cal Tech was explaining diagrams of a multi-stage rocket.

After a bit, I got up and said, "I have something out in the lab I want to check on."

"Hey, wait a minute," Guy objected. "They're about to show the shots of the launching."

My wife gave me a look; you know the kind. I sat down. Then I got up and poured myself another martini and freshened Em's up, too. I sat down again.

The scene had changed to a desert launching site. There was old Guy himself explaining that when he pressed the button before him, the hatch on the third stage of the great rocket in the background would close and, five minutes later, the ship would fire itself.

Guy, on the screen, pushed the button, and I heard Guy, beside me, give a sort of little sigh. We watched the hatch slowly close.

"You look real good," I said. "A regular Space Ranger. What are you shooting at?"

"Darling, will you please—be—*quiet?*"

"Yeah, Dad. Can it, will you? You're always gagging around."

On the screen, Guy's big dead-earnest face was explaining more about the project and suddenly I realized that this was an instrument-bearing rocket they hoped to land on the Moon. It would broadcast from there. Well, now—say, that *would* be something! I began to feel a little ashamed of the way I had been acting and I reached out and slapped old Guy on the shoulder. For just a moment, I thought of telling him about my volplas. But only for a moment.

A ball of flame appeared at the base of the rocket. Miraculously, the massive tower lifted, seemed for a moment merely to stand there on a flaming pillar, then was gone.

The screen returned to a studio, where an announcer explained that the film just shown had been taken day before yesterday. Since then, the rocket's third stage was known to have landed successfully at the south shore of Mare Serenitatis. He indicated the location on a large lunar map behind him.

"From this position the telemeter known as Rocket Charlie will be broadcasting scientific data for several months. But now, ladies and gentlemen, we will clear the air for Rocket

Charlie's only general broadcast. Stand by for Rocket Charlie."

A chronometer appeared on the screen and, for several seconds, there was silence.

I heard my boy whisper, "Uncle Guy, this is the biggest!"

My wife said, "Em, I think I'll just faint."

Suddenly there was a lunar landscape on the screen, looking just as it's always been pictured. A mechanical voice cut in.

"This is Rocket Charlie saying, 'Hello, Earth,' from my position in Mare Serenitatis. First I will pan the Menelaus Mountains for fifteen seconds. Then I will focus my camera on Earth for five seconds."

The camera began to move and the mountains marched by, stark and awesomely wild. Toward the end of the movement, the shadow of the upright third stage appeared in the foreground.

Abruptly the camera made a giddy swing, focused a moment, and we were looking at Earth. At that time, there was no Moon over California. It was Africa and Europe we were looking at.

"This is Rocket Charlie saying, 'Good-by, Earth.'"

Well, when that screen went dead, there was pandemonium around our terrace. Big old Guy was so happy, he was wiping tears from his eyes. The women were kissing him and hugging him. Everybody was yelling at once.

I used the metabolic accelerator to cut the volplas' gestation down to one week. Then I used it to bring the infants to maturity in one month. I had luck right off. Quite by accident, the majority of the early infants were females, which sped things up considerably.

By the next spring, I had a colony of over a hundred volplas and I shut down the accelerator. From now on, they could have babies in their own way.

I had devised the language for them, using Basic English as my model, and during the months while every female was busy in the metabolic accelerator, I taught the language to the males. They spoke it softly in high voices and the eight hundred words didn't seem to tax their little skulls a bit.

My wife and the kids went down to Santa Barbara for a week and I took the opportunity to slip the oldest of the males and his two females out of the lab.

I put them in the jeep beside me and drove to a secluded little valley about a mile back in the ranch.

They were all three wide-eyed at the world and jabbered continuously. They kept me busy relating their words for "tree," "rock," "sky" to the objects. They had a little trouble with "sky."

Until I had them out in the open country, it had been impossible to appreciate fully what lovely little creatures they were. They blended perfectly with the California landscape. Occasionally, when they raised their arms, the spars would open and spread those glorious planes.

Almost two hours went by before the male made it into the air. His playful curiosity about the world had been abandoned momentarily and he was chasing one of the girls. As usual, she was anxious to be caught and stopped abruptly at the bottom of a little knoll.

He probably meant to dive for her. But when he spread his arms, the spars snapped out and those golden planes sheared into the air. He sailed over her in a stunning sweep. Then he rose up and up until he hung in the breeze for a long moment, thirty feet above the ground.

He turned a plaintive face back to me, dipped worriedly, and skimmed straight for a thorn bush. He banked instinctively, whirled toward us in a golden flash, and crashed with a bounce to the grass.

The two girls reached him before I did and stroked and fussed over him so that I could not get near. Suddenly he laughed with a shrill little whoop. After that, it was a carnival.

They learned quickly and brilliantly. They were not fliers; they were gliders and soarers. Before long, they took agilely to the trees and launched themselves in beautiful glides for hundreds of feet, banking, turning and spiraling to a gentle halt.

I laughed out loud with anticipation. Wait till the first pair of these was brought before a sheriff! Wait till reporters from the *Chronicle* motored out into the hills to witness this!

Of course, the volplas didn't want to return to the lab. There was a tiny stream through there and at one point it formed a sizable pool. They got into this and splashed their long arms about and they scrubbed each other. Then they got out and lay on their backs with the planes stretched to dry.

I watched them affectionately and wondered about the advisability of leaving them out here. Well, it had to be done sometime. Nothing I could tell them about surviving would help them as much as a little actual surviving. I called the male over to me.

He came and squatted, conference fashion, the elbows resting on the ground, the wrists crossed at his chest. He spoke first.

"Before the red men came, did we live here?"

"You lived in places like this all along these mountains. Now there are very few of you left. Since you have been staying at my place, you naturally have forgotten the ways of living outdoors."

"We can learn again. We want to stay here." His little face was so solemn and thoughtful that I reached out and stroked the fur on his head reassuringly.

We both heard the whir of wings overhead. Two mourning doves flew across the stream and landed in an oak on the opposite hillside.

I pointed. "There's your food, if you can kill it."

He looked at me. "How?"

"I don't think you can get at them in the tree. You'll have

to soar up above and catch one of them on the wing when they fly away. Think you can get up that high?"

He looked around slowly at the breeze playing in the branches and dancing along the hillside grass. It was as if he had been flying a thousand years and was bringing antique wisdom to bear. "I can get up there. I can stay for a while. How long will they be in the tree?"

"Chances are they won't stay long. Keep your eye on the tree in case they leave while you are climbing."

He ran to a nearby oak and clambered aloft. Presently he launched himself, streaked down-valley a way and caught a warm updraft on a hillside. In no time, he was up about two hundred feet. He began crisscrossing the ridge, working his way back to us.

The two girls were watching him intently. They came over to me wonderingly, stopping now and then to watch him. When they were standing beside me, they said nothing. They shaded their eyes with tiny hands and watched him as he passed directly above us at about two hundred and fifty feet. One of the girls, with her eyes fast on his soaring planes, reached out and grasped my sleeve tightly.

He flashed high above the stream and hung behind the crest of the hill where the doves rested. I heard their mourning from the oak tree. It occurred to me they would not leave that safety while the hawklike silhouette of the volpla marred the sky so near.

I took the girl's hand from my sleeve and spoke to her, pointing as I did so. "He is going to catch a bird. The bird is in that tree. You can make the bird fly so that he can catch it. Look here." I got up and found a stick. "Can you do this?"

I threw the stick up into a tree near us. Then I found her a stick. She threw it better than I had expected.

"Good, pretty one. Now run across the stream and up to that tree and throw a stick into it."

She climbed skillfully into the tree beside us and launched herself across the stream. She swooped up the opposite hillside and landed neatly in the tree where the doves rested.

The birds came out of the tree climbing hard with their graceful strokes.

I looked back, as did the girl remaining beside me. The soaring volpla half closed his planes and started dropping. He became a golden flash across the sky.

The doves abruptly gave up their hard climbing and fell away with swiftly beating wings. I saw one of the male planes open a little. He veered giddily in the new direction and again dropped like a molten arrow.

The doves separated and began to zigzag down the valley. The volpla did something I would not have anticipated—he opened his planes and shot lower than the bird he was after, then swept up and intercepted the bird's crossward flight.

I saw the planes close momentarily. Then they opened again and the bird plummeted to a hillside. The volpla landed gently atop the hill and stood looking back at us.

The volpla beside me danced up and down shrieking in a language all her own. The girl who had raised the birds from the tree volplaned back to us, yammering like a bluejay.

It was a hero's welcome. He had to walk back, of course—he had no way to carry such a load in flight. The girls glided out to meet him. Their lavish affection held him up for a time, but eventually he strutted in like every human hunter.

They were raptly curious about the bird. They poked at it, marveled at its feathers, and danced about it in an embryonic rite of the hunt. But presently the male turned to me.

"We *eat* this?"

I laughed and took his tiny four-fingered hand. In a sandy spot beneath a great tree that overhung the creek, I built a small fire for them. This was another marvel, but first I wanted to teach them how to clean the bird. I showed them how to spit it and turn it over their fire.

Later, I shared a small piece of the meat in their feast. They were gleeful and greasily amorous during the meal.

When I had to leave, it was dark. I warned them to stand

watches, keep the fire burning low and take to the tree above if anything approached. The male walked a little away with me when I left the fire.

I said again, "Promise me you won't leave here until we've made you ready for it."

"We like it here. We will stay. Tomorrow you bring more of us?"

"Yes. I will bring many more of you, if you promise to keep them all here in this woods until they're ready to leave."

"I promise." He looked up at the night sky and, in the firelight, I saw his wonder. "You say we came from there?"

"The old ones of your kind told me so. Didn't they tell you?"

"I can't remember any old ones. You tell me."

"The old ones told me you came long before the red men in a ship from the stars." Standing there in the dark, I had to grin, visioning the Sunday supplements that would be written in about a year, maybe even less.

He looked into the sky for a long time. "Those little lights are the stars?"

"That's right."

"Which star?"

I glanced about and presently pointed over a tree. "From Venus." Then I realized I had blundered by passing him an English name. "In your language, Pohtah."

He looked at the planet a long time and murmured, "Venus. Pohtah."

That next week, I transported all of the volplas out to the oak woods. There were a hundred and seven men, women, and children. With no design on my part, they tended to segregate into groups consisting of four to eight couples together with the current children of the women. Within these groups, the adults were promiscuous, but apparently not outside the group. The group thus had the appearance of a superfamily and the males indulged and cared for all the children without reference to actual parenthood.

By the end of the week, these super-families were scattered over about four square miles of the ranch. They had found a new delicacy, sparrows, and hunted them easily as they roosted at night. I had taught the volplas to use the fire drill and they were already utilizing the local grasses, vines and brush to build marvelously contrived tree houses in which the young, and sometimes the adults, slept through midday and midnight.

The afternoon my family returned home, I had a crew of workmen out tearing down the animal rooms and lab building. The caretakers had anesthetized all the experimental mutants, and the metabolic accelerator and other lab equipment were being dismantled. I wanted nothing around that might connect the sudden appearance of the volplas with my property. It was already apparent that it would take the volplas only a few more weeks to learn their means of survival and develop an embryonic culture of their own. Then they could leave my ranch and the fun would be on.

My wife got out of the car and looked around at the workmen hurrying about the disemboweled buildings and she said, "What on earth is going on here?"

"I've finished my work and we no longer need the buildings. I'm going to write a paper about my results."

My wife looked at me appraisingly and shook her head. "I thought you meant it. But you really ought to. It would be your first."

My son asked, "What happened to the animals?"

"Turned them over to the university for further study," I lied.

"Well," he said to her, "you can't say our pop isn't a man of decision."

Twenty-four hours later, there wasn't a sign of animal experimentation on the ranch.

Except, of course, that the woods were full of volplas. At

night, I could hear them faintly when I sat out on the terrace. As they passed through the dark overhead, they chattered and laughed and sometimes moaned in winged love. One night a flight of them soared slowly across the face of the full Moon, but I was the only one who noticed.

I made daily trips out to the original camp to meet the oldest of the males, who had apparently established himself as a chief of all the volpla families. He assured me that the volplas were staying close to the ranch, but complained that the game was getting scarce. Otherwise things were progressing nicely.

The males now carried little stone-tipped spears with feathered shafts that they could throw in flight. They used them at night to bring down roosting sparrows and in the day to kill their biggest game, the local rabbits.

The women wore bluejay feathers on their heads. The men wore plumes of dove feathers and sometimes little skirts fashioned of rabbit down. I did some reading on the subject and taught them crude tanning of their rabbit and squirrel hides for use in their tree homes.

The tree homes were more and more intricately wrought with expert basketry for walls and floor and tight thatching above. They were well camouflaged from below, as I suggested.

These little creatures delighted me more and more. For hours, I could watch the adults, both the males and females, playing with the children or teaching them to glide. I could sit all afternoon and watch them at work on a tree house.

So one day my wife asked, "How *does* the mighty hunter who now returns from the forest?"

"Oh, fine. I've been enjoying the local animal life."

"So has our daughter."

"What do you mean?"

"She has two of them up in her room."

"Two what?"

"I don't know. What do *you* call them?"

I went up the stairs three at a time and burst into my daughter's room.

There she sat on her bed reading a book to two volplas.

One of the volplas grinned and said in English, "Hello there, King Arthur."

"What's going on here?" I demanded of all three.

"Nothing, Daddy. We're just reading like we always do."

"Like *always?* How long has this been going on?"

"Oh, weeks and weeks. How long has it been since you came here that first time to visit me, Fuzzy?"

The impolite volpla who had addressed me as King Arthur grinned at her and calculated. "Oh, weeks and weeks."

"But you're teaching them to read English."

"Of course. They're such good pupils and so grateful. Daddy, you won't make them go away, will you? We love each other, don't we?"

Both volplas nodded vigorously.

She turned back to me. "Daddy, did you know they can fly? They can fly right out of the window and way up in the sky."

"Is that a fact?" I said testily. I looked coldly at the two volplas. "I'm going to speak to your chief."

Back downstairs again, I raved at my wife. "Why didn't you tell me a thing like this was going on? How could you let such an unusual thing go on and not discuss it with me?"

My wife got a look on her face that I don't see very often. "Now you listen to me, mister. Your whole life is a secret from us. Just what makes you think your daughter can't have a little secret of her own?"

She got right up close to me and her blue eyes snapped little sparks all over me. "The fact is that I was wrong to tell you at all. I promised her I wouldn't tell *anyone*. Look what happened when I did. You go leaping around the house like a raving maniac just because a little girl has a secret."

"A fine secret!" I yelled. "Didn't it occur to you this might be dangerous? Those creatures are oversexed and—" I stumbled into an awful silence while she gave me the dirtiest smile since the days of the Malatestas.

"How did *you* . . . . suddenly get to *be* . . . the palace eunuch? Those are sweet lovable little creatures without a harm in their furry little bodies. But don't think I don't realize what's been going on. You created them yourself. So, if they have any dirty ideas, I know where they got them."

I stormed out of the house. I spun the jeep out of the yard and ripped off through the woods.

The chief was sitting at home as comfortable as you please. He was leaning back against the great oak that hid his tree house. He had a little fire going and one of the women was roasting a sparrow for him. He greeted me in volpla language.

"Do you realize," I blurted angrily, "that there are two volplas in my daughter's bedroom?"

"Why, yes," he answered calmly. "They go there every day. Is there anything wrong with that?"

"She's teaching them the words of men."

"You told us some men may be our enemies. We are anxious to know their words, the better to protect ourselves."

He reached around behind the tree and, right there in broad daylight, that volpla pulled a copy of the San Francisco *Chronicle* out of hiding. He held it up apologetically. "We have been taking it for some time from the box in front of your house."

He spread the paper on the ground between us. I saw by the date that it was yesterday's. He said proudly, "From the two who go to your house, I have learned the words of men. As men say, I can 'read' most of this."

I just stood there gaping at him. How could I possibly recoup this situation so that the stunning joke of the volplas wouldn't be lost? Would it seem reasonable that the volplas, by observing and listening to men, had learned their language? Or had they been taught it by a human friend?

That was it—I would just have to sacrifice anonymity. My family and I had found a colony of them on our ranch and taught them English. I was stuck with it because it was the truth.

The volpla waved his long thin arm over the front page. "Men are dangerous. They will shoot us with their guns if we leave here."

I hastened to reassure him. "It will not be like that. When men have learned about you, they will leave you alone." I stated this emphatically, but for the first time I was beginning to see this might not be a joke to the volplas. Nevertheless, I went on. "You must disperse the families at once. You stay here with your family so we remain in contact, but send the other families to other places."

He shook his head. "We cannot leave these woods. Men would shoot us."

Then he stood and looked squarely at me with his nocturnal eyes. "Perhaps you are not a good friend. Perhaps you have lied to us. Why are you saying we should leave this safety?"

"You will be happier. There will be more game."

He continued to stare directly at me. "There will be men. One has already shot one of us. We have forgiven him and are friends. But one of us is dead."

"You are friends with *another* man?" I asked, stunned.

He nodded and pointed up the valley. "He is up there today with another family."

"Let's go!"

He had the advantage of short glides, but the volpla chief couldn't keep up with me. Sometimes trotting, sometimes walking fast, I got way ahead of him. My hard breathing arose as much out of my anxiety about the manner of handling this stranger as it did out of the exertion.

I rounded a bend in the creek and there was my son sitting on the grass near a cooking fire playing with a baby volpla and talking in English to an adult volpla who stood beside him. As I approached, my son tossed the baby into the air. The tiny planes opened and the baby drifted down to his waiting hands.

He said to the volpla beside him, "No, I'm sure you didn't come from the stars. The more I think about it, the more I'm sure my father—"

I yelled from behind them, "What business do you have telling them that?"

The male volpla jumped about two feet. My son turned his head slowly and looked at me. Then he handed the baby to the male and stood up.

"You haven't any business out here!" I was seething. He had destroyed the whole store of volpla legends with one small doubt.

He brushed the grass from his trousers and straightened. The way he was looking at me, I felt my anger turning to a kind of jelly.

"Dad, I killed one of these little people yesterday. I thought he was a hawk and I shot him when I was out hunting. I wouldn't have done that if you had told me about them."

I couldn't look at him. I stared at the grass and my face got hot.

"The chief tells me that you want them to leave the ranch soon. You think you're going to play a big joke, don't you?"

I heard the chief come up behind me and stand quietly at my back.

My son said softly, "I don't think it's much of a joke, Dad. I had to listen to that one crying after I hit him."

There were big black trail ants moving in the grass. It seemed to me there was a ringing sound in the sky. I raised my head and looked at him. "Son, let's go back to the jeep and we can talk about it on the way home."

"I'd rather walk." He sort of waved to the volpla he had been talking to and then to the chief. He jumped the creek and walked away into the oak woods.

The volpla holding the baby stared at me. From somewhere far up the valley, a crow was cawing. I didn't look at the chief. I turned and brushed past him and walked back to the jeep alone.

At home, I opened a bottle of beer and sat out on the terrace to wait for my son. My wife came toward the house with some cut flowers from the garden, but she didn't speak to me. She snapped the blades of the scissors as she walked.

A volpla soared across the terrace and landed at my daughter's bedroom window. He was there only briefly and relaunched himself. He was followed from the window in moments by the volplas I had left with my daughter earlier in the afternoon. I watched them with a vague unease as the three veered off to the east, climbing effortlessly.

When I finally took a sip of my beer, it was already warm. I set it aside. Presently my daughter ran out onto the terrace.

"Daddy, my volplas left. They said good-by and we hadn't even finished the TV show. They said they won't see me again. Did you make them leave?"

"No. I didn't."

She was staring at me with hot eyes. Her lower lip protruded and trembled like a pink tear drop.

"Daddy, you did so." She stomped into the house, sobbing.

My God! In one afternoon, I had managed to become a palace eunuch, a murderer, and a liar!

Most of the afternoon went by before I heard my son enter the house. I called to him and he came out and stood before me. I got up.

"Son, I can't tell you how sorry I am for what happened to you. It was my fault, not yours at all. I only hope you can forget the shock of finding out what sort of creature you had hit. I don't know why I didn't anticipate that such things would happen. It was just that I was so intent on mystifying the whole world that I . . ."

I stopped. There wasn't anything more to say.

"Are you going to make them leave the ranch?" he asked.

I was aghast. "After what has happened?"

"Gee, what *are* you going to do about them, Dad?"

"I've been trying to decide. I don't know what I should do

that will be best for them." I looked at my watch. "Let's go back out and talk to the chief."

His eyes lighted and he clapped me on the shoulder, man to man. We ran out and got into the jeep and drove back up to the valley. The late afternoon sun glared across the landscape.

We didn't say much as we wound up the valley between the darkening trees. I was filled more and more with the unease that had seized me as I watched the three volplas leave my terrace and climb smoothly and purposefully into the east.

We got out at the chief's camp and there were no volplas around. The fire had burned down to a smolder. I called in the volpla language, but there was no answer.

We went from camp to camp and found dead fires. We climbed to their tree houses and found them empty. I was sick and scared. I called endlessly till I was hoarse.

At last, in the darkness, my son put a hand on my arm. "What are you going to do, Dad?"

Standing there in those terribly silent woods, I trembled. "I'll have to call the police and the newspapers and warn everybody."

"Where do you suppose they've gone?"

I looked to the east where the stars, rising out of the great pass in the mountains, glimmered like a deep bowl of fireflies.

"The last three I saw were headed that way."

We had been gone from the house for hours. When we stepped out onto the lighted terrace, I saw the shadow of a helicopter down on the strip. Then I saw Guy sitting near me in a chair. He was holding his head in his hands.

Em was saying to my wife, "He was beside himself. There wasn't a thing he could do. I had to get him away from there and I thought you wouldn't mind if we flew over here and stayed with you till they've decided what to do."

I walked over and said, "Hello, Guy. What's the matter?"

He raised his head and then stood and shook hands. "It's a mess. The whole project will be ruined and we don't dare go near it."

"What happened?"

"Just as we set it off——"

"Set what off?"

"The rocket."

"Rocket?"

Guy groaned.

"The *Venus* rocket! Rocket Harold!"

My wife interjected. "I was telling Guy we didn't know a thing about it because they haven't delivered our paper in weeks. I've complained——"

I waved her to silence. "Go on," I demanded of Guy.

"Just as I pushed the button and the hatch was closing, a flock of owls circled the ship. They started flying through the hatch and somehow they jammed it open."

Em said to my wife, "There must have been a hundred of them. They kept coming and coming and flying into that hatch. Then they began dumping out all the recording instruments. The men tried to run a motor-driven ladder up to the ship and those owls hit the driver on the head and knocked him out with some kind of instrument."

Guy turned his grief-stricken face to me. "Then the hatch closed and we don't dare go near the ship. It was supposed to fire in five minutes, but it hasn't. Those damned owls could have——"

There was a glare in the east. We all turned and saw a brief streak of gilt pencil its way up the black velvet beyond the mountains.

"That's it!" Guy shouted. "That's the ship!" Then he moaned. "A total loss."

I grabbed him by the shoulders. "You mean it won't make it to Venus?"

He jerked away in misery. "Sure, it will make it. The automatic controls can't be tampered with. But the rocket is on its way without any recording instruments or TV aboard. Just a load of owls."

My son laughed. "Owls! My dad can tell you a thing or two."

I silenced him with a scowl. He shut up, then danced off across the terrace. "Man, man! This is the biggest! The most —the greatest—the end!"

The phone was ringing. As I went to the box on the terrace, I grabbed my boy's arm. "Don't you breathe a word."

He giggled. "The joke is on you, Pop. Why should I say anything? I'll just grin once in a while."

"Now you cut that out."

He held onto my arm and walked toward the phone box with me, half convulsed. "Wait till men land on Venus and find Venusians with a legend about their Great White Father in California. That's when I'll tell."

The phone call was from a screaming psychotic who wanted Guy. I stood near Guy while he listened to the excited voice over the wire.

Presently Guy said, "No, no. The automatic controls will correct for the delay in firing. It isn't that. It's just that there aren't any instruments. . . What? What just happened? Calm down. I can't understand you."

I heard Em say to my wife, "You know, the strangest thing occurred out there. I *thought* it looked like those owls were carrying things on their backs. One of them dropped something and I saw the men open a package wrapped in a leaf. You'd never believe what was in it—three little birds roasted to a nice brown!"

My son nudged me. "Smart owls. Long trip."

I put my hand over his mouth. Then I saw that Guy was holding the receiver limply away from his ear.

He spluttered. "They just taped a radio message from the rocket. It's true that the radio wasn't thrown out. But we didn't have a record like *this* on that rocket."

He yelled into the phone. "Play it back." He thrust the receiver at me.

For a moment there was only a gritty buzz from the receiver. Then the tape started playing a soft, high voice. "This is Rocket Harold saying everything is well. This is Rocket Harold saying good-by to men." There was a pause and then, in clear volpla language, another voice spoke. "Man who made us, we forgive you. We know we did not come from the stars, but we go there. I, chief, give you welcome to visit. Good-by."

We all stood around too exhausted by the excitement to say anything. I was filled with a big, sudden sadness.

I stood for a long time and looked out to the east, where the sprawling mountain range held a bowl of dancing fireflies between her black breasts.

Presently I said to old Guy, "How long do you think it will be before you have a manned rocket ready for Venus?"

Honorable Opponent

By CLIFFORD D. SIMAK

No general ever had a worse assignment . . . to be dignified with Earth's conquerors . . . a race of unmilitary clowns!

The Fivers were late.

Perhaps they had misunderstood.

Or this might be another of their tricks.

Or maybe they never had intended to stick to their agreement.

"Captain," asked General Lyman Flood, "what time have we got now?"

Captain Gist looked up from the chessboard. "Thirty-seven oh eight, galactic, sir."

Then he went back to the board again. Sergeant Conrad had pinned his knight and he didn't like it.

"Thirteen hours late!" the general fumed.

"They may not have got it straight, sir."

"We spelled it out to them. We took them by the hand and we went over it time and time again so they'd have it clear in mind. They couldn't possibly misunderstand."

But they very possibly could, he knew.

The Fivers misunderstood almost everything. They had been confused about the armistice—as if they'd never heard of an armistice before. They had been obtuse about the prisoner exchange. Even the matter of setting a simple time had involved excruciating explanation—as if they had never heard of the measurement of time and were completely innocent of basic mathematics.

"Or maybe they broke down," the captain offered.

The general snorted. "They don't break down. Those ships of theirs are marvels. They'd live through anything. They whipped us, didn't they?"

"Yes, sir," said the captain.

"How many of them, Captain, do you estimate we destroyed?"

"Not more than a dozen, sir."

"They're tough," the general said.

He went back across the tent and sat down in a chair.

The captain had been wrong. The right number was eleven. And of those, only one had been confirmed destroyed. The others had been no better than put out of action.

And the way it figured out, the margin had been more than ten to one in favor of the Fivers. Earth, the general admitted to himself, had never taken such a beating. Whole squadrons had been wiped out; others had come fleeing back to base with their numbers cut in half.

They came fleeing back to base and there were no cripples. They had returned without a scratch upon them. And the ships that had been lost had not been visibly destroyed—they had simply been wiped out, leaving not a molecule of wreckage.

How do you beat a thing like that? he asked himself. How do you fight a weapon that cancels out a ship in its entirety?

Back on Earth and on hundreds of other planets in the Galactic Confederacy, thousands of researchers were working day and night in a crash-priority program to find an answer to the weapon—or at least to find the weapon.

But the chance of success ran thin, the general knew, for there was not a single clue to the nature of it. Which was understandable, since every victim of the weapon had been lost irretrievably.

Perhaps some of the human prisoners would be able to provide a clue. If there had been no such hope, he knew, Earth never would have gone to all the trouble to make this prisoner exchange.

He watched the captain and the sergeant hunched above the chessboard, with the captive Fiver looking on.

He called the captive over.

The captive came, like a trundling roly-poly.

And once again, watching him, the general had that strange, disturbing sense of outrage.

For the Fiver was a droll grotesque that held no hint of the martial spirit. He was round and jolly in every feature, expression, and gesture, dressed in a ribald clash of colors, as though designed and clad deliberately to offend any military man.

"Your friends are late," the general told him.

"You wait," the Fiver said and his words were more like whistling than talk. One had to listen closely to make out what he said.

The general held himself in check.

No use in arguing.

No point blowing up.

He wondered if he—or the human race—would ever understand the Fivers.

Not that anyone really wanted to, of course. Just to get them combed out of Earth's hair would be enough.

"You wait," the Fiver whistled. "They come in middle time from now."

And when in hell, the general wondered, would be a middle time from now?

The Fiver glided back to watch the game.

The general walked outside.

The tiny planet looked colder and more desolate and forbidding than it ever had before. Each time he looked at it, the general thought, the scene was more depressing than he had remembered it.

Lifeless, worthless, of no strategic or economic value, it had qualified quite admirably as neutral territory to carry out the prisoner exchange. Neutral mostly because it wasn't worth the trouble for anyone to grab it.

The distant star that was its sun was a dim glow in the sky. The black and naked rock crept out to a near horizon. The icy air was like a knife inside the general's nostrils.

There were no hills or valleys. There was absolutely nothing—just the smooth flatness of the rock stretching on all sides, for all the world like a great space-field.

It had been the Fivers, the general remembered, who had suggested this particular planet and that in itself was enough to make it suspect. But Earth, at that point in the negotiations, had been in no position to do much haggling.

He stood with his shoulders hunched and he felt the cold breath of apprehension blowing down his neck. With each passing hour, it seemed, the place felt more and more like some gigantic trap.

But he must be wrong, he argued. There was absolutely nothing in the Fivers' attitude to make him feel like that. They had, in fact, been almost magnanimous. They could have laid down their terms—almost any terms—and the Confederacy would have had no choice but to acquiesce. For Earth must buy time, no matter what the price. Earth had to be ready next time—five years or ten or whatever it might be.

But the Fivers had made no demands, which was unthinkable.

Except, the general told himself, one could never know what they might be thinking or what they might be planning.

The exchange camp huddled in the dimness—a few tents, a portable power plant, the poised and waiting ship and, beside it, the little scouter the captive Fiver had been piloting.

The scouter in itself was a good example of the gulf which separated the Fivers and the humans. It had taken three full days of bickering before the Fivers had been able to make clear their point that the scouter as well as its pilot must be returned to them.

No ship in all the Galaxy had ever gotten so thorough a study as that tiny craft. But the facts that it had yielded had been few indeed. And the captive Fiver, despite the best efforts of the experts in Psych, had furnished even fewer.

The area was quiet and almost deserted. Two sentries strode briskly up and down. Everyone else was under cover, killing time, waiting for the Fivers.

The general walked quickly across the area to the medic tent. He stooped and went inside.

Four men were sitting at a table, drearily playing cards. One of them put down his hand and rose.

"Any word, General?"

The general shook his head. "They should be coming soon, Doc. Everything all set?"

"We've been ready for some time," said the psychiatrist. "We'll bring the boys in here and check them over as soon as they arrive. We've got the stuff all set. It won't take us long."

"That's fine. I want to get off this rock as quickly as I can. I don't like the feel of it."

"There's just one thing . . ."

"What's that?"

"If we only knew how many they are handing back?"

The general shook his head. "We never could find out. They're not so hot on figures. And you'd think, wouldn't you, that math would be universal?"

"Well," said Doc resignedly, "we'll do the best we can."

"There can't be many," the general said. "We're only giving back one Fiver and one ship. How many humans do you figure a ship is worth to them?"

"I wouldn't know. You really think they'll come?"

"It's hard to be certain that they understood. When it comes to sheer stupidity——"

"Not so stupid," Doc replied, quietly. "We couldn't learn their language, so they learned ours."

"I know," the general said impatiently. "I realize all that. But that armistice business—it took days for them to get what we were driving at. And the time-reckoning system still more days. Good Lord, man, you could do better using sign language with a Stone Age savage!"

"You should," said Doc. "The savage would be human."

"But these Fivers are intelligent. Their technology, in many ways, has us beaten seven ways from Sunday. They fought us to a standstill."

"They licked us."

"All right, then, they licked us. And why not? They had this weapon that we didn't have. They were closer to their bases. They had no logistics problem to compare with ours. They licked us, but I ask you, did they have the sense to know it? Did they take advantage of it? They could have wiped us out. They could have laid down peace terms that would have crippled us for centuries. Instead, they let us go. Now how does that make sense?"

"You're dealing with an alien race," said Doc.

"We've dealt with other aliens. And we always understood them. Mostly, we got along with them."

"We dealt with them on a commercial basis," Doc reminded him. "Whatever trouble we might have had with them came after a basic minimum of understanding had been achieved. The Fivers are the first that ever came out shooting."

"I can't figure it," the general said. "We weren't even heading for them. We might have passed them by. They couldn't have known who we were. Point is, they didn't care. They just came piling out and opened up on us. And it's been the same with everyone else who came within their reach. They take on every comer. There's never a time when they aren't fighting someone—sometimes two or three at once."

"They have a defensive complex," said Doc. "Want to be left alone. All they aim to do is keep others off their planets. As you say, they could have wiped us out."

"Maybe they get hurt real easy. Don't forget we gave them a bloody nose or two—not as much as they busted us, but we hurt them some. I figure they'll come out again, soon as they can cut in."

He drew a deep breath. "Next time, we have to be ready for them. Next time, they may not stop. We have to dope them out."

It was tough work, he thought, to fight an enemy about which one knew next to nothing. And a weapon about which one knew absolutely nothing.

There were theories in plenty, but the best no more than educated guesses.

The weapon might operate in time—hurling its targets back into unimagined chaos. Or it might be dimensional. Or it might collapse the atoms in upon themselves, reducing a spaceship to the most deadly massive dust-mote the Universe had known.

One thing for certain—it was not disintegration, for there was no flash and there was no heat. The ship just disappeared and that was the end of it—the end and all of it.

"There's another thing that bothers me," said Doc. "Those other races that fought the Fivers before they jumped on us. When we tried to contact them, when we tried to get some help from them, they wouldn't bother with us. They wouldn't tell us anything."

"This is a new sector of space for us," the general said. "We are strangers here."

"It stands to reason," argued Doc, "they should jump at the chance to gang up on the Fivers."

"We can't depend on alliances. We stand alone. It is up to us."

He bent to leave the tent.

"We'll get right on it," said Doc, "soon as the men show up. We'll have a preliminary report within an hour, if they're in any shape at all."

"That's fine," the general said and ducked out of the tent.

It was a bad situation, blind and terrifying if one didn't manage to keep a good grip on himself.

The captive humans might bring back some information, but even so, you couldn't buy it blind, for there might be a gimmick in it—as there was a gimmick in what the captive Fiver knew.

This time, he told himself, the Psych boys might have managed to outsmart themselves.

It had been a clever trick, all right—taking the captive Fiver on that trip and showing him so proudly all the barren, no-good planets, pretending they were the showplaces of the Confederacy.

Clever—if the Fiver had been human. For no human would have fought a skirmish, let alone a war, for the kind of planets he'd been shown.

But the Fiver wasn't human. And there was no way of knowing what kind of planet a Fiver might take a fancy to.

And there always was the chance that those crummy planets had given him the hunch that Earth would be easy prey.

The whole situation didn't track, the general thought. There was a basic wrongness to it. Even allowing for all the differences which might exist between the Fiver and the human cultures, the wrongness still persisted.

And there was something wrong right here.

He heard the sound and wheeled to stare into the sky. The ship was close and coming in too fast.

But even as he held his breath, it slowed and steadied and came to ground in a perfect landing not more than a quarter of a mile from where the Earth ship stood.

The general broke into a run toward it, then remembered and slowed to a stiff military walk.

Men were tumbling out of tents and forming into lines. An order rang across the area and the lines moved with perfect drill precision.

The general allowed himself a smile. Those boys of his were good. You never caught them napping. If the Fivers had expected to sneak in and catch the camp confused and thus gain a bit of face, it was a horse on them.

The marching men swung briskly down the field. An ambulance moved out from beneath its tarp and followed. The drums began to roll and the bugles sounded clear and crisp in the harsh, cold air.

It was men like these, the general told himself with pride, who held the expanding Confederacy intact. It was men like these who kept the peace across many cubic light-years. It was men like these who some day, God willing, would roll back the Fiver threat.

There were few wars now. Space was too big for it. There were too many ways to skirt around the edge of war for it to come but seldom. But something like the Fiver threat could not be ignored. Some day, soon or late, either Earth or Fiver must go down to complete defeat. The Confederacy could never feel secure with the Fivers on its flank.

Feet pounded behind him and the general turned. It was Captain Gist, buttoning his tunic as he ran. He fell in beside the general.

"So they finally came, sir."

"Fourteen hours late," the general said. "Let us, for the moment, try to look our best. You missed a button, Captain."

"Sorry, sir," the captain said, fastening the button.

"Right, then. Get those shoulders back. Smartly, if you will. Right, left, hup, hup!"

Out of the corner of his eye, he saw that Sergeant Conrad had his squad moving out with precision, escorting the captive Fiver most correctly forward, with all the dignity and smartness that anyone might wish.

The men were drawn up now in two parallel lines, flanking the ship. The port was swinging open and the ramp was rumbling out and the general noted with some satisfaction that he and Captain Gist would arrive at the foot of the ramp about the time it touched the ground. The timing was dramatic and superb, almost as if he himself had planned it down to the last detail.

The ramp snapped into position and three Fivers came sedately waddling down it.

A seedy-looking trio, the general thought. Not a proper uniform nor a medal among the lot of them.

The general seized the diplomatic initiative as soon as they reached the ground.

"We welcome you," he told them, speaking loudly and slowly and as distinctly as he could so they would understand.

They lined up and stood looking at him and he felt a bit uncomfortable because there was that round jolly expression in their faces. Evidently they didn't have the kind of faces that could assume any other expression. But they kept on looking at him.

The general plunged ahead. "It is a matter of great gratification to Earth to carry out in good faith our obligations as agreed upon in the armistice proceedings. It marks what we sincerely hope will be the beginning of an era . . ."

"Most nice," one of the Fivers said. Whether he meant the general's little speech or the entire situation or was simply trying to be gracious was not at once apparent.

Undaunted, the general was ready to go on, but the spokesman Fiver raised a short round arm to halt him.

"Prisoners arrive briefly," he whistled.

"You mean you didn't bring them?"

"They come again," the Fiver said with a glorious disregard for preciseness of expression.

He continued beaming at the general and he made a motion with the arm that might have been a shrug.

"Shennanigans," the captain said, close to the general's ear.

"We talk," the Fiver said.

"They're up to something," warned the captain. "It calls for Situation Red, sir."

"I agree," the general told the captain. "Set it up quietly." He said to the Fiver delegation: "If you gentlemen will come with me, I can offer you refreshments."

He had a feeling that they were smiling at him, mocking him, but one could never tell. Those jolly expressions were always the same. No matter what the situation.

"Most happy," said the Fiver spokesman. "These refresh—"

"Drink," the general said and made a motion to supplement the word.

"Drink is good," the Fiver answered. "Drink is friend?"

"That is right," the general said.

He started for the tent, walking slowly so the Fivers could keep up.

He noted with some satisfaction that the captain had carried on most rapidly, indeed. Corporal Conrad was marching his squad back across the area, with the captive Fiver shambling in the center. The tarps were coming off the guns and the last of the crew was clambering up the ladder of the ship.

The captain caught up with them just short of the tent.

"Everything all set, sir," Corporal Conrad reported in a whisper.

"Fine," the general said.

They reached the tent and went inside. The general opened a refrigerating unit and took out a gallon jug.

"This," he explained, "is a drink we made for your compatriot. He found it very tasty."

He set out glasses and sipping straws and uncorked the jug, wishing he could somehow hold his nose, for the drink smelled like something that had been dead too long. He didn't even like to guess what might have gone into it. The chemists back on Earth had whomped it up for the captive Fiver, who had consumed gallon after gallon of it with disconcerting gusto.

The general filled the glasses and the Fivers picked them up in their tentacles and stuck the straws into their drawstring mouths. They drank and rolled their eyes in appreciation.

The general took the glass of liquor the captain handed him and gulped half of it in haste. The tent was getting just a little thick. What things a man goes through, he thought, to serve his planets and his peoples.

He watched the Fivers drinking and wondered what they might have up their sleeves.

Talk, the spokesman had told him, and that might mean almost anything. It might mean a reopening of negotiations or it might be nothing but a stall.

And if it was a negotiation, Earth was across the barrel. For there was nothing he could do but negotiate. Earth's fleet was crippled and the Fivers had the weapon and a renewal of the war was unthinkable. Earth needed five years at the minimum and ten years would be still better.

And if it was attack, if this planet was a trap, there was only one thing he could do—stand and fight as best he could, a thoroughly suicidal course.

Either way, Earth lost, the general realized.

The Fivers put down their glasses and he filled them up again.

"You do well," one of the Fivers said. "You got the paper and the marker?"

"Marker?" the general asked.

"He means a pencil," said the captain.

"Oh, yes. Right here." The general reached for a pad of paper and a pencil and laid them on the desk.

One of the Fivers set down his glass and, picking up the pencil, started to make a laborious drawing. He looked for all the world like a five-year-old printing his first alphabet.

They waited while the Fiver drew. Finally he was finished. He laid the pencil down and pointed to the wiggly lines.

"Us," he said.

He pointed to the sawtoothed lines.

"You," he told the general.

The general bent above the paper, trying to make out what the Fiver had put down.

"Sir," the captain said, "it looks like a battle diagram."

"Is," said the Fiver proudly.

He picked the pencil up.

"Look," he said.

He drew directional lines and made a funny kind of symbol for the points of contact and made crosses for the sections where the battle lines were broken. When he was done, the Earth fleet had been shattered and sliced into three segments and was in headlong flight.

"That," the general said, with the husk of anger rising in his throat, "was the engagement in Sector 17. Half of our Fifth Squadron was wiped out that day."

"Small error," said the Fiver and made a deprecatory gesture.

He ripped the sheet of paper off the pad and tossed it on the floor. He laboriously drew the diagram again.

"Attend," he said.

The Fiver drew the directional lines again, but this time he changed them slightly. Now the Earth line pivoted and broke and became two parallel lines that flanked the Fiver drive and turned and blunted it and scattered it in space.

The Fiver laid the pencil down.

"Small matter," he informed the general and the captain. "You good. You make one thin mistake."

Holding himself sternly in hand, the general filled the glasses once again.

What are they getting at, he thought. Why don't they come flat out and say it?

"So best," one of the Fivers said, lifting his glass to let them know that he meant the drink.

"More?" asked the Fiver tactician, picking up the pencil.

"Please," said the general, seething.

He walked to the tent flap and looked outside. The men were at the guns. Thin wisps of vapor curled from the ship's launching tubes; in just a little while, it would be set to go, should the need arise. The camp was quiet and tense.

He went back to the desk and watched as the Fiver went on gaily with his lesson on how to win a battle. He filled page after page with diagrams and occasionally he was generous—he sometimes showed how the Fivers lost when they might have won with slightly different tactics.

"Interesting!" he piped enthusiastically.

"I find it so," the general said. "There is just one question."

"Ask," the Fiver invited.

"If we should go to war again, how can you be sure we won't use all of this against you?"

"But fine," the Fiver enthused warmly. "Exactly as we want."

"You fight fine," another Fiver said. "But just too slightly hard. Next time, you able to do much better."

"Hard!" the general raged.

"Too roughly, sir. No need to make the ship go poof."

Outside the tent, a gun cut loose and then another one and above the hammering of the guns came the full-throated, ground-shaking roar of many ship motors.

The general leaped for the entrance, went through it at a run, not bothering with the flap. His cap fell off and he staggered out, thrown slightly off his balance. He jerked up his head and saw them coming in, squadron after squadron, painting the darkness with the flare of tubes.

"Stop firing!" he shouted. "You crazy fools, stop firing!"

But there was no need of shouting, for the guns had fallen silent.

The ships came down toward the camp in perfect flight

formation. They swept across it and the thunder of their motors seemed to lift it for a moment and give it a mighty shake. Then they were climbing, rank on serried rank, still with drill precision—climbing and jockeying into position for regulation landing.

The general stood like a frozen man, with the wind ruffling his iron-gray hair, with a lump, half pride, half thankfulness, rising in his throat.

Something touched his elbow.

"Prisoners," said the Fiver. "I told you bye and bye."

The general tried to speak, but the lump was there to stop him. He swallowed it and tried once again.

"We didn't understand," he said.

"You did not have a taker," said the Fiver. "That why you fight so rough."

"We couldn't help it," the general told him. "We didn't know. We never fought this way before."

"We give you takers," said the Fiver. "Next time, we play it right. You do much better with the takers. It easier on us."

No wonder, the general thought, they didn't know about an armistice. No wonder they were confused about the negotiations and the prisoner exchange. Negotiations are not customarily needed to hand back the pieces one has won in a game.

And no wonder those other races had viewed with scorn and loathing Earth's proposal to gang up on the Fivers.

"An unsporting thing to do," the general said aloud. "They could have told us. Or maybe they were so used to it."

And now he understood why the Fivers had picked this planet. There had to be a place where all the ships could land.

He stood and watched the landing ships mushing down upon the rock in clouds of pinkish flame. He tried to count them, but he became confused, although he knew every ship Earth had lost would be accounted for.

"We give you takers," said the Fiver. "We teach you how

to use. They easy operate. They never hurt people or ships."

And there was more to it, the general told himself, than just a silly game—though maybe not so silly, once one understood the history and the cultural background and the philosophic concepts that were tied into it. And this much one could say for it: it was better than fighting actual wars.

But with the takers, there would be an end of war. What little war was left would be ended once for all. No longer would an enemy need to be defeated; he could be simply taken. No longer would there be years of guerrilla fighting on newly settled planets; the aborigines could be picked up and deposited in cultural reservations and the dangerous fauna shunted into zoos.

"We fight again?" the Fiver asked with some anxiety.

"Certainly," said the general. "Any time you say. Are we really as good as you claim?"

"You not so hot," the Fiver admitted with disarming candor. "But you the best we ever find. Play plenty, you get better."

The general grinned. Just like the sergeant and the captain and their eternal chess, he thought.

He turned and tapped the Fiver on the shoulder.

"Let's get back," he said. "There's still some drinking in that jug. We mustn't let it go to waste."

The Game of Rat and Dragon

By CORDWAINER SMITH

Only partners could fight this deadliest of wars—and the one way to dissolve the partnership was to be personally and eternally dissolved!

THE TABLE

Pinlighting is a hell of a way to earn a living. Underhill was furious as he closed the door behind himself. It didn't make much sense to wear a uniform and look like a soldier if people didn't appreciate what you did.

He sat down in his chair, laid his head back in the headrest, and pulled the helmet down over his forehead.

As he waited for the pin-set to warm up, he remembered the girl in the outer corridor. She had looked at it, then looked at him scornfully.

"Meow." That was all she had said. Yet it had cut him like a knife.

What did she think he was—a fool, a loafer, a uniformed nonentity? Didn't she know that for every half hour of pinlighting, he got a minimum of two months' recuperation in the hospital?

By now the set was warm. He felt the squares of space around him, sensed himself at the middle of an immense grid, a cubic grid, full of nothing. Out in that nothingness, he could sense the hollow aching horror of space itself and could feel the terrible anxiety which his mind encountered whenever it met the faintest trace of inert dust.

As he relaxed, the comforting solidity of the Sun, the clockwork of the familiar planets and the Moon rang in on him. Our own solar system was as charming and as simple as an ancient cuckoo clock filled with familiar ticking and with reassuring noises. The odd little moons of Mars swung around their planet like frantic mice, yet their regularity was itself an assurance that all was well. Far above the plane of the ecliptic, he could feel half a ton of dust more or less drifting outside the lanes of human travel.

Here there was nothing to fight, nothing to challenge the mind, to tear the living soul out of a body with its roots dripping in effluvium as tangible as blood.

Nothing ever moved in on the Solar System. He could wear the pin-set forever and be nothing more than a sort of telepathic astronomer, a man who could feel the hot, warm protection of the Sun throbbing and burning against his living mind.

Woodley came in.

"Same old ticking world," said Underhill. "Nothing to report. No wonder they didn't develop the pin-set until they began to planoform. Down here with the hot Sun around us, it feels so good and so quiet. You can feel everything spinning and turning. It's nice and sharp and compact. It's sort of like sitting around home."

Woodley grunted. He was not much given to flights of fantasy.

Undeterred, Underhill went on, "It must have been pretty good to have been an Ancient Man. I wonder why they burned up their world with war. They didn't have to planoform. They didn't have to go out to earn their livings among the stars. They didn't have to dodge the Rats or play the Game. They couldn't have invented pinlighting because they didn't have any need of it, did they, Woodley?"

Woodley grunted, "Uh-huh." Woodley was twenty-six years old and due to retire in one more year. He already had a farm picked out. He had gotten through ten years of hard work pinlighting with the best of them. He had kept his sanity by not thinking very much about his job, meeting the strains of the task whenever he had to meet them and thinking nothing more about his duties until the next emergency arose.

Woodley never made a point of getting popular among the Partners. None of the Partners liked him very much. Some of them even resented him. He was suspected of thinking ugly thoughts of the Partners on occasion, but since none of the Partners ever thought a complaint in articulate form, the other pinlighters and the Chiefs of the Instrumentality left him alone.

Underhill was still full of the wonder of their job. Happily he babbled on, "What does happen to us when we planoform? Do you think it's sort of like dying? Did you ever see anybody who had his soul pulled out?"

"Pulling souls is just a way of talking about it," said Woodley. "After all these years, nobody knows whether we have souls or not."

"But I saw one once. I saw what Dogwood looked like when he came apart. There was something funny. It looked wet and sort of sticky as if it were bleeding and it went out of him—and you know what they did to Dogwood? They took him away, up in that part of the hospital where you and I never go—way up at the top part where the others are, where the others always have to go if they are alive after the Rats of the Up-and-Out have gotten them."

Woodley sat down and lit an ancient pipe. He was burning something called tobacco in it. It was a dirty sort of habit, but it made him look very dashing and adventurous.

"Look here, youngster. You don't have to worry about that

stuff. Pinlighting is getting better all the time. The Partners are getting better. I've seen them pinlight two Rats forty-six million miles apart in one and a half milliseconds. As long as people had to try to work the pin-sets themselves, there was always the chance that with a minimum of four hundred milliseconds for the human mind to set a pinlight, we wouldn't light the Rats up fast enough to protect our planoforming ships. The Partners have changed all that. Once they get going, they're faster than Rats. And they always will be. I know it's not easy, letting a Partner share your mind——"

"It's not easy for them, either," said Underhill.

"Don't worry about them. They're not human. Let them take care of themselves. I've seen more pinlighters go crazy from monkeying around with Partners than I have ever seen caught by the Rats. How many of them do you actually know of that got grabbed by Rats?"

Underhill looked down at his fingers, which shone green and purple in the vivid light thrown by the tuned-in pin-set, and counted ships. The thumb for the *Andromeda,* lost with crew and passengers, the index finger and the middle finger for *Release Ships 43* and *56,* found with their pin-sets burned out and every man, woman, and child on board dead or insane. The ring finger, the little finger, and the thumb of the other hand were the first three battleships to be lost to the Rats—lost as people realized that there was something out there *underneath space itself* which was alive, capricious, and malevolent.

Planoforming was sort of funny. It felt like——

Like nothing much.

Like the twinge of a mild electric shock.

Like the ache of a sore tooth bitten on for the first time.

Like a slightly painful flash of light against the eyes.

Yet in that time, a forty-thousand-ton ship lifting free above Earth disappeared somehow or other into two dimensions and appeared half a light-year or fifty light-years off.

At one moment, he would be sitting in the Fighting Room,

the pin-set ready and the familiar Solar System ticking around inside his head. For a second or a year (he could never tell how long it really was, subjectively), the funny little flash went through him and then he was loose in the Up-and-Out, the terrible open spaces between the stars, where the stars themselves felt like pimples on his telepathic mind and the planets were too far away to be sensed or read.

Somewhere in this outer space, a gruesome death awaited, death and horror of a kind which Man had never encountered until he reached out for interstellar space itself. Apparently the light of the suns kept the Dragons away.

Dragons. That was what people called them. To ordinary people, there was nothing, nothing except the shiver of planoforming and the hammer blow of sudden death or the dark spastic note of lunacy descending into their minds.

But to the telepaths, they were Dragons.

In the fraction of a second between the telepaths' awareness of a hostile something out in the black, hollow nothingness of space and the impact of a ferocious, ruinous psychic blow against all living things within the ship, the telepaths had sensed entities something like the Dragons of ancient human lore, beasts more clever than beasts, demons more tangible than demons, hungry vortices of aliveness and hate compounded by unknown means out of the thin tenuous matter between the stars.

It took a surviving ship to bring back the news—a ship in which, by sheer chance, a telepath had a light beam ready, turning it out at the innocent dust so that, within the panorama of his mind, the Dragon dissolved into nothing at all and the other passengers, themselves non-telepathic, went about their way not realizing that their own immediate deaths had been averted.

From then on, it was easy—almost.

Planoforming ships always carried telepaths. Telepaths had their sensitiveness enlarged to an immense range by the pin-sets, which were telepathic amplifiers adapted to the mammal mind. The pin-sets in turn were electronically geared into small dirigible light bombs. Light did it.

Light broke up the Dragons, allowed the ships to reform three-dimensionally, skip, skip, skip, as they moved from star to star.

The odds suddenly moved down from a hundred to one against mankind to sixty to forty in mankind's favor.

This was not enough. The telepaths were trained to become ultrasensitive, trained to become aware of the Dragons in less than a millisecond.

But it was found that the Dragons could move a million miles in just under two milliseconds and that this was not enough for the human mind to activate the light beams.

Attempts had been made to sheath the ships in light at all times.

This defense wore out.

As mankind learned about the Dragons, so too, apparently, the Dragons learned about mankind. Somehow they flattened their own bulk and came in on extremely flat trajectories very quickly.

Intense light was needed, light of sunlike intensity. This could be provided only by light bombs. Pinlighting came into existence.

Pinlighting consisted of the detonation of ultra-vivid miniature photonuclear bombs, which converted a few ounces of a magnesium isotope into pure visible radiance.

The odds kept coming down in mankind's favor, yet ships were being lost.

It became so bad that people didn't even want to find the ships because the rescuers knew what they would see. It was sad to bring back to Earth three hundred bodies ready for burial and two hundred or three hundred lunatics, damaged beyond repair, to be wakened, and fed, and cleaned, and put to sleep, wakened and fed again until their lives were ended.

Telepaths tried to reach into the minds of the psychotics

who had been damaged by the Dragons, but they found nothing there beyond vivid spouting columns of fiery terror bursting from the primordial id itself, the volcanic source of life.

Then came the Partners.

Man and Partner could do together what Man could not do alone. Men had the intellect. Partners had the speed.

The Partners rode their tiny craft, no larger than footballs, outside the spaceships. They planoformed with the ships. They rode beside them in their six-pound craft ready to attack.

The tiny ships of the Partners were swift. Each carried a dozen pinlights, bombs no bigger than thimbles.

The pinlighters threw the Partners—quite literally threw—by means of mind-to-firing relays direct at the Dragons.

What seemed to be Dragons to the human mind appeared in the form of gigantic Rats in the minds of the Partners.

Out in the pitiless nothingness of space, the Partners' minds responded to an instinct as old as life. The Partners attacked, striking with a speed faster than Man's, going from attack to attack until the Rats or themselves were destroyed. Almost all the time it was the Partners who won.

With the safety of the interstellar skip, skip, skip of the ships, commerce increased immensely, the population of all the colonies went up, and the demand for trained Partners increased.

Underhill and Woodley were a part of the third generation of pinlighters and yet, to them, it seemed as though their craft had endured forever.

Gearing space into minds by means of the pin-set, adding the Partners to those minds, keying up the mind for the tension of a fight on which all depended—this was more than human synapses could stand for long. Underhill needed his two months' rest after half an hour of fighting. Woodley needed his retirement after ten years of service. They were young. They were good. But they had limitations.

So much depended on the choice of Partners, so much on the sheer luck of who drew whom.

THE SHUFFLE

Father Moontree and the little girl named West entered the room. They were the other two pinlighters. The human complement of the Fighting Room was now complete.

Father Moontree was a red-faced man of forty-five who had lived the peaceful life of a farmer until he reached his fortieth year. Only then, belatedly, did the authorities find he was telepathic and agree to let him late in life enter upon the career of pinlighter. He did well at it, but he was fantastically old for this kind of business.

Father Moontree looked at the glum Woodley and the musing Underhill. "How're the youngsters today? Ready for a good fight?"

"Father always wants a fight," giggled the little girl named West. She was such a little little girl. Her giggle was high and childish. She looked like the last person in the world one would expect to find in the rough, sharp dueling of pinlighting.

Underhill had been amused one time when he found one of the most sluggish of the Partners coming away happy from contact with the mind of the girl named West.

Usually the Partners didn't care much about the human minds with which they were paired for the journey. The Partners seemed to take the attitude that human minds were complex and fouled up beyond belief, anyhow. No Partner ever questioned the superiority of the human mind, though very few of the Partners were much impressed by that superiority.

The Partners liked people. They were willing to fight with them. They were even willing to die for them. But when a Partner liked an individual the way, for example, that Captain Wow or the Lady May liked Underhill, the liking had nothing to do with intellect. It was a matter of temperament, of feel.

Underhill knew perfectly well that Captain Wow regarded his, Underhill's, brains as silly. What Captain Wow liked was Underhill's friendly emotional structure, the cheerfulness and glint of wicked amusement that shot through Underhill's unconscious thought patterns, and the gaiety with whch Underhill faced danger. The words, the history books, the ideas, the science—Underhill could sense all that in his own mind, reflected back from Captain Wow's mind, as so much rubbish.

Miss West looked at Underhill. "I bet you've put stickum on the stones."

"I did not!"

Underhill felt his ears grow red with embarrassment. During his novitiate, he had tried to cheat in the lottery because he got particularly fond of a special Partner, a lovely young mother named Murr. It was so much easier to operate with Murr and she was so affectionate toward him that he forgot pinlighting was hard work and that he was not instructed to have a good time with his Partner. They were both designed and prepared to go into deadly battle together.

One cheating had been enough. They had found him out and he had been laughed at for years.

Father Moontree picked up the imitation-leather cup and shook the stone dice which assigned them their Partners for the trip. By senior rights he took first draw.

He grimaced. He had drawn a greedy old character, a tough old male whose mind was full of slobbering thoughts of food, veritable oceans full of half-spoiled fish. Father Moontree had once said that he burped cod liver oil for weeks after drawing that particular glutton, so strongly had the telepathic image of fish impressed itself upon his mind. Yet the glutton was a glutton for danger as well as for fish. He had killed sixty-three Dragons, more than any other Partner in the service, and was quite literally worth his weight in gold.

The little girl West came next. She drew Captain Wow. When she saw who it was, she smiled.

"I *like* him," she said. "He's such fun to fight with. He feels so nice and cuddly in my mind."

"Cuddly, hell," said Woodley. "I've been in his mind, too. It's the most leering mind in this ship, bar none."

"Nasty man," said the little girl. She said it declaratively, without reproach.

Underhill, looking at her, shivered.

He didn't see how she could take Captain Wow so calmly. Captain Wow's mind *did* leer. When Captain Wow got excited in the middle of a battle, confused images of Dragons, deadly Rats, luscious beds, the smell of fish, and the shock of space all scrambled together in his mind as he and Captain Wow, their consciousnesses linked together through the pin-set, became a fantastic composite of human being and Persian cat.

That's the trouble with working with cats, thought Underhill. It's a pity that nothing else anywhere will serve as Partner. Cats were all right once you got in touch with them telepathically. They were smart enough to meet the needs of the fight, but their motives and desires were certainly different from those of humans.

They were companionable enough as long as you thought tangible images at them, but their minds just closed up and went to sleep when you recited Shakespeare or Colegrove, or if you tried to tell them what space was.

It was sort of funny realizing that the Partners who were so grim and mature out here in space were the same cute little animals that people had used as pets for thousands of years back on Earth. He had embarrassed himself more than once while on the ground saluting perfectly ordinary non-telepathic cats because he had forgotten for the moment that they were not Partners.

He picked up the cup and shook out his stone dice.

He was lucky—he drew the Lady May.

The Lady May was the most thoughtful Partner he had ever met. In her, the finely bred pedigree mind of a Persian cat had reached one of its highest peaks of development. She was more complex than any human woman, but the complexity was all one of emotions, memory, hope, and discriminated experience—experience sorted through without benefit of words.

When he had first come into contact with her mind, he was astonished at its clarity. With her he remembered her kittenhood. He remembered every mating experience she had ever had. He saw in a half-recognizable gallery all the other pinlighters with whom she had been paired for the fight. And he saw himself radiant, cheerful, and desirable.

He even thought he caught the edge of a longing—

A very flattering and yearning thought: *What a pity he is not a cat.*

Woodley picked up the last stone. He drew what he deserved—a sullen, scarred old tomcat with none of the verve of Captain Wow. Woodley's Partner was the most animal of all the cats on the ship, a low, brutish type with a dull mind. Even telepathy had not refined his character. His ears were half chewed off from the first fights in which he had engaged.

He was a serviceable fighter, nothing more.

Woodley grunted.

Underhill glanced at him oddly. Didn't Woodley ever do anything but grunt?

Father Moontree looked at the other three. "You might as well get your Partners now. I'll let the Scanner know we're ready to go into the Up-and-Out."

THE DEAL

Underhill spun the combination lock on the Lady May's cage. He woke her gently and took her into his arms. She humped her back luxuriously, stretched her claws, started to purr, thought better of it, and licked him on the wrist instead. He did not have the pin-set on, so their minds were closed to each other, but in the angle of her mustache and in the movement of her ears, he caught some sense of the gratification she experienced in finding him as her Partner.

He talked to her in human speech, even though speech meant nothing to a cat when the pin-set was not on.

"It's a damn shame, sending a sweet little thing like you whirling around in the coldness of nothing to hunt for Rats that are bigger and deadlier than all of us put together. You didn't ask for this kind of fight, did you?"

For answer, she licked his hand, purred, tickled his cheek with her long fluffy tail, turned around and faced him, golden eyes shining.

For a moment, they stared at each other, man squatting, cat standing erect on her hind legs, front claws digging into his knee. Human eyes and cat eyes looked across an immensity which no words could meet, but which affection spanned in a single glance.

"Time to get in," he said.

She walked docilely into her spheroid carrier. She climbed in. He saw to it that her miniature pin-set rested firmly and comfortably against the base of her brain. He made sure that her claws were padded so that she could not tear herself in the excitement of battle.

Softly he said to her, "Ready?"

For answer, she preened her back as much as her harness would permit and purred softly within the confines of the frame that held her.

He slapped down the lid and watched the sealant ooze around the seam. For a few hours, she was welded into her projectile until a workman with a short cutting arc would remove her after she had done her duty.

He picked up the entire projectile and slipped it into the

ejection tube. He closed the door of the tube, spun the lock, seated himself in his chair, and put his own pin-set on.

Once again he flung the switch.

He sat in a small room, *small, small, warm, warm,* the bodies of the other three people moving close around him, the tangible lights in the ceiling bright and heavy against his closed eyelids.

As the pin-set warmed, the room fell away. The other people ceased to be people and became small glowing heaps of fire, embers, dark red fire, with the consciousness of life burning like old red coals in a country fireplace.

As the pin-set warmed a little more, he felt Earth just below him, felt the ship slipping away, felt the turning Moon as it swung on the far side of the world, felt the planets and the hot, clear goodness of the Sun which kept the Dragons so far from mankind's native ground.

Finally, he reached complete awareness.

He was telepathically alive to a range of millions of miles. He felt the dust which he had noticed earlier high above the ecliptic. With a thrill of warmth and tenderness, he felt the consciousness of the Lady May pouring over into his own. Her consciousness was as gentle and clear and yet sharp to the taste of his mind as if it were scented oil. It felt relaxing and reassuring. He could sense her welcome of him. It was scarcely a thought, just a raw emotion of greeting.

At last they were one again.

In a tiny remote corner of his mind, as tiny as the smallest toy he had ever seen in his childhood, he was still aware of the room and the ship, and of Father Moontree picking up a telephone and speaking to a Scanner captain in charge of the ship.

His telepathic mind caught the idea long before his ears could frame the words. The actual sound followed the idea the way that thunder on an ocean beach follows the lightning inward from far out over the seas.

"The Fighting Room is ready. Clear to planoform, sir."

THE PLAY

Underhill was always a little exasperated the way that Lady May experienced things before he did.

He was braced for the quick vinegar thrill of planoforming, but he caught her report of it before his own nerves could register what happened.

Earth had fallen so far away that he groped for several milliseconds before he found the Sun in the upper rear right-hand corner of his telepathic mind.

That was a good jump, he thought. This way we'll get there in four or five skips.

A few hundred miles outside the ship, the Lady May thought back at him, "O warm, O generous, O gigantic man! O brave, O friendly, O tender and huge Partner! O wonderful with you, with you so good, good, good, warm, warm, now to fight, now to go, good with you . . ."

He knew that she was not thinking words, that his mind took the clear amiable babble of her cat intellect and translated it into images which his own thinking could record and understand.

Neither one of them was absorbed in the game of mutual greetings. He reached out far beyond her range of perception to see if there was anything near the ship. It was funny how it was possible to do two things at once. He could scan space with his pin-set mind and yet at the same time catch a vagrant thought of hers, a lovely, affectionate thought about a son who had had a golden face and a chest covered with soft, incredibly downy white fur.

While he was still searching, he caught the warning from her.

We jump again!

And so they had. The ship had moved to a second planoform. The stars were different. The Sun was immeasurably far behind. Even the nearest stars were barely in contact. This was good Dragon country, this open, nasty, hollow kind of space. He reached farther, faster, sensing and looking for danger, ready to fling the Lady May at danger wherever he found it.

Terror blazed up in his mind, so sharp, so clear, that it came through as a physical wrench.

The little girl named West had found something—something immense, long, black, sharp, greedy, horrific. She flung Captain Wow at it.

Underhill tried to keep his own mind clear. "Watch out!" he shouted telepathically at the others, trying to move the Lady May around.

At one corner of the battle, he felt the lustful rage of Captain Wow as the big Persian tomcat detonated lights while he approached the streak of dust which threatened the ship and the people within.

The lights scored near misses.

The dust flattened itself, changing from the shape of a sting ray into the shape of a spear.

Not three milliseconds had elapsed.

Father Moontree was talking human words and was saying in a voice that moved like cold molasses out of a heavy jar, "C-a-p-t-a-i-n." Underhill knew that the sentence was going to be "Captain, move fast!"

The battle would be fought and finished before Father Moontree got through talking.

Now, fractions of a millisecond later, the Lady May was directly in line.

Here was where the skill and speed of the Partners came in. She could react faster than he. She could see the threat as an immense Rat coming direct at her.

She could fire the light-bombs with a discrimination which he might miss.

He was connected with her mind, but he could not follow it.

His consciousness absorbed the tearing wound inflicted by the alien enemy. It was like no wound on Earth—raw, crazy pain which started like a burn at his navel. He began to writhe in his chair.

Actually he had not yet had time to move a muscle when the Lady May struck back at their enemy.

Five evenly spaced photonuclear bombs blazed out across a hundred thousand miles.

The pain in his mind and body vanished.

He felt a moment of fierce, terrible, feral elation running through the mind of the Lady May as she finished her kill. It was always disappointing to the cats to find out that their enemies whom they sensed as gigantic space Rats disappeared at the moment of destruction.

Then he felt her hurt, the pain and the fear that swept over both of them as the battle, quicker than the movement of an eyelid, had come and gone. In the same instant there came the sharp and acid twinge of planoform.

Once more the ship went skip.

He could hear Woodley thinking at him. "You don't have to bother much. This old son-of-a-gun and I will take over for a while."

Twice again the twinge, the skip.

He had no idea where he was until the lights of the Caledonia space board shone below.

With a weariness that lay almost beyond the limits of thought, he threw his mind back into rapport with the pin-set, fixing the Lady May's projectile gently and neatly in its launching tube.

She was half dead with fatigue, but he could feel the beat of her heart, could listen to her panting, and he grasped the grateful edge of a "Thanks" reaching from her mind to his.

THE SCORE

They put him in the hospital at Caledonia.

The doctor was friendly but firm. "You actually got touched by that Dragon. That's as close a shave as I've ever seen. It's all so quick that it'll be a long time before we know what happened scientifically, but I suppose you'd be ready for the insane asylum now if the contact had lasted several tenths of a millisecond longer. What kind of cat did you have out in front of you?"

Underhill felt the words coming out of him slowly. Words were such a lot of trouble compared with the speed and the joy of thinking, fast and sharp and clear, mind to mind! But words were all that could reach ordinary people like this doctor.

His mouth moved heavily as he articulated words, "Don't call our Partners cats. The right thing to call them is Partners. They fight for us in a team. You ought to know we call them Partners, not cats. How is mine?"

"I don't know," said the doctor contritely. "We'll find out for you. Meanwhile, old man, you take it easy. There's nothing but rest that can help you. Can you make yourself sleep, or would you like us to give you some kind of sedative?"

"I can sleep," said Underhill. "I just want to know about the Lady May."

The nurse joined in. She was a little antagonistic. "Don't you want to know about the other people?"

"They're okay," said Underhill. "I knew that before I came in here."

He stretched his arms and sighed and grinned at them. He could see they were relaxing and were beginning to treat him as a person instead of a patient.

"I'm all right," he said. "Just let me know when I can go see my Partner."

A new thought struck him. He looked wildly at the doctor. "They didn't send her off with the ship, did they?"

"I'll find out right away," said the doctor. He gave Underhill a reassuring squeeze of the shoulder and left the room.

The nurse took a napkin off a goblet of chilled fruit juice.

Underhill tried to smile at her. There seemed to be something wrong with the girl. He wished she would go away. First she had started to be friendly and now she was distant again. It's a nuisance being telepathic, he thought. You keep trying to reach even when you are not making contact.

Suddenly she swung around on him.

"You pinlighters! You and your damn cats!"

Just as she stamped out, he burst into her mind. He saw himself a radiant hero, clad in his smooth suede uniform, the pin-set crown shining like ancient royal jewels around his head. He saw his own face, handsome and masculine, shining out of her mind. He saw himself very far away and he saw himself as she hated him.

She hated him in the secrecy of her own mind. She hated him because he was—she thought—proud and strange and rich, better and more beautiful than people like her.

He cut off the sight of her mind and, as he buried his face in the pillow, he caught an image of the Lady May.

"She *is* a cat," he thought. "That's all she is—a *cat!*"

But that was not how his mind saw her—quick beyond all dreams of speed, sharp, clever, unbelievably graceful, beautiful, wordless and undemanding.

Where would he ever find a woman who could compare with her?